"How do you Adam up?"

"The best way I ca

"And what's that?"

Cade stared at her hard. "I love him. He's mine. I'll go the whole nine yards for him."

"He's not a possession," Megan countered, remembering the way she had been a possession of her father's, something to get him what he wanted. "He's a human being who deserves a good life."

"Listen, Doc—" he reached out without warning, cupping her chin in a calloused hand "—let's get one thing straight between us."

She stared up at him, stunned by the sudden contact and the heat of his touch on her skin. She could barely focus on what he was saying. "What?"

His hold tightened just a fraction as he spoke in a rough, tight voice. "Reality is that I will do *anything* to have my son with me."

Dear Reader:

We at Silhouette are very excited to bring you this reading **Sensation**. *Look out for the four books which appear in our Silhouette* **Sensation** *series every month. These stories will have the high quality you have come to expect from Silhouette, and their varied and provocative plots will encourage you to explore the wonder of falling in love – again and again!*

Emotions run high in these drama-filled novels. Greater sensual detail and an extra edge of realism intensify the hero and heroine's relationship so that you cannot help but be caught up in their every change of mood.

We hope you enjoy this **Sensation** *– and will go on to enjoy many more.*

We would love to hear your comments and encourage you to write to us:

Jane Nicholls
Silhouette Books
PO Box 236
Thornton Road
Croydon
Surrey
CR9 3RU

MARY ANNE WILSON
Child of Mine

Silhouette Sensation

*First published in Great Britain in 1994
by Silhouette Books, Eton House, 18-24 Paradise Road,
Richmond, Surrey TW9 1SR*

© Mary Anne Wilson 1991

Silhouette, Silhouette Sensation and Colophon are
Trade Marks of Harlequin Enterprises B.V.

ISBN 0 373 59101 2

18-9402

Made and printed in Great Britain

Other novels by Mary Anne Wilson

Silhouette Sensation

Brady's Law
Liar's Moon

For Jeff—
my firstborn
and favorite son
Welcome back—I missed you
All my love

Prologue

Cade Daniels stared intently at the floor-to-ceiling wall of windows across the bare, concrete floor. He saw nothing else in the unfinished office on the top story of the deserted high rise in downtown Los Angeles.

He took several deep breaths, watching the sheets of glass shimmer in front of his eyes. Then he braced his solid, six-foot frame as he tried to clear his mind and force his concentration on what he had to do—jump through the closed windows and plunge to the parking lot, twelve floors below.

But try as he would, he couldn't block out the memories of last night, the painful fact that Lori had turned on him.

"I'm leaving, Cade," she'd said in a low voice as she'd faced him on the terrace at Jack Reynolds's home in Brentwood Heights. Her gray eyes had been narrowed with anger and intensity. *"And I'm going alone."*

"Hey, Cade?"

He didn't look behind him at the owner of the male voice that cut through his thoughts. He just kept staring at the windows and called over his shoulder, "What?"

"Is everything all right?"

Cade gave the thumbs-up sign, not saying anything more as the memories grew stronger with each passing moment. He closed his eyes tightly, but that didn't stop the voices ringing in his mind.

"All right, we'll go home," he'd said, too tired to endure another argument. He'd known the pattern all too well. Lori bored with his friends. Lori issuing ultimatums. Lori running out on him. He'd had no emotional reserves last night to go through that routine again. *"We'll leave. Your parents are keeping the baby overnight, so we can go right home. I've got to get up early for work in the morning."*

Jack, Bobby Slate and Leon McCann, the stunt crew, had been inside, going over details of the next job, while the women visited in the den. But not Lori. *"I don't want to leave with you. I don't want to be with you. You're boring, Cade, really boring. I never thought I'd say that, but it's true. I married you because I thought we'd have fun. But all you do is work and hang out with people like these men."*

He could remember staring at her face, framed by a wild tumble of blond curls, a face he would at one time have called beautiful. But right then it had been twisted into an ugly expression. His only clear thought then had been to question what he had ever seen in Lori Sinclair. Why had he looked at Lori that second time? Why had he approached her at that party and eventually left with her?

He opened his eyes to the glare of the Los Angeles sun streaming through the dirt-streaked glass. But Lori's voice still echoed inside him. *"It's over, Cade, really over. I want out. I want free of you and this life."*

He hated the mistakes he'd made. And he hated the fact that Lori had said out loud what he'd been thinking for a long time. He'd known right then the marriage had been over almost before it began.

"If I have to spend one more minute with those people, I think I'll scream." She'd waved her hand at the house, including all the people inside, people who were his friends—Jack, a veteran who had been a mentor of sorts to Cade when he started in the business, Leon, a journeyman stunt performer who'd never made it big, but stayed in there, and Bobby, a new kid, just out of stunt school.

"I'm sick to death of them all," Lori had finished.

In the cold light of day Cade realized now that he'd never really known Lori, not even after a year of marriage. And when she'd turned from him last night and walked away, heading across the terrace onto the grass and around to the front of the house toward their car, he hadn't even been sure he liked her anymore.

As he'd watched her go, he hadn't been able to help thinking that giving birth to Adam just six months before had made Lori look even more terrific—leggy, blond and what most men would call stunning. But he had felt close to hating her right then.

Why hadn't he gone after her when she'd taken off in their car? he wondered now, but knew the answer before the question was formed. She'd walked out one time too many, even staying away for a few days, always counting on him to track her down. So he'd walked back inside, told everyone the lie that Lori hadn't felt well and had gone home. Then he'd called a taxi for himself and returned home to find an empty house. He hadn't even been surprised when he woke this morning to find Lori still wasn't there.

His hands clenched into fists so tightly that they ached. Lori had played havoc with him from the first. After thirty-four years of being on his own, she'd changed everything by announcing she was pregnant, only two months after they'd met.

When he'd called Lori's parents a few hours ago to see if he could leave the baby with them for the day, they had assumed that Lori was with him. He'd had a flash of uneasiness, even thought of calling the police, but had pushed that away. Lori was playing one of her games, and he wasn't going to go along with it.

The marriage was over. That wasn't a game.

He blinked rapidly, then deliberately opened his hands and shook them, while he rotated his head slowly to ease his bunching muscles.

"Cade, they said it's ready whenever you are," the man behind him called out.

Cade nodded and narrowed his eyes to the May sun streaming through the glass.

Marriage was supposed to be for better or worse, forever. All he had to do was look at his family. His parents had been married for forty-two years, his brother Ethan for ten. Cade was the one who couldn't get it right, who made bad, destructive choices. Maybe love was an illusion for some people. Maybe the lucky ones found it, while the others just had to do without. He knew he'd never come close.

"Hey," the voice called to him again, "any last words?"

"Life sucks," Cade muttered as he opened his eyes.

"Amen to that," the other man agreed.

"Let's do it."

"All right," the man behind him said, then shouted, "Counting down! Five, and four, and three, two, one. Now!"

Cade ran full tilt toward the far wall. Just before contact, he spun around and hurled himself backward through the window, shattering the breakaway glass as he flew out and into the air.

For a heartbeat he was free, unencumbered by life and its problems, then started waving his arms and legs wildly as he plummeted like a stone toward the earth.

"One thousand one, one thousand two, one thousand three, one thousand four, one thousand five," he muttered to himself, then spread his limbs and hit the huge air bag squarely on his back.

He felt his body sink to the bottom, then start back up. When he finally stilled on the cushion of air, he took inventory to make sure nothing was broken, starting with his neck and working his way down to his feet.

He'd wanted to use a larger bag, but it would have taken too much time to find one, and time was money in this industry. So he'd gone with the small bag. Twelve stories into this had been a gamble, a very slight risk compared to the one he'd taken with his marriage, but at least this chance had paid off. The fall had been just right.

He felt a twinge where he had separated his shoulder last spring. Nothing new. As he rolled to the edge of the forty-by-forty-foot bag, he grabbed the side and did an expert tuck and roll to the ground.

When he landed squarely on his feet and gave the thumbs-up sign, the crew broke into applause and the director, sitting in a basket high on a crane lift, yelled, "Great, Cade, perfect! It's a print."

Cade brushed at the tight black pants he was wearing with a black T-shirt, then drew himself up and tugged a false mustache off his upper lip. As he turned to go to his trailer, he felt a sudden stab of pain in his knee. It stopped him dead.

"Damn," he muttered. Not such a perfect gag. He touched the pain site with his fingertips, prodding at it. A strain. Maybe a pulled ligament. An injury, just because he hadn't been concentrating the way he should have been, but nothing serious.

"Mr. Daniels?"

Cade straightened and looked to his left as a heavyset man in a rumpled, gray suit strode toward him. In the clear, spring sunlight, the middle-aged man looked haggard, his fleshy face pulled into tense lines.

"Cade Daniels?" he asked as he stopped in front of him.

Cade wanted to get back to his trailer and ice his knee. He had no desire to chat with anyone. "That's me, but if you want anything, you'll have to talk to my business manager, Evan Rice. You can get his number—"

"No, sir, Mr. Daniels, I need to talk to you."

Cade tossed the mustache to a waiting crew member and raked both hands through his shaggy, brown hair. Then, being careful not to put his weight squarely onto his bad knee, he looked at the man in front of him. "All right, what do you want?"

The man shifted from one foot to the other. "I'm Detective Carlson with the Los Angeles Police Department. I'm afraid there's been an accident—"

"What?"

"We would have gotten to you sooner, but we had a hard time finding you. I'm sorry. I need you to come with me."

Cade felt his chest tighten so horribly that he could barely get air into his lungs to manage one word. "Accident?"

The man took a harsh breath, then said bluntly, "I'm afraid your wife's been killed."

Chapter 1

Six months later

The clamor came down a long, dark tunnel, pulling Cade from a heavy, dreamless sleep. It echoed painfully through his being, and he groped for a pillow, pulling it tightly over his head. Yet that didn't stop the torment or stop him from waking enough to name the sound—a mixture of someone pounding on the front door and ringing the doorbell at the same time.

Even though the master bedroom in his two-story, adobe home in the hills above Hollywood was upstairs and at the back of the house, the racket cut right through his head. It was waking him as effectively as if someone were running a jackhammer within two feet of his king-size bed.

Snarling a violent oath, he finally tossed the pillow away, flopped onto his back and opened his eyes just a slit to the shadowy room. With the drapes pulled and all the lights off, he could barely make out the domed ceiling and the heavy light fixture that hung above the huge bed.

He flinched at the noise and pressed a hand to his eyes. "All right, all right," he muttered, reluctantly aware that his speech was thickened by the combination of clinging sleep and a hangover he could only call all encompassing.

He rolled slowly to his right across the bed, then his bare feet touched the thick carpeting. With the help of one hand braced flat against the nightstand, he managed to lever himself to a standing position. For a split second he felt as if his head would explode, then the world settled into a dull ache that seemed to throb in cadence with the noise downstairs.

Cade didn't bother reaching for the bathrobe that had been discarded on the floor by the door. Instead, wearing only his Jockey shorts, he padded into the hall and along to the spiral staircase, his steps noiseless on the soft carpeting.

By the time he felt the jarring cold of quarry tile in the two-story entry under his feet, his mood had gone from bad to worse. "This had better be good," he grumbled, imagining the tortures he was going to put the intruder through when he managed to stop the horrendous noise the person was inflicting on him.

He raked his hands through his unkempt brown hair, then down over the bristling of beard on his jaw. God, his mouth felt as if someone had stuffed cotton balls into it while he slept, and his eyes were having a devil of a time just focusing with any clarity. All in all, this was just about the worst hangover he'd had since . . . He remembered. The day after Lori died.

As he stopped by the heavy double doors, a single knock came, literally shaking the dark carved wood. Enough was enough. Cade reached for the knob and jerked back the door. A barrage of brilliant sunlight stunned him for a moment, then he narrowed his eyes and was able to make out the blurred image of someone outside, who might or might not be a man dressed in dark colors.

"What in the hell do you want?" Cade managed, his voice a raspy croak.

"You," a familiar voice said out of the brightness.

Cade rubbed at his gritty eyes with his knuckles, then focused on Evan Rice. The sight of the slight man, his narrow face dominated by a perfectly trimmed beard and dark eyes, and looking painfully neat in a three-piece suit, stark white shirt and polished black oxfords, only added to Cade's aggravation. Probably because he knew how awful *he* looked right now.

"What in the hell—?"

"I came to see you," Evan said in a low, even voice as he moved past Cade and into the foyer. "I've been trying to get a hold of you for almost two weeks. I hope you don't have plans for today."

Actually Cade didn't even know what day "today" was, or, for that matter, what time it was. He turned from the sight of Evan's BMW parked alongside his own dusty Jeep, and closed the door slowly, making very sure he didn't slam it. He took a moment to lean against the cool wood before he looked at Evan and asked, "What's going on?"

He saw Evan stare at him, then turn without a word and walk to the step that led down into the living room to the right of the doors. Cade muttered a low curse, then padded after the other man into the large room, which was in shadow. He heard a rustling, then brilliant sun poured in as Evan opened the heavy drapes on the bank of windows along the back wall. The shock of the sudden sunlight intensified Cade's headache, and he turned away. He couldn't remember the last time he'd bothered to pull back the heavy, woven drapes to expose the house or himself to the sunlight. Right now it didn't feel good at all.

He crossed the carpet, sidestepping discarded newspapers and clothes, and sank onto the linen-covered sofa to one side of the windows with his back to the light. He inhaled, taking in the staleness of the room, of the whole house—an odor of something closed, abandoned—then looked at Evan, who had made himself comfortable in a chair opposite.

He'd thought for a moment when he opened the door that Evan was a process server, that someone was suing him for something. It wouldn't have surprised him or been the first time it had happened. He'd caused his share of problems in his life when he got out on his own, away from his parents' home. He'd learned most things the hard way, even his profession, though in the past couple of years he'd tried to be more stable. At least until six months ago.

Since then there'd been blank spots in his memory when he'd been drinking, spots that could have been filled with just about anything, good or bad. A while ago he'd gotten a letter from some bar near Malibu, telling him he would never be welcome in their establishment again. He didn't know of the bar, let alone remember ever being there.

He sank into the couch, resting his head on the softness of the back cushions and closed his eyes. "What do you want, Evan?" he muttered.

"Where have you been?"

"Sante Fe."

"Why?"

"Visiting Jack Reynolds. He's working there on a Derey movie." He ran a hand over his face. "I got sidetracked at the wrap party." Sidetracked was putting it mildly. He didn't remember too much about it, either, though he vaguely recalled getting to the airport and stumbling up a boarding ramp. Then there was nothing—until a flashing image of coming into this house at night. The sun was out now, so it had to be at least the next day, but he really didn't know how long he'd been home.

"You look sidetracked."

Cade opened his eyes just enough to glance at Evan. "What do you want?"

"Don't you ever check your answering machine?"

He glanced at the machine near the phone on the end table, not more than three feet away, and saw the light blinking frantically. He'd been in no condition to check messages when he came home. "Not unless I have to," he muttered.

"Obviously. I've been leaving messages for over two weeks."

Cade closed his eyes and exhaled harshly. "Can this wait?"

"I wouldn't be here if it could."

Being careful not to jar his head, Cade levered himself off the couch and straightened slowly. "All right. All right." He waited only long enough for the dizziness to subside, then walked past Evan to the wet bar on the opposite wall and reached for the closest bottle of alcohol—whiskey. "Hair of the dog," he muttered as his fingers closed around the cold glass of the container.

"Cade. Don't."

He hesitated, then asked, "Give me one good reason not to."

"Doris and Leo have started legal proceedings to get permanent custody of Adam."

The words stopped him dead. *Permanent custody?* His son? They wanted his son? He'd told them just a week ago, no, more like a month ago, that he wasn't about to let them have Adam. He'd be ready to take the boy back in a while. Just a bit longer, when he'd gotten his life in order, when he could make his life stable. He never wanted them to have Adam forever.

Cade thought about Adam, a tiny bundle with a shock of dark hair and lungs that could have brought down the walls of Jericho. He'd been asleep the last time Cade had been to Doris and Leo's house. Peacefully asleep. And Cade hadn't wanted to wake him. He'd just wanted to see him, to feel his presence, then leave.

His hand clenched tightly on the bottle, but he didn't pour a drink. Instead he stared at the amber liquid and acknowledged a reality he'd been avoiding for half a year. Alcohol didn't make anything better.

It never had, not in his youth, when his parents had been horrified by his life-style, and it didn't now. It just dulled the pain, the memories, the need to face life.

He knew he finally had to confront his world, deal with it, a world that crumbled more with each passing day. He let go of the bottle, pushing it away, then pressed his hands flat on the polished bar top. "What have they done?" he asked without turning.

"Got everything in motion. You'll be getting the papers any day now. As your lawyer, I can tell you you've got an uphill battle. As your friend, I can tell you that you're going to lose your son, unless you get your life back on track."

Cade stared at the image that was bouncing back at him from the wall of mirrors behind the bar. That sight, the first deliberate look he'd taken in a long time, was a real shock. Down at least ten pounds from his usual hundred and seventy-five pounds, he knew his six-foot frame looked bony. His bare shoulders seemed squarer, sharper, and the scar that hooked over his left shoulder and down to his breastbone stood out pearly white against his naturally dark, smooth skin.

Brown eyes that were normally deep set looked sunken and shadowed. His hair, usually just long enough to brush the nape of his neck, now rested on his shoulders in an unkempt tangle, and a scruffy beard darkened his square jaw, hiding the cleft.

He'd always been an ordinary-looking person as far as he was concerned—ordinary height, size, coloring—and that had made him good at his profession, able to double for most actors with just the addition of a wig at times, a mustache or a beard. Now he looked anything but ordinary. And he doubted that anyone would take him for one of the top stuntmen in Hollywood, though that was what he'd been for the past ten years.

Obviously Doris and Leo didn't think he could even be a good father. He knew he should be angry at that, but had to admit he'd never had the time to really be a father. He had always thought he could when Adam grew older, when the baby was more of a human being instead of a wiggly, squirming infant. After all, Adam *was* his, just about the only good thing in his life. That much was sure.

Lori had been a mistake, a terrible error of judgment. Now it seemed it had also been a mistake to let Doris and Leo keep Adam for "a while," until Cade could sort out his life, get onto his feet.

He frowned. It had been about a month since his last visit to Adam. And Leo and Doris had had Adam for six months. He couldn't blame his in-laws for what they were doing, but that didn't mean he'd accept it. The problem was he couldn't zero in on anything right now, not when his brain and thought processes felt so thick and sluggish.

"Cade?"

"I'm listening," he murmured, closing his eyes to the sight of himself.

"You've also got a Dr. Lewis looking all over town for you."

"Dr. who?"

"Lewis."

He couldn't remember ever knowing anyone called Lewis, especially a doctor. And he knew a lot of those. He had enough scars on his body to testify to that fact.

Evan kept talking. "Listen, Cade. We have to discuss a lot of things. One of them is your money situation."

One more nail in his coffin? "Take what you need, Evan. You've got power of attorney."

"Damn straight I do. That's how I know if you keep going on like this, you'll be broke in six months."

Cade couldn't begin to comprehend what Evan was saying. He licked his dry lips. "Evan, listen, we'll talk tomorrow. Right now I need—" he looked again at his reflection in the mirror "—I need to do some things."

When the phone rang, he jerked his head in the direction of the shrill sound; the room did a sickening flip before it settled. When the phone rang a second time, Evan asked, "Are you going to get it?"

"Yeah." Cade reached for the extension on the bar, then picked it up. "Hello?"

"Cade Daniels, please?"

The sound of a decidedly feminine voice on the other end stunned him. It was soft and touched with a certain gentleness that made him want to reach out and wrap it around himself. The reaction was so sudden and so intense that it almost took his breath away. His nerves were raw, too sensitive, he admitted. He'd been too long without any real connection with other human beings, beyond drinking with the guys and getting crazy. Now this voice was making him think of wounds being healed and tenderness he'd almost forgotten existed in this world. It took him a long moment to reply. "I'm Cade Daniels."

"Mr. Daniels, this is Dr. Lewis," the owner of the voice said. "I need to see you."

The voice seemed to surround Cade, to seep into his pores. A certain healing could be there for him, he thought. The woman must have been born to be a doctor.

"I don't know you, do I?" he asked, already aware that if he had heard this voice before, he would never have forgotten it.

"No, we've never met. There's been a request from the Los Angeles Family Court for evaluation of all parties concerned in the custody case of Adam Emerson Daniels. I need to set up an appointment with you at your earliest convenience."

Family Court? Cade felt as if he'd been broadsided. He hadn't expected the voice to belong to a "head doctor," or that the doctor would be all tangled up in Adam's custody fight. "I don't understand."

She began speaking rapidly, as if reading the words off a cue card. "I've been asked to evaluate all the parties concerned in the custody of—"

"I understand *that*," he said, almost hating to cut off the sound of her words.

"Then you understand that I need to give my opinion of who is best fit to bring up the child, Adam Daniels."

"You're a psychiatrist?"

"A psychologist specializing in family services. I'm a fully accredited psychologist and have been affiliated with the Los Angeles Court system for two years, doing evaluation on dysfunctional family matters."

A shrink, a head doctor. And she wanted to see him to find out if he was father material. The idea made Cade sick, maybe because he knew he didn't have the slightest idea what sort of father material he really was. Or maybe because he sensed that the owner of this voice would be evaluating him psychologically instead of being the stuff dreams were made of. "How about the Sinclairs? Will you be seeing them?" he asked.

"Yes, but I would like to meet with you first. I'll have to talk to everyone involved in the custody suit. That's the only way to give an impartial evaluation, Mr. Daniels. And I would like to meet with you at your home as soon as possible."

At first he wanted to tell her to forget it. The house looked like hell, just the way he felt, then he realized that he didn't want to be in some office, lying on a couch, telling this woman about his repressed childhood. A doctor could have a field day with his intrafamilial relationships. "That can be arranged, I guess," he said.

"When?"

He closed his eyes for a long moment. "When do you want to do it?"

"Today."

"No," he said quickly.

"We don't have much time. I want to stress how important it is to get started on this, and—"

"Tomorrow. How about then? Around two o'clock." That would give him time to get the house in order and get himself straightened out, too.

The woman hesitated, then agreed. "Tomorrow at two."

"My address—"

"I have your address, Mr. Daniels," the doctor said, then, "I'll see you tomorrow at your house at two o'clock." The next sound he heard was the click of the connection breaking.

Cade put the phone back, then looked into the mirrors once more and saw the reflection of Evan, still sitting in the chair. "Dr. Lewis is a head doctor, and she's coming to see me tomorrow to see if I'm a fit father for Adam." He raked his fingers through his shaggy hair and spoke to Evan's reflection. "Can we talk later?"

"No, I need to get things straight now." When Cade would have argued that he wasn't human right now, that he was having trouble just concentrating on standing up, Evan said bluntly, "You're in terrible shape financially. You're close to being broke. We *need* to talk and we need to talk *now*."

Cade focused on his own reflection and grimaced. "And I need a shower and some clothes."

"Take a shower and get dressed. I'll wait. I can use your phone to make some calls while you do that, then we'll talk."

Cade didn't have the energy to argue with Evan. With a shrug he turned from the wall of mirrors and headed for the door. "Suit yourself," he said over his shoulder as he stepped up and out, onto the cold tile of the entry. He took his time going back upstairs, through the bedroom and into the bathroom-dressing room area. Without snapping on the overhead lights, he passed through the dressing room, went past the Jacuzzi and turned the control knob on the outside of the sauna to High.

Dr. Megan Lewis stared at the phone for a long time after she hung up from talking to Cade Daniels.

It had shocked her when he answered, instead of the answering machine she'd been leaving messages on for the past three days. It had also shocked her that he sounded educated, with a deep, husky voice that was edged with impatience.

She shook her head and looked out the window at the Pacific in the distance. The office complex was on a hill, high above Malibu in a very exclusive area, but that had mattered little to her when she had rented the space. It had been rented for the view. She loved it. The ocean, soothing, sure, dependable. It took the edge off her frayed nerves, and the sound of the incoming and outgoing surf in the distance was a constant reassurance to her.

A refuge, she thought, surprised that that word came to her in connection with the ocean. Then she understood. When she was a child it had been just about the only place where she had been able to block out her life, to pretend she was normal, that her family was like those of all the other kids who went in and out of her existence.

She spread her hand on the case folder in front of her. They'd lived by the ocean for three months once, then moved on. Not normal at all. She'd never been normal, or what she had always thought of as normal, not as long as Frank had been in her life.

She brushed distractedly at her hair, the loose tumble of curls that fell below her shoulders, not confined in the usual French braid or twist. She had no appointments today, so she'd forgone her sensible clothes and hairstyle for jeans, an oversize sweatshirt and running shoes.

She stared at the view, realizing she felt restless today, uneasy; it didn't sit well with her. For a moment she considered a vacation, getting away, maybe driving up the coast until she found a peaceful place to stop.

Time away from the office, from her practice, from patients, from people's problems. Time to sit on a California beach that wouldn't be too crowded in November, to soak up the sun and relax. Then she turned and glanced at the files piled on her desk and knew a vacation would have to wait for a while.

Maybe she could get away in January. She stopped at that thought. January was when Frank came up for parole. He'd stand before the parole board and try to convince them he was rehabilitated, ready to go back into the world. That meant one thing. He would come back into her world, too.

The telephone on her desk rang, and Megan jerked slightly at the sudden noise. She turned and stared at the phone, each ring increasing the tension in her. She'd let her service pick it up. Then she realized that was a stupid reaction here, now; she'd been thrown back to a time when a ringing phone had meant she would have to lie to someone, to put off bill collectors or other people looking for Frank.

She felt relieved when it stopped ringing. The flashing light at the base of her phone let Megan know Rose MacKay, her assistant, was back from lunch and had answered it. There was silence for a long moment, then the door opened and Rose hurried into the room.

"That was Brad Carlin, checking to see if you made contact with the parties in the Adam Daniels case."

Megan could feel herself releasing her breath. What had she expected, bill collectors? Men calling to get to Frank or to threaten his life? Then she knew whom she'd expected to be on the line—Frank. *You're paranoid,* she told herself. A paranoid psychologist.

"Is he still on the line?"

Rose came farther into the room, a tiny sprite of a woman, wearing a simple dress in an improbable shade of purple, and shook her head. "No, he said to give him a call back when you're free."

Megan motioned to the file open in front of her. "As a matter of fact, I just got off the phone with Mr. Daniels." She massaged her temples with the tips of her fingers. "I have a two o'clock appointment with him tomorrow, a home evaluation visit."

Rose came closer, her face pulled into a frown of concern. "Are you feeling all right? You don't have one of those headaches, do you?"

"I'm fine," Megan lied. "I'm just a bit tired. I was even thinking that a vacation would be pretty welcome now." She looked at the stack of pending cases she was carrying for the family court system. "But I can't leave the work right now."

"Too bad. You deserve a vacation. It's a shame the Adam Daniels case is already behind schedule, because of some glitch in the system that kept it from getting here earlier."

"Yes, that's why I was trying so hard to contact him. And I got lucky. I got the appointment with Mr. Daniels, and after I meet with him, I'll set up an appointment with the maternal grandparents."

"Anyone else to talk to on it?"

Megan leaned forward, resting her elbows on the desk top and pressing her fingers to her temples as she scanned the top page of the Daniels file. *Father, Cade Emerson Daniels.* The father's parents had an out-of-state address and phone number, but a notation had been made not to bother them. That left one sibling, a brother, Ethan Jon Daniels, a professor of archaeology at a university on the East Coast. But he was out of the country until March.

Megan kept reading and came to *Evan Rice, attorney and business manager.* "I don't think so. I talked to Mr. Rice yesterday, and he didn't seem to know too much. This might be a very simple case." She sank back in her chair. "I can only hope." Exhaling slowly, she looked up at Rose. "Did anyone call when I was in L.A. yesterday?"

"No." The other woman studied her. "You weren't really expecting Frank to call, were you?"

Megan had always thought that mind reading was one of Rose's gifts, along with being the glue that held the office together. "I asked him not to contact me, to leave me out of his life, but you know he's due to go in front of the parole board pretty soon."

"And you figure he's going to forget what you said and call to ask you to be a character witness for him?"

"It wouldn't hurt to have a psychologist testify that he's stable, rehabilitated and ready for the outside world, would it?"

"How about a psychologist who happens to be his daughter?"

She wished she could laugh at that, but there was no humor in her. "I'm sure he's considered that angle. Frank knows all of the angles."

"Would you do it?"

"Do what?"

"Testify for him, if he asked you to."

Megan had asked herself that question so many times during the two years her father had been in prison that her head spun from it. She still had no answer. On a gut level, her first response was to do what it took to get him out of prison. She'd always been the mender, the one to try and make things right. But as a professional she knew what her father was and what he was capable of doing.

"I haven't talked to him for over two years. I have no idea what he's like now. If he's the same person, I couldn't, yet a part of me..." She sighed. "Some psychologist I am. I tell people not to be enablers, not to be the one to take the pain, while the person with the compulsive habit goes on blithely in their addiction, then I find myself falling into that role over and over again."

"*I* remember how hard it was on you when he was arrested."

In truth it had almost killed her, but Megan had made herself refuse his calls and letters. She hadn't put up bail, having decided to let him suffer the consequences of his actions. There had been the option of a deal, probation, if Frank made restitution, and Megan had had the money. But she hadn't paid up for him. On the one hand it had felt good to stop enabling him, yet on the other it had torn her apart.

"No harder than looking forward to him getting out. At least with him locked up, there aren't any calls in the middle of the night, begging for money because someone's going to break his legs."

"Hard to believe you're his daughter," Rose said softly.

Frank had often said the very same thing. "But I am. You can't divorce a parent."

"Too bad. It would make life easier if a person could turn off loving someone."

"I just don't think about it," Megan murmured, knowing she'd loved her father once; now she was close to hating him. One thing she knew. She wouldn't be his salvation again. Over the years he'd taken a lot from her—her childhood, her peace of mind—and her money. He'd also robbed her of the ability to trust anyone, or to even believe that love made all things right.

Nothing could make Frank right. He'd been sentenced to five years for embezzlement and fraud. But his real crime had been gambling, needing money for that addiction. It had ruled their existence when Megan's mother had been alive, and had only grown in intensity after her death. Megan had been six.

She'd learned while still a child to cover for her father and make excuses, to lie, to take care of moving when they lost their house or apartment. She'd never kept count, but wouldn't doubt they had moved at least once for every year she'd been alive. That made twenty-eight times.

"If he calls, no matter what, tell him I'm not here. Tell him . . . tell him I'm out of town for an indefinite period of time."

"Could he call you at home?"

Changing her number had been more of a psychological salve for her than a real deterrent to him. "Yes. If he's pushed, he'll find my new number. I know that."

"And?"

"I'll take care of it." She glanced down at the file and did what she'd learned to do over the past few years—center her thoughts on her work. "Now I want to go over this file and get a handle on the situation before my meeting tomorrow. Call Brad back and update him on the progress in the Daniels case."

"All right," Rose said, then turned and left, closing the door softly behind her.

Megan leaned forward once again, resting her elbows on the desk and began to reread the Adam Daniels file. "Father: Cade Emerson Daniels. Special physical effects expert in the entertainment industry." In brackets: "stuntman."

"A stuntman," she murmured; it was all she could do not to pick up a pencil and write "Dangerous, unsettled, risky, unstable and chancy" next to it.

She remembered one of her first cases for the court. The father had been a boxer, and she had had to work hard to remain objective about the custody recommendations. She would have to do the same this time, to really find out what was best for the child.

What's best for the child? How many times had she heard that while she was growing up? About as often as her father had taken her and skipped town to get away from social workers, about as often as he had let her be a buffer against the realities of life, so he could go on with his fantasies.

About as many times as people had called her "perky" or "cute." She grimaced at that. At five foot nothing, she knew she could look young, especially when she wore no makeup and dressed as she had today. Having a turned-up nose and huge blue eyes only added to the illusion. She knew that was why she tried so hard to look competent and in control at work.

She refocused and kept reading.

Thirty-six years old, married for just over a year. Wife killed in an automobile accident. Maternal grandparents, Leo and Doris Sinclair, living in Bel Air. Primary caretakers of the child in question for past six months.

Megan knew the Sinclair name. Money from plastics and laser technology. She'd never heard of Cade Daniels, but then again, even though she lived and worked in Malibu, she didn't really know anyone in the entertainment industry.

Had the excitement of Hollywood drawn the daughter of Leo Sinclair to marry Cade Daniels? Lori Sinclair-Daniels had died so young, just twenty-six years of age. Why had Cade Daniels given his son to the Sinclairs for six months, then decided he wanted the boy back now?

Obviously Cade Daniels was a grieving widower. Maybe he was just now able to think about taking care of his son. She could feel a degree of sympathy for his plight, then re-read the designation "stuntman" and grimaced. A stuntman was just another name for a gambler, one who didn't use money to bet.

A stuntman bet his own life.

cotton cloth on the rack by his side and began to scrub it over his skin until he could feel an uncomfortable tingling.

Concentrate, concentrate, he told himself and felt the fuzzy thinking leave, replaced by more solid, sharper thought.

He didn't need a woman. He needed to get his life out of the tailspin he'd put it in. He had to find some way to change the hard, cold facts that he was losing his son and that it was his fault.

Less than half an hour later Cade walked into the living room and felt annoyed, yet not surprised, to find Evan sitting on the couch with the phone pressed to his ear. Evan looked up as Cade entered, then nodded and kept talking into the receiver.

Cade walked past Evan and went to the windows that exposed the view of Hollywood, lying under a thin veil of smog far below. The sun seemed a bit less offensive to him now, but the ache behind his eyes wasn't lessening. He took several steadying breaths and wondered if he had the capacity to be rational anymore. His reactions to Dr. Lewis over the phone hadn't even been close.

"Cade?"

He closed his eyes for a fraction of a second, then turned to Evan and watched the slender man laying the phone receiver back into its cradle. "All right, Evan, since you insisted on staying, say what you have to say."

The man settled back in the pale cushions of the couch and with a vague shrug of his narrow shoulders studied Cade, pulling his bearded face into a frown of concentration. "Near as I can figure, you're six months away from being in a serious state of deficit."

"Since when?" Cade asked.

"Since I looked at your quarterlies. I've been trying to get in touch to tell you, leaving messages anywhere I could think you might be. Until you answered the door today, looking like death warmed over, I had begun to think you'd fallen off the face of the earth."

Cade tugged nervously at the cuffs of the black pullover he was wearing with faded Levi's and a pair of well-worn Western boots. "I almost did."

"So I've been hearing. News gets around fast in this town."

Cade knew about rumors. Most of the industry people probably thought he was in a bad way. It was closer to the truth than he cared to admit at this moment. One thing he knew for sure, it was damned hard to live down a bad reputation in this—or any other—business. "While I was upstairs getting cleaned up, I decided that's the first thing I need to fix. I need a job, a good, respectable piece of work."

Evan nodded. "Good thinking. Something that brings in some money instead of something that guarantees a good wrap party."

Cade couldn't tell if Evan was being sarcastic or not, so he turned his back on the man and stared down at the distant city. So, Evan knew about New Mexico. "If you knew where I was . . ."

"I didn't, not until this morning, when Scalla called to tell me what a sport you were to do a gag on his film for scale. Dirt cheap, Cade, dirt cheap."

"It seemed like a good idea at the time," he muttered, knowing that when he was drunk "a good idea" could be anything. After the argument he'd had with Doris, the last time he'd gone to see Adam, he'd been open to any "good idea." New Mexico had been far enough away to fill the bill.

He tucked the tips of his fingers into the pockets of his Levi's and stared at his reflection in the window glass. It was a reflection that bore little resemblance to the man he'd been less than an hour ago. Gone were the scruffy beginnings of a beard, and his thick hair was combed straight back from his face and caught into a ponytail with a rubber band.

He'd call in the cleaning service to get the house in order before tomorrow at two o'clock and get his hair cut, but the problems that had taken so long to develop certainly weren't going to go away just with a good cleaning, a sobering up and a trip to the barber.

"I'll take any jobs you can get for me, no questions, no complaints," he said.

"Isn't an out-of-condition stuntman more dangerous than he's worth?"

Evan's thinly veiled reproach made the thudding behind Cade's eyes grow more intense, and nausea twisted his stomach. He closed his eyes for a moment before he said, "I know I can still do the work and do a good job."

"And what about the child? What are you going to do about that mess?"

He'd fight. It was that simple. He'd thought about it over and over again upstairs. On a gut level he wanted the boy; he needed him. Yet he couldn't help wondering if he could be a real father. Did he have it in him? Even when Doris had told him they wanted Adam, that they'd go to court to get him, Cade hadn't believed it. He'd walked out of their house, telling them he'd be back soon to get his son. Well, they obviously hadn't been bluffing.

"Doris and Leo aren't giving me a chance." He turned to Evan. "I want to say what I said to Doris and Leo, that I'll fight like hell for him, but if I'm honest, I wonder what I'm going to do with a year-old baby. God, I can hardly run my own life right now. I'm sober enough to admit that Doris and Leo can give him everything I can't. They're stable and they love him."

Evan sat forward, his eyes unblinking. "Is that what you want for your son?"

His son. His child. A tiny creature that was a part of him. He didn't have to think over his answer. "No, it isn't, not for a child of mine."

Evan rested his elbows on his knees, then formed a tent with his thin fingers and peered intently over them at Cade. "Then we'll fight it, Cade."

"We?"

"I'm your lawyer as well as your business manager. We'll do whatever it takes, starting with your appointment with the good doctor tomorrow."

Cade exhaled in a rush. "What a place to start! How can I convince a professional that I'm stable and that I'm the best thing for Adam?"

"Be honest with her."

"Tell her that I've taken bad jobs for peanuts, that I've probably had a death wish, that I'm about to go broke?"

Evan smiled, a wry expression that lifted the corners of his mouth. "Just tell her about Rick Walters."

Cade leaned back against the window and crossed his arms on his chest as he looked across the room at Evan. "What are you talking about?"

"I ran into Walters a week ago. Seems he's working on a new project."

Cade knew Rick Walters, a combination director-producer—the hottest ticket in town. Failure wasn't in his vocabulary. Cade could remember running into Walters himself a while back, but couldn't begin to figure out where or when.

He tried to think, but all he got was the image of the man himself—long, red hair worn in braids, a five-foot-six-inch frame, carrying more than its share of weight, and pale blue eyes.

"What does he need?"

"A specialist. He was wondering if you might be up to doing serious work soon."

A picture with Walters could be his salvation right now. Cade straightened, trying to think past the pounding headache. "What did you tell him?"

"I stalled him and let him think you were considering other offers. I said I'd talk to you as soon as I could."

One job with Walters could put him right with the industry again. Word of mouth was a powerful force in Hollywood. "Who's coordinating?"

"Ross Barnette."

"A good man."

"Actually Ross recommended you for the special."

Cade had worked with Ross over the years and knew the man respected what he could do. "They really want me?"

"I know he's talked with McCallister and Rainer, but he said he'd like you to consider it. You know he's really particular, and the things he usually wants can't be done by just anyone in town."

"What is it?"

"A modified cannon roll, over a fence, and an end crash."

"What kind of money was he talking?"

"Double what you made on Zular's last film for the special."

Cade crossed the room and sank into a chair that faced the couch. He leaned forward, forearms on knees, mimicking Evan's posture. He felt vaguely unnerved when he saw unsteadiness in his hands. Deliberately he laced his fingers and pressed the tip of one thumb against the other for stability. "I could sure use the money, couldn't I?"

"Yes, you could. Enough to pay for legal expenses." Evan's expression tightened. "And enough to pay for extra medical expenses." He shook his head. "You're out of shape, and at your age..." The words trailed off, leaving the implied accusation hanging in the air.

Cade kept himself from rubbing his left arm; he had broken it in two places on the Zular film. He knew he was lighter than his fighting weight, that he hadn't kept up any exercise routine, but he had time to change all that. And as far as his age was concerned, even at thirty-six he could still do better gags than ninety percent of the other stuntmen out there—kids included. "I can be in shape, and my age isn't relevant." He changed the subject. "Who's the main actor?"

"Two of them. Peter Shaw and Lincoln Steele."

"Good. Good. Get in touch with Walters, and if it's still open, tell him I want to do it." He looked at Evan intently. "Sell me to him, Evan. I'll make you look good, I swear. Call him now."

"Are you sure?"

"I don't have to think about it. Walters is the best, the pay's right, and I *can* do it—if he'll give me the chance. God knows what he thinks of me now, but he obviously hasn't forgotten how good I've been before."

"He hasn't forgotten. And he was pretty concerned about you after the accident, calling and asking about you. Actually I think he understands better than most what you've been through these past months. He lost his wife years back, suddenly, no warning. A bit like you."

Cade could feel his whole being tighten, now that the alcoholic haze had worn off. He sat back in the chair, clenching his hands into fists on his thighs. He was sure Rick Walters hadn't felt the way he had—stunned disbelief, then regret and pain, all overlaid with horrible guilt. Guilt for not going after her, for not caring enough to go, for actually wanting out of the marriage. Then she'd been dead.

Guilt. That was why he'd made good use of the alcohol after the accident. He'd known he'd do more harm than good if he tried to keep the baby with him. But he'd never meant to turn his back on Adam. Never.

"Cade?"

He glanced at Even. "I'm sorry. What did you say?"

"The fight with Leo and Doris is going to be hard."

Damn hard, he admitted to himself, since Lori's parents knew the truth, that he hadn't wanted a marriage, that he'd only gone ahead with it because of Lori's pregnancy, that the idea of fatherhood for a man who had stayed single for thirty-four years had really put him off. They knew that the marriage had never been good, and had rapidly become worse. Even that last night. They knew there had been an argument. Ammunition, and he'd handed it to them on a silver platter.

"I'll think about that later. Right now, tell me what sort of picture Walters is doing."

Cade felt as nervous and anxious as he'd been before doing his first stunt years ago, when he heard the door chimes at one minute to two o'clock the next day. Before he opened the door, he tugged at the cuffs of the gray jacket he wore with a white shirt and deep red tie. He took several deep breaths, braced himself, then reached for the knob and pulled back the heavy, wooden barrier.

"Mr. Daniels?"

It was the slightly breathless, female voice he'd heard over the phone yesterday. The same voice that had seemed to drift through the maze of dreams he'd endured during the long night just past . . . when he'd been able to get to sleep.

Then he saw its owner, and saw no gray hair in a knot, nor a substantial figure. In front of him, backed by the afternoon sun, was a petite woman, dressed in a perfectly tailored navy jacket and straight skirt, matched by a leather shoulder bag and simple pumps.

Brilliant auburn hair was skimmed back and confined in a twist, but soft curls had managed to escape at the temples and neck. Huge eyes, the color of the skies on a clear day and framed by dark lush lashes, dominated a perfectly oval face accented by a scattering of freckles on a small straight nose. A mouth free of lipstick, yet still a soft, yielding pink, was pulled into a vaguely impatient line.

Cade knew a response was expected of him, a verbal response, not this physical awareness that tugged at every fiber of his being. "Yes, I'm Cade Daniels." Then he made himself ask, "Dr. Lewis?" although he had no doubt as to who this woman was.

"Yes," she said. "We have a two o'clock appointment."

His nerves seemed too raw, and it didn't help that even though he'd always preferred tall, blond, leggy women like Lori, the subtle sensuality of this one brought back the undeniable realization that he'd been a man alone for too long.

But this woman was the person who would decide what his life would be like from now on. That cold fact helped Cade focus on the reality of what he faced. "I'm sorry. Come in."

As the doctor stepped past him into the silent foyer, he glanced outside, not surprised to see a sleek Mercedes-Benz coupé parked beside his Jeep in the circle of the driveway. Then he turned, coming face-to-face with the doctor, who was only two feet away. He was thankful that Evan had called moments ago to tell him Walters had agreed to let him do the special. At least he had something substantial and positive to back him up.

When he inhaled, he took in freshness and delicate flowers that seemed to cling to the woman and fill the air. The scents contrasted sharply with the lingering pungency of cleaning materials from the efforts of the service that had finished less than an hour ago.

As the stranger stared at him, the blueness of her eyes seemed even more intense. "I'd like to start by saying I don't want you to think of this as an interrogation, Mr. Daniels," she said quickly. "I simply need to talk to you, to get some idea of you as a person, to see your house, the home you have for the child."

He felt himself tighten at the word "interrogation" and found himself experiencing anger. That was exactly what this was—an interrogation. Words he shouldn't let slip past his lips were out before he could stop them. "You're going to play judge and jury and tell me if I can have my son back. Isn't that what this is all about?"

He saw the frown expose a fine line between her blue eyes and her hands tighten on the leather strap of her shoulder bag. Tiny, delicate hands, yet they held his future with Adam.

Megan stared at the man in front of her, trying to ignore his tone, the edge to his words. She knew he was nervous, that having the fate of his son at stake was unnerving. It would be to anyone. In a way it helped her to shift a bit toward a more positive reaction. At least he cared. From her brief conversation with Doris Sinclair and the fact that there had been little contact with his son for half a year, she'd begun to wonder if he was a caring person at all.

"No, of course I'm not judge and jury," she said, unsettled by the realization that her preconceived idea of how a Hollywood stuntman would look could be so wrong.

In an immaculate, gray business suit and deep red tie, Cade Daniels could have passed for a professional, maybe an attorney or doctor. Definitely upscale, not even close to her image of a man with a broken nose, torn jeans, rundown boots, and a can of beer clutched in his hand.

About six feet tall, he was trim, almost thin, but obviously in condition and tanned at a time of year when the sun, even in Los Angeles, wasn't very strong. Despite the perfect fit of the suit, she was aware of muscular thighs and the width of strong shoulders.

It was as hard for her to assimilate his general appearance as it was to really evaluate his face. He certainly wasn't Hollywood handsome, yet something about him was striking. Maybe it was his eyes, the color of deep, rich chocolate, the sharply defined cheekbones that hinted at possible Indian ancestry, or a mouth that had a sensuously full bottom lip. Or maybe she was put off by the dimples that didn't need a smile to make themselves evident at either side of his mouth.

Right now he wasn't smiling.

In that instant she knew that everything about him added up to controlled, sexy maleness. That observation bothered her most of all. In no way should she be regarding a participant in this evaluation as "a man," let alone a disturbingly sexy one. Yet she knew there wouldn't be too many women who could look at this particular example and not feel the same way.

She touched her tongue to her lips, for a fleeting moment thinking how fortunate his late wife had been. This man had loved her. That was something Megan had never known.

She brought herself up short. She wasn't here to do a self-analysis—especially while the man in front of her seemed to be analyzing her, skimming his eyes over her in a way that made heat seep up under her skin.

"Then what are you?" he asked.

She spoke in a rush. "An appointee of the court. My opinion is only one of several aspects taken into consideration by the judge in determining the custody of your son."

At last his eyes met hers, eyes so brown they could have been black. "And you're qualified to do that?" he asked in a low voice.

She stood straighter, aware that her hand was twisting the strap of her purse. "I can assure you, I am."

She could sense a softening in his expression, a shifting that might have come from a touch of wry humor, and found herself welcoming it with great relief. "And you're a real doctor?" he asked.

She knew she didn't look like a doctor, and that usually annoyed her when someone brought it up. But not with this man. "A real doctor," she echoed, feeling something begin to ease inside her.

"Good," he said, then motioned to an arched entry on her left. "Let's go in the living room and get this over with."

She followed his suggestion and stepped down into a large, whitewashed room that seemed to sprawl the length of the house. Thick, off-white carpeting flowed into every corner, and the soft colors of the Southwest style touched everything—an overstuffed couch and chairs in natural linen, ceramic lamps and bleached wood accents.

Curtains along the far side were drawn back to show a stunning view of the city far below. Megan looked around at the perfect order, the white on white, then turned and watched Cade follow her into the room. But he stopped halfway, his weight on the balls of his feet, his presence strong and disturbing.

"So, what do you think?" he asked abruptly.

"About what?"

"About the house. I can see your mind working, analyzing everything."

She felt the heat rise again into her face, knowing she had thought he was referring to her reactions to him. The house was definitely a safe subject. "It's lovely."

"And?"

She spoke honestly. "I don't see any signs of a child living here."

"Adam didn't."

"What?"

"Not really. There's a nursery upstairs in what used to be an office, and when he...when he left, he was only six months old." He gestured with one hand. "No bikes, no baseballs, no catcher's mitts. Just bottles and diapers."

She turned from the tightness in his expression and glanced again at the windows before looking back at him. "You have a wonderful view from here."

"I know," was all Cade said as he moved to his left to a bar backed by mirrors. "Can I offer you a drink?"

"No, no thanks, but you go ahead if you like."

He stopped and turned. "I'm fine." He motioned to the couch. "Have a seat."

She settled on the couch, laying her purse beside her, then made herself cross her legs and sit back, instead of sitting forward on the edge, the way she wanted to.

Cade settled into a chair directly opposite, undoing the buttons on his jacket, but never took his eyes off her. "Go ahead, ask me whatever you want," he said. "Start dissecting me."

She changed her mind and sat forward after all. "Mr. Daniels, this isn't a test you either pass or don't pass. I don't have a set list of questions with right and wrong answers. I don't give a grade at the end."

He leaned forward and rested his forearms on his knees. "Oh, you don't? Then tell me what this is all about."

"Your son, Adam, and what's best for him."

"And that brings us back to the same old question. What makes you qualified to judge my fitness?"

This was getting worse with each passing moment. "I'm a psychologist. I'm trained in family counseling. That's my specialty."

He looked at her hard. "How many children do you have, Dr. Lewis?"

She could see immediately where he was going. "I don't have any children."

"Married?"

"No."

"Then what makes you an expert on deciding people's lives?"

She looked right at him. "Mr. Daniels, it isn't necessary to be able to build a car to be able to change a bad spark plug."

There was an abrupt burst of laughter from the man; it brought a brightness to his face that almost took her breath away.

She spoke quickly. "Everyone who's alive has to deal with family one way or another, whether as a child, a parent or a sibling. We all do, married or not."

"All right," he said, holding up one hand as the smile faded rapidly. "Ask me what you want to know, Doc."

Megan sat back, feeling as if she had just cleared a hurdle she hadn't even seen coming. She wanted to take a deep breath, but settled for exhaling softly. "We can just talk. Maybe…maybe you can start by telling me about what you do for a living."

"I'm in the movie industry."

"Doing what?"

He slanted her a glance. "Coordinating specialized physical effects for specific movie projects."

"Oh?"

"I'm a stuntman," he said, "and you already knew that."

"Yes, I did. It's in your file." She reached into her purse, took out a small notebook and flipped it open to the notes that she'd made while she had gone over the files. She decided to ask a few general questions next. "Where do you work?"

"Wherever my work takes me. I've worked in Spain, France, Mexico, Alaska and right around here."

"Lots of travel?"

"Some. I'm going out of town in a few days on a new project."

"Why would you do that right now?"

"Why not?"

"I mean, you're in the middle of this custody case and you're—"

"Working. I was just hired onto the new Rick Walters film, and the exteriors are being shot on location. I'll only be gone a few weeks at the most. I'll be back for Christmas."

"What sort of movie is it?" she asked, really interested.

"A prison movie, being shot in Texas. Rick Walters's company found a prison that was phased out of the penal system years ago, and they're going to use it. A small town nearby that depended on the prison while it was working has been practically deserted since the prison pulled out, and the people are glad to have some money coming into the town coffers. They probably think making a movie there would be glamorous."

"And it won't be?"

A smile came again, this time a wry, knowing expression. "There's very little in this business that's glamorous and exciting. Not even the travel. But my job is the only way I have to make a living."

That brought up another question. "And if you had Adam with you, what would happen to him while you fly off somewhere to do your job?"

Chapter 3

Cade kept his eyes on the woman across from him. Dr. Megan Lewis. Beyond the delicate beauty that was obvious, he knew there was real intelligence. It made him wish he was as smart right now. But he could feel nerves robbing him of coherent thought.

He kept eye contact with her pure blue gaze, while he tried to come up with some rational answer. What would he do with Adam? What was logical? He knew he needed to say the right words to this woman.

He bought more time by settling back in the chair. The doctor might say this wasn't a test, but it was worse. No real score, but there definitely was going to be a winner and a loser. He didn't want to be the loser.

He wanted to make her understand that just because he was a stuntman, that didn't mean he wasn't any less rational or dependable than any other man, when it came to his son.

He took a breath as he realized the obvious answer, even though most stuntmen didn't take their families with them on location. "Adam could come with me, if I had to travel. As long as he's not in school, that wouldn't be a problem." She listened without commenting, then looked down at her book and wrote quickly. Cade told himself she was just a woman, a person, a human being, as flawed as the next. Maybe she could be rational about his job. Maybe she was as human as the signs he could see indicated—the slightly vulnerable sweep of her jaw, the way she caught the tip of her tongue between her teeth while she wrote. He ran a hand over his face, and braced himself when she looked up at him.

"And how would you do that?" she asked.

He blinked, embarrassed he didn't know what she was talking about. "Do what?"

"Take the child with you."

Of course. "I would need live-in help, a nanny to go along with us. She can be with Adam when I can't. But he'll be where I am. I think that's important."

She wrote some more, then sat back and looked at him again for a long moment before asking, "When he gets older, what do you think Adam will think about your job?"

He remembered how he had been as a child, going to the movies, marveling at what stunt people could do. Nowadays the stunt business was even more remarkable, more stunning. If he were a child right now, he doubted he'd ever leave the movie theater. But he knew she wouldn't want to hear that. "I don't know. Being a boy, I suspect he'll think it's great, but..."

"But?" she prodded intently, her pen poised over the notebook page.

"I guess what's important is what *you* think about it, isn't it?"

Wrong thing to say, he told himself, as soon as he saw the way her finely arched brows tugged together in a frown. "Mr. Daniels, what I think personally isn't the point right now."

"But it is." He sat forward. "Dr. Lewis, what you think is *all*-important. You're the professional, the one the court trusts. What do *you* think about my job?"

He saw the way her tongue darted out to touch her lips and moisten them—a nervous gesture that in some way echoed his own tension. With a snap she closed her notebook. "I'll be honest with you, Mr. Daniels. I—"

He held up one hand, palm out. "Cade. Please call me Cade. I never think of anyone as Mr. Daniels, except my father, or my brother, when he's talking to one of his students."

She laid the pen on the notebook. "All right. I see the job of a stuntman as dangerous, risk-taking, chancy...a minute by minute gamble with your life...and your child's future and happiness."

He stood abruptly. What little optimism he'd allowed himself to feel died a surprisingly quick death. "Is that all, or do you want to add that I'm a maniac, too?"

Color rose into her cheeks as she scrambled to her feet and tossed the notebook and pen onto the cushions by her purse. "I never said that you—"

"You don't have to, Doc. I can see I've got as much chance of getting my son as I do of surviving a thousand-foot free-fall without a parachute."

Even higher color stained her skin. "Listen to me," she said in a breathless voice. "I never meant—"

"I know what you meant. And I'm sorry you feel that way. All I want is my son and to do what I do best to make money to support him. The two things aren't mutually exclusive. At least, I don't believe they are."

He heard her take one deep breath and saw the way the action tugged her jacket across her high breasts. "Mr. Dan...Cade. I came here to be an impartial observer, to listen, to learn. I'm sorry if I said the wrong thing." She paused, then finished in a rush. "But you had no right to get so angry."

Angry? He was totally frustrated. He wanted his child, and he knew he had to get through to this woman to obtain Adam. He took a mental step back and regrouped. Even though Evan had said they could do this together, he was really on his own; this was all up to him, the way everything had been in his life. "I'm sorry," he murmured. "You have to understand how important this is to me. I'd do anything for Adam, but the only thing I do well that makes money is stunt work. That's it. The bottom line. And I need money to be able to provide for my son."

"I do understand that."

He faced her across the low coffee table, hit by how tiny, yet how strong she was. He could almost see her gathering her professional control around her like armor. "You must have this happen all the time," he said, hoping that was the truth. "People getting upset and saying things that they shouldn't say."

"It's happened before," she conceded.

"And?"

"And what?"

"Did everything work out with those people, or did you write them off?"

She met his gaze directly, the blueness so intense that he had an urge to look away. But he didn't. "I stayed and did my best," she said.

He exhaled in a rush and raised both hands toward her, palms out. "All right. That's all I'm asking of you. To stay and do your best."

She hesitated for only a moment before slowly sitting down again and casting him a look from under her dark lashes. "It's my job. I'll stay."

Cade sat down, too, but on the edge of his seat. He leaned toward her. "And Adam *is* my child."

"Exactly," she responded.

Cade could feel a growing unsteadiness in his hands and pressed them on his knees for support. "Can we start again, Doc?"

"Yes, I think we should." She reached for the notebook and pen, then looked at Cade. "My name's Megan. Now, where were we?"

"At my job. I think I need to convince you that most stuntmen aren't a bunch of crazy, demented risk takers."

That brought a hesitant smile to her pale pink lips, an expression not fully realized, yet Cade could guess at the way it would enhance this lady's beauty. "You have to understand that everything I've heard and seen about stuntmen—"

"You got from the movie and television image of our profession, what the media gives out. Not the reality."

"What is the reality?"

How could he make her understand there were risks in the job, grave risks at times, but usually nothing greater than most people took every day? How could he explain that for him to fall out a window was as much of a gamble as someone else crossing the street in traffic? "Let me explain something to you, if I can. Everything is calculated. Everything is timed and choreographed down to the split second, with every precaution taken."

She sat forward, her blue eyes intent. "And if anything goes wrong when you're doing a stunt?"

"I improvise. I'm a professional. I have the knowledge to go in another direction or use another technique."

"There was a stuntman killed a few years ago—I remember reading about it—when he was doing a simple stunt, something on a motorcycle, and a stuntwoman was paralyzed and brought suit over it."

"There aren't any guarantees, and I admit this is a risky business. There's a chance of failure, but the odds are stacked in favor of success." He felt tension pulling at his shoulders and middle. "Isn't life really a series of chances, Doc? There are so-called normal people, lawyers and doctors, killed on the freeways or falling as they get out of the shower."

"But that's not job related. What I'm trying to say is, their children don't have to live with the idea that they might not see their dad again when he leaves the house in the morning."

"I know, and I understand what you're saying. No one wants to die, unless they're suicidal or crazy, and I'm neither. I don't plan on dying until I'm very old, after I've seen Adam's children and their children. If I could just show you..." His words trailed off as the answer came to him. He *could* show her. "I've got an idea. If you really want to do this right, if you really want to give the best-considered opinion you can?"

"Of course I do."

"I'm going on location with the new movie I told you about, and I'll be leaving in a week. You could come and see firsthand every phase of my work, how much thought goes into it, how the risks are minimized." He spoke more quickly when he saw the hesitation in her expression. "That would give you a chance to be totally informed and impartial in your recommendations to the court."

Megan watched Cade, feeling the intensity radiating from him, and knew he was right. She could really get to understand what he did, and it was a sensible, professional decision to do just that. But the idea of going away with him for any amount of time made her uneasy. "How long would it be for?"

"A day, two days, a week. Whatever amount of time it takes for you to see what you need to see. I'll be there until near Christmas probably, in a little town north of Dallas called Dedrick."

She looked at Cade and could literally feel the need in him to have her do this. But for her to leave right now, with the caseload she had, wasn't practical. "I don't know if I—"

"Doc, it's important," he cut in. "Just a day. Fly in and fly out. Or make it a vacation. Get away from your office for a while."

That struck a chord in Megan. This would be an excuse for her to get away, away from the chance of Frank contacting her. She did need to see this man in action, to understand what she could of his profession, and it would be work. "I suppose I could do that, for a day or two."

"Good, good," Cade breathed, the relief in his voice so obvious that Megan felt guilty about her real motives. "Why don't you fly out with me? It would save you money on the trip, and it would give me extra time, so I could explain things more completely to you."

Cade literally held his breath until Megan finally said, "Yes, I guess that would be all right. When would you leave?"

He felt slightly giddy with relief. She was at least going to give him a chance. "Friday." He felt as if he'd finally made some sort of passing grade with her, the concession to accompany him leaving a taste of victory, however slight, in his mouth. "I'll have to get back to you after I make the arrangements."

"Call my office and leave a message." She picked up her purse, took out a business card and handed it to Cade. "The number's on there."

He looked at the black-on-white card, then at the woman across from him. How much of a victory would there be, if she didn't change her mind once she saw the business first-hand? "I'll call you as soon as I can." He tucked her card into the pocket of his jacket, then sat back in his chair. "Tell me, does everything about Adam's custody ride on my career?"

She shook her head. "No, not everything. There's finances and emotional stability to be considered."

Whether *she* knew it or not, Cade knew she had him on every count. His sense of victory was completely gone as he grasped the arms of the chair. "What else do you need to know, Doc?"

"It was in the files that you've let Adam stay with the Sinclairs for over six months."

"That's right. From the end of May. Memorial Day weekend."

"And you've seen him two or three times since then, brief visits, in and out, no real quality time spent with him?"

"Quality time." He exhaled. "No, there hasn't been quality time, but you have to understand, there are some things that happen in this life that are so devastating, so all-encompassing that you don't have room for any more emotions right then. You can't function. You're drained, empty, with nothing left for anyone else."

Megan heard his words and the emotional edge in his deep voice. Doris Sinclair had insinuated that Cade hadn't loved her daughter, that he had never even wanted to be married, to have a child, but this man sounded as if he had cared so much that he had ceased to live when Lori Daniels died. What would it be like to have another person care so much for you that the rest of the world ceased to exist for him or her when you were gone? She couldn't begin to comprehend that.

No one had ever loved her like that, especially Frank, and she never wanted to feel like that about anyone herself. She could see the vulnerability in Cade, the pain. No, she didn't want that—ever.

Cade was staring at her, waiting, and she murmured, "I see," to skim past the awkward moment. "But why is it different now?"

His dark brows drew together over his hooded eyes. "I guess it's time to take a good, long look at what's left for me, and that includes my son. I need to get on with living. Having him with me is part of that process."

"But he doesn't even know you."

She regretted the comment when she saw the way Cade's face tightened. "I'm going to correct that as soon as I can."

"How?"

"I guess a start would be to spend some time with him before I leave for the Walters job." Without another word, he stood and crossed to a phone on a polished bar along the side of the room. He picked up the receiver and punched in a number, waited, then said, "Doris, it's Cade."

When Megan saw the way his hand tightened on the receiver, she felt like an intruder. So she looked out the windows at the distant city. But she couldn't shut out his voice. "I know, I know. I don't want to get into that. I just called to find out when I can see Adam again."

The silence on his end of the line went on for such a long time that Megan finally turned back to Cade. She wished she hadn't. She could see the muscle working in his jaw, while his knuckles whitened where his hand held the receiver. He pressed his free hand to his eyes, then exhaled on a harsh rush of air. "Doris, listen to me. I just want to see my son again. No, I want to spend some time with him, time alone. Just Adam and me, and—''

He stopped abruptly and slowly lowered the receiver. When he turned and saw Megan, he almost seemed surprised, as if he had forgotten all about her being there. Then he shrugged, a sharp motion of his shoulders. ''She won't let me see him again.'' He slipped off his jacket and laid it on the bar. ''She said that she didn't have to let me see him until the court case is settled.'' He tugged at his tie, freeing it from his collar. ''Is that true?''

Megan stood, very aware of the man's confusion and pain. ''Yes, I'm afraid it is, but if you go to court, you'll be sure to get visitation rights. The problem is, it would take as much time to get it through the courts as it would for the hearing to come up on the calendar.''

His mouth tightened into a grim line. ''Why can't I just go in that house and walk out with him?''

''The Sinclairs wouldn't let you do that without a terrible fight.''

''I know, but don't I have some inherent right to be with my child?''

She almost said he hadn't really been with the boy for half a year, and that a few more weeks could hardly make much of a difference. Then she saw the pain in his dark eyes. Although she dealt with people in varying degrees of pain in her work, she knew that most of this man's pain wasn't necessary. He'd obviously had enough of it since his wife died. He didn't need any more. She went closer, not knowing what she was going to do until she got within two feet of him.

Impulsively Megan reached out to him, her hand touching his arm. She could feel the tension vibrating in his muscles under the fine material of the shirt, and knew the contact was a mistake. It might have given him some comfort, but the gesture only made her thoughts get tangled up in the body heat she felt under her fingertips. She drew back quickly, unable to deal with that right now. "I think I can get you in to see him, if you want me to," she offered.

His eyes, dark and brooding, met hers. "Doc, do whatever it takes."

"I need to see Adam in his present home environment, and, if I think it would be beneficial to see you with him, I can take you with me to the Sinclair house. Actually I need to see interchange between all the parties concerned."

"All right, Doc, when can you get me in?" he asked.

"I need to make a call and find out."

Without another word, Cade tossed the tie on top of his jacket and reached for the receiver. He held it out to Megan, and she took it quickly to avoid further contact. With only a quick, slanting glance at the tense Cade, she pushed the Redial button.

When Cade drove his Jeep through the open, wrought iron gates onto the grounds of Doris and Leo's colonial-style home two days later, he saw Megan's Mercedes parked near the expanse of brick steps that led up to the formal entry. He pulled up next to the sleek, blue car, then stepped out into the chill of the November afternoon. With just a cursory glance around, he turned to the front of the three-story house.

A pretentious mansion, he'd always thought. That idea hadn't changed. With ten bedrooms and as many baths, and antiques that would do a museum proud, the brick and white wood structure was more of a showplace than a home. With all its formality he'd never felt comfortable in the house, and had no idea how a little boy could grow up here.

Almost before he had left the Jeep, the leaded-glass door opened and the maid, a small, Spanish girl, looked out at him.

"Ah, Mr. Daniels, they are expecting you."

He wanted to see Adam, but since Megan had made the appointment, he'd begun to wonder if making this visit was the right thing to do. Why was he going willingly into the lion's den? Doris and Leo were certainly not going to welcome him with open arms. And Megan had been right. Adam wouldn't even remember him.

Yet that was why he was here. His son didn't even know him. He strode toward the entry, ignoring the nervousness that tied a knot in his stomach. He'd go inside, ignore whatever Doris and Leo said and be with his child. He'd hold Adam—feel the reality of his son in his arms. He swallowed hard. He just hoped he would be able to be rational and walk away when he had to leave. Ideas of grabbing Adam and running flitted through his mind, then he killed them. He had to be so careful if he wanted to legally get Adam back into his world.

Cade had to swallow hard to ease the tightness in his throat, then he took the brick steps two at a time, went through the door the maid held open and into the cavernous foyer. He barely glanced at the sweeping, circular stairway or the crystal and marble as he turned to the maid. "Where are they, Rosa?"

"In the sun room, sir," she said. "I'll take you—"

"Never mind. I know the way," he murmured and turned to the left. He strode across the black and white marble floor, stepped down into the leather and oak library and went through it to a short hallway that led to the south side of the house.

With just a few more steps he was at the louvered doors of the sun room. There he stopped and using a prestunt relaxation technique, he slowly rotated his head and took a few, cleansing breaths. So much was riding on the next few minutes.

Then he pushed back the door and stepped onto the stone floor of the large, glass and wood room that was filled with plants and light and heat. As he entered, the first person he saw was Megan. She sat in one of the high, circular-backed, wicker chairs, and the thought that she looked like a ray of sunlight in a land that held nothing but gloom came without warning. The pure light in the room had turned the highlights in her hair to a rich copper, and her skin, almost translucent, took on a luminous tone.

The drab suit was gone in favor of a soft yellow silk blouse with long sleeves and a calf-length black pleated skirt. Her hair, falling in soft curls to her shoulders, was restrained only by two silver combs above her ears. When she looked up at him and smiled, he almost stopped in his tracks. The expression of spontaneous welcome hit him right behind his breastbone, radiating a shock wave of heat through every part of his body.

When she stood and held out her hand to him as he kept moving toward her, he almost didn't touch her. He had no idea why he thought that if he made that physical contact, he would cross some unseen boundary. He didn't understand what that would mean or where it would lead him. But he was acutely aware of the gamble he was taking.

You've been too long without a woman, he told himself, grasping at a simple physical reason for the effect Megan was having on him. He knew if he tried too hard to make sense of it, he couldn't, so he took the easy way out and accepted his own, simple rationale as he held his hand out to her.

Then she spoke in the soft voice that always played havoc with his already raw nerves. "Hello. We'd just about given up on you." Her fingers closed around his rough calluses with a comforting, supportive pressure, and he found himself stammering.

"I—I had to stop for gas. I'm sorry...if I'm late."

"Well," she said, drawing back, leaving a sense of loss in him as the contact was broken. "We're certainly glad you came." She looked to her left. "Aren't we, Adam?"

It took Cade a full heartbeat to focus on what she was saying, then he turned to the mesh playpen to his right and saw his child. A tiny human being in blue shorts over bulky diapers, a white T-shirt and high-topped, white boots, Adam stood on his toes. His chocolate-brown eyes stared solemnly up at Cade. Cade was stunned at how welcome the sight of his child was to him—and how strongly the urge to scoop up Adam and run was at that moment.

Suddenly Adam crinkled his nose and lifted a chubby fist that held what could once have been a cookie. Now it was mashed and oozing between the tiny fingers. "Ga, ga, ga," he chanted, waving the mess in Cade's direction.

Cade moved slowly to the playpen and dropped to his haunches. He touched the side and had to try twice to get words past the lump in his throat. "Hi, Adam. I came to see you."

"Ga, ga, gak!" the boy squealed.

"Yeah, I know," Cade said, wondering how he could feel so much like a father, when he didn't have the first idea of what to do.

While Cade tried to sort through his reactions, the child jerked his hand open and upward, and in the process tossed the destroyed cookie into the air. Crumbs and chunks rained down onto his dark curls and into the playpen, then he let out a piercing squeal and promptly flopped down, landing solidly on his bottom.

He looked again at Cade with his deep brown eyes. "Ga, ga, gak!" He smiled a huge smile that showed four, snowy-white teeth, two on the top and two on the bottom. Cade hadn't known that Adam had teeth already. The impact of realizing what he *should* know about this child and what he *did* know almost left him light-headed.

Adam cocked his head to one side, then scrambled on his knees to the mesh side and pulled himself up again. "Ga, ga, gak!" he screamed again.

"I heard the baby—?"

Not now, not now, Cade thought, but knew he had to face his mother-in-law. Awkwardly patting Adam's hand, he stood and turned as Doris hurried into the room. The tall, thin woman looked as perfect as ever, her silver hair styled in a cap cut that accentuated her narrow face, now pulled into an intense frown. If Lori had lived, he figured she would eventually have looked a lot like her mother. Strange he could think that now and not flinch from it.

Then he felt Adam hit his leg and looked down at his son. The youngster held out his arms, clearly wanting to be picked up, and it seemed so natural for Cade to reach down and pull the child into his arms. Adam felt solid and heavy, nothing like the feathery-light infant he'd been, and it was an oddly comforting sensation until Doris spoke again.

"Playing Daddy?" she asked in a particularly strident tone of voice.

Cade felt a tiny hand press against his cheek, the hand that still had mashed cookie clinging to it, but he made himself focus on the older woman. "Hello, Doris," he said, aware of Megan coming to stand at his side. For the length of a heartbeat he had the urge to reach out his free hand and hold on to her, almost the way a drowning man would reach out to a rescuer. Then he brought himself up short. Not only could she not rescue him, she was more likely to be the one throwing him overboard, if he blew this custody suit for Adam. He was in this alone.

Megan had been surprised by how much the child looked like his father when she first saw Adam. Now, with the toddler in his father's arms, she wondered if Cade had looked like that when he was a year old. The brown eyes, the silky, dark curls, the smile with the dimples were all there.

Cade held Adam but seemed to be paying no attention to the tiny bits of cookie that were being rubbed into his cheek and onto the shoulder of his impeccable, beige suit.

"I was wondering if you would really show up," Doris said.

Megan looked from Cade to Doris, then back again. She could see the way his jaw was working, yet his voice stayed even and controlled. "I almost ran out of gas," he replied.

Doris came farther into the room, never taking her eyes off Cade. "You've run out of more than gas, Cade," she declared, her voice low and vibrating with intensity.

"So I have," he agreed without an argument.

"And now you really intend to drag this poor baby into your life?"

As if he could sense the tension in the room, Adam began to squirm and without warning, let out a loud, piercing cry of distress. His hands flailed, hitting his father squarely on the cheek. Cade looked shocked, then suddenly awkward and out of place holding a crying child.

Megan's first instinct was to reach out and take the youngster to comfort him and help Cade. But before she could do anything, Doris was calling, "Thelma! Thelma!" A heavyset woman dressed in white hurried into the room. "Take the child upstairs," Doris told her. "And see to it that he gets his nap. He's had a difficult time today."

Cade made no effort to fight her command, and Megan thought he even seemed relieved to hand the boy to the woman in white. "See you later, champ," he said, ruffling the dark curls and ignoring the child's increased crying.

As the nanny left the room and the screams faded, Megan saw Doris take a step closer to Cade. "He doesn't need you. He doesn't want you. He probably doesn't even like you. Why, in heaven's name, do you think you have to play at being Daddy now?"

Megan had figured Cade's mother-in-law would have hard feelings, but she hadn't expected this pure, raging anger in the older woman.

"He's my son, Doris," Cade said in a low, intense voice.

Megan looked at the woman, stunned by the cold hatred she could see in her eyes. "He's nothing to you, Cade. You go on a six-month binge, drop by a few times to do little more than look at Adam, then you sober up and decide, 'Hey, I think I might want to be a daddy for a while.' Well, that doesn't cut it. You're nothing to him. Nothing!"

Cade took a deep, unsteady breath and grunted, "He's my son, my child, not yours."

Before Megan knew what was happening, Doris was striking out at Cade, but in one swift movement Cade caught her by the wrist, stopping the slap before it had really begun.

"Oh, no, you don't," he growled, then slowly lowered her hand and let it go. "We have to get on with life, Doris. We have to put the past behind us. God knows, I'm trying to."

"Oh, wouldn't you like that, to turn your back on everything." Doris Sinclair rubbed her wrist, the same tears that choked her voice welling up into her eyes. "Wouldn't you like to forget you killed our Lori."

Megan turned to Cade, waiting for the denials. His wife had died in a car crash—alone. There hadn't been anyone with her. Cade had been on the set of a movie he was working on. Megan knew that and waited for Cade to deal with the woman's irrational attack.

But instead she saw a spasm of pain twist his face, then he closed his eyes for a moment. When he looked at Doris again, his dark eyes were bleak, and he spoke in a low, rough voice. "No, I can never forget that."

Chapter 4

After Cade uttered the words, Megan looked at Doris. It was as if whatever had supported the woman since she'd entered the room had been taken from her. The slender woman groped behind her with one hand, grasping the white rattan arm of the nearest chair, then slowly sank onto the floral cushion.

"See the boy, then leave," she said, her eyes on the flagstone floor and her voice so low that Megan could hardly make out the words. "I don't want you in this house any longer than you have to be."

Cade stared at her, his jaw working, but didn't say anything to her. Instead he turned to Megan; she saw that a tinge of paleness had overlaid his tan. "Are you coming with me?"

"Yes...of course," she said and went to get her purse and jacket that she'd left by her chair. By the time she turned, Cade was walking out of the room and she hurried after him. When she drew abreast of Doris, the woman stopped her by uttering her name.

"Dr. Lewis?"

Megan paused and saw Cade step through the door and disappear from view. She turned to Doris. "Yes?"

"Do what you have to do, then get him out of here... please."

Megan watched Doris, who never looked up from the floor while she spoke. "What...did you mean by saying Cade killed your daughter?"

The older woman's hands, heavy with the flash of diamonds, slowly balled into fists on the fine material of her elegant black dress. "The man ruins everything he touches. That's why I won't let him get a hold of this child. He mustn't." Doris looked up at Megan with overly bright eyes, and intensity made the woman's voice shake. "Do you understand, Doctor? He mustn't."

"That's for the courts to decide, Mrs. Sinclair. It's not up to me."

"But you are the one who can tell them that the child is better here than with that man. Surely there must be some way you can make sure he doesn't get the baby. We are wealthy people, and there must be something I can do to help you see..."

Megan shook her head to stop the woman from saying any more. "I'll evaluate the situation fairly. I promise you that, and that's all I can do."

Doris flicked one hand at Megan. "Then get on with it. I don't want that man in this house longer than necessary."

Megan knew then that Doris Sinclair really hated Cade. But enough to accuse him of killing her daughter? The irrational rantings of a bereaved parent? "We'll be out of here soon, and I'll be in touch with you tomorrow," she murmured, then turned and headed for the door.

She stepped into the next room and was surprised to find Cade standing there at the windows, not more than ten feet from the door of the sun room. He was very still, both hands pressed, palms flat, against the glass, his head bowed. Had he heard what Doris had said about him? He must have. Every line and angle in his body screamed with tension, and she found herself doing the same thing she'd done at his house yesterday, after he'd talked to Doris on the phone.

She went closer and reached out, touching him on the shoulder. She felt him jerk, then his hands dropped and she drew back as Cade turned to look at her, his eyes narrowed.

"Are you all right?"

"So, you didn't go for it, eh?"

"Go for it?"

"The bribe."

"There wasn't any bribe." But Megan knew that Doris's words had been heading in that direction, and they only underscored the woman's determination to keep Cade away from Adam. "We don't have much time..."

"I know. She wants me out of here. Actually, she felt the same way when Lori was alive, but then she tolerated me for Lori's sake. Now she doesn't have to." He glanced down at her purse. "Is your notebook ready?"

"For what?"

"Isn't that what this is all about? You observing me with Adam and taking copious notes?"

"I'll depend on my memory this time," she said, putting her jacket over her arm and adjusting her purse strap. "Are you ready?"

No, Cade wasn't. That was why he'd been late getting to the Sinclair house. The possibility of running out of gas on the way had looked like a blessing—for a few minutes. This had gone worse than he'd imagined, down to the fact that Adam really had no idea who he was. That hurt most of all. "Sure, I'm ready," he lied. "Let's go.'

He heard Doris call out to her maid in the sun room and headed away from the echo of her voice. He knew where he was going, and he didn't want to wait around for the old lady to send an escort. He could hear Megan behind him, her heels clicking on the tiles, then they were in the foyer at the bottom of the stairs.

"Cade?" Megan gasped in a soft voice.

As he stopped and turned, she almost ran into him and he touched her shoulders, steadying her. The contact shot fire through him, the reaction coming from nowhere to center in his chest. Quickly he drew back. "What is it?"

"Can we go slower? I feel as if I'm running the hundred-yard dash."

"Sorry," he murmured, pushing his hands behind his back before he reached to touch her again, to test, to see if the same thing would happen again. "I guess my legs are a bit longer than yours."

"A lot longer," she said with a suggestion of a smile.

The fleeting expression was as much of a jolt to him as the contact had been moments earlier. But totally different. It hinted at softness and gentleness, something in this life that was honest and direct. "Let's go...slowly," he said, turning from her before he did something foolish like reaching out to touch her cheek, to feel the softness under his hand.

He headed for the stairs, taking them slowly, sensing Megan beside him, but not looking. He kept his eyes on each step he took as he went higher. When he got to the top and stepped onto the balcony that looked over the foyer, he paused for just a moment, then caught the delicate scent of Megan's perfume to his right. He turned away from it and headed down the wide hall, lined with exquisite, original oil paintings. The tapestry runner underfoot muffled any noise their shoes would make.

He headed for the last door, then pushed it open and looked into Adam's room. Red, white and blue were the dominant colors, and toys were everywhere; the twenty-by-forty-foot space seemed filled to overflowing with the things of a child.

The brass crib sat in the middle of everything under a round canopy, suspended from a vaulted ceiling that had been painted to look exactly like the sky on a clear, summer's day. Disney Babies murals in bright, primary colors ran around the perimeter, and the windows opposite the door were shaded with scalloped blinds in red, white and blue stripes. A plush giraffe, at least ten feet tall, stood in a pile of stuffed toys by the door, his head hanging just a bit.

A child's delight, Cade had to concede, but really overkill. "Thelma," he said to the nanny standing over the crib, "we won't need you for now."

The dark-haired woman looked at him, then at Megan, who'd come up beside him. "Doctor?" she asked.

"It's all right. We're going to visit for a while. Go and see to Mrs. Sinclair. I think she might need you."

The woman cast Cade an uncertain look, then left, closing the door behind her.

Cade crossed to the crib and looked down at Adam, who lay on his stomach, his diapered bottom in the air, his eyes closed. He'd fallen asleep. The crying episode obviously hadn't had any lasting effect. Cade reached out, gently ruffling the silky curls that lay against the child's delicate skin. But he was totally aware of Megan moving to the other side of the crib, and a sudden thought rocked through him. Would Megan's skin feel as soft and silky as it looked, if he dared touch her?

Today was all out of balance for him; his emotions were obviously distorted. Adam looked so innocent, so peaceful. How Cade wished he had an iota of that peace in his own life. "I don't remember him crying so hard then going to sleep this quickly, but . . ." His voice trailed off before he admitted that he'd seldom seen Adam when he was an infant. Location shoots had kept him away from home more days than he cared to think about now.

"Babies are very resilient. They're a lot stronger than people give them credit for," Megan said in a low voice.

Megan was watching Adam. "How much does Adam know right now?" Cade asked her.

She looked up at him, her incredible eyes partially veiled by her long lashes. At least he was getting used to the impact he felt when their gazes met. That was something. "A child knows when he's loved, when he's safe, when he's cared for. And he knows when he's not loved or safe or cared for."

"But he doesn't have a clue who I am, does he?"

She shrugged, a fluttery motion of her slender shoulders under her silky, yellow blouse. "Children learn who loves them by being with that person. You've admitted that you haven't spent a great deal of time with him, and his memory's pretty short."

He hated to have her lay out his deficiencies with such unerring accuracy. "Thank goodness for that," he said. "Maybe he won't remember all of this, when it's over and done."

"Can I ask you something?"

"Go ahead," he said, straightening up and drawing his hand back to close his fingers around the smooth coolness of the side rail. "You're the doctor."

That didn't bring any suggestion of a smile from Megan, just a direct question. "Why do you want Adam?"

He had thought that was obvious, but apparently she needed it spelled it. "I'm his father. He's my son. I want to have him with me."

"But why?" she persisted, her gaze never faltering.

"Why would any parent want his or her child with them?" he countered.

She exhaled softly. "There are lots of reasons parents want their children. The nice ones are loving and caring and nurturing. Then the not so nice ones are greedy, selfish, vengeful, trying to cause others pain."

The way her elegantly lashed eyes grew hard and cold shocked Cade. Then he thought about what she must deal with on a day-to-day basis. The misery of broken families and the reasons behind the breaks. "Your business is pretty rough, isn't it?"

She blinked, as if shocked by his statement, yet it seemed logical to him. "My business? Yes, it can be really hard. But life's hard."

He had the urge to tell her he'd make sure that her life wasn't like that, that she'd always have sun and roses and happiness. But the foolishness of the impulse rendered him speechless. Nothing was making sense to him right now. "Yes, life's hard, but it's even harder on a child without a father."

He could have sworn that his words, spoken just to fill spaces, just to agree with her and not to say something he'd regret, had actually caused her pain.

She moved away from the crib, put her purse and jacket on a stool, then crossed to the pile of stuffed toys. She didn't speak again until she reached out to touch the brown-spotted giraffe. "Having a father doesn't guarantee happiness," she said in a flat tone. Then she turned to him. "Why do you want Adam?"

He wished he knew what she wanted him to say, but had no clue, so he spoke as honestly as he could. "Because I need him. And I think he needs me."

"Why does he need you?"

He studied her. There was a professionally neutral expression on her face now, and it made him edgy. As if she were hiding behind that mask, not about to let him know what she was thinking. "Is this where I'm supposed to lie on a couch and bare my soul?" he asked, nerves making his stomach hurt.

"No, just be as honest as you can be."

"I thought I was being honest."

"I didn't say you weren't." She came back to the crib, but never looked at Adam. Her gaze held Cade's. "I was just trying to figure out why Adam is suddenly important to you. A child needs to be wanted for himself, not for what he can do for the parent. It's the worst thing in the world to be used by the one person in this world who should love you unconditionally."

The professional mask slipped, just enough for Cade to think he saw pain in her eyes, before she looked down at Adam. This wasn't just a business to her, obviously. She was emotionally involved. "I imagine it would be," he said.

She was still for a very long time before she finally drew in a breath and spoke, without looking again at Cade. "It is. At least, I imagine it is. Probably as painful for a child as being an orphan."

"Are you an orphan?"

That brought her eyes up; he saw that the mask was back in place. "As good as," she muttered and let go of the crib. "But we aren't talking about me. We're talking about you and your child. And the Sinclairs."

Doris had accused him of killing Lori. As guilty as Cade felt, he knew he couldn't let that go. And he knew Megan wasn't about to. He had to tell her things he hadn't wanted to when this all started, things he had wanted to ignore, hide from. But he couldn't. He took a breath. "My business manager told me to be completely honest with you. And I think that's the way it has to be. There are things I need to explain, but I don't want to do it at your office, on a couch, while you answer my questions with questions."

"Would you feel better if I told you I don't have a couch?"

He looked at the way the diffused light in the room cast gentle shadows onto her cheeks and throat. She was a beautiful woman, too beautiful to be a doctor who played God with people's lives. He had to make her understand what he was and what he wasn't. And he had to get past his reactions to her. They weren't relevant to any of this. He had to concentrate on Adam.

Megan was thankful to push away the memories that this discussion was stirring up, memories of Frank wanting her with him for his own reasons. She was glad to forget the time when he'd actually put her between himself and a man who had come "collecting." *"You wouldn't hurt a child, would you?"* Frank had asked. The other man had looked down at the eight-year-old Megan, disgust for Frank clear in his eyes. He'd reached out and touched Megan on the head.

She could still feel the weight of his hand resting there while he spoke to Frank. *"This is a new low, Lewis. I'll be back after the kid's gone."* Frank had made very sure Megan went everywhere with him for over a week, until that man had been replaced by another and another and another, men who didn't care if a child got caught in the middle of their sordid dealings.

"What things?" she asked Cade.

He looked at her, then crossed his arms on his chest. "Did you ever get in the car and just drive? Just take off and go, without any idea of where you were going or what you wanted to see?''

Megan was angry that his words kept conjuring up the past. There had been a day when she'd done that very thing to get away from Frank. He'd been in jail a month, calling her collect, writing letters to her that she'd never opened. She'd made her escape and ended up driving almost to San Francisco, before she'd realized she was letting him run her life again.

"Of course I have," she said. "Why?"

"That's the way I've been most of my life. My parents are teachers, staid, solid, reliable, dependable. I love them, but their life suffocated me. My brother is an archaeologist. He can spend years on a fragment of bone, trying to date it and figure out where it came from."

"So?" she prodded.

He raked his fingers through his thick hair. "So, I'm trying to figure out how to say the rest."

"Just say it."

"All right. You can see that Doris hates me."

Megan touched the cold brass of the crib rail. "She's been through a lot."

"Yes, she has. And she's got every right to hate me."

Megan could feel the tightness in her chest. She had to swallow hard before she could manage to ask the question that had to be answered. "How on earth are you responsible for your wife's death?"

Cade turned abruptly and walked to the bank of windows at the rear of the room. He stared outside and when he spoke, it wasn't an answer to her question. "I never wanted to be married," he said. "I'm sure, if Doris hasn't told you this by now, she soon will. I met Lori at a party, thought she was beautiful, and didn't think much about anything past that."

He turned to Megan. "Go ahead, Doc. You can label it. I was irresponsible, probably stupid, and not thinking about much past the moment. Eat, drink and be merry, et cetera."

"I don't label people. That's not my job."

"Everyone else does," he countered.

"Let's forget labels. Just tell me what you wanted to say."

"Sure, why not? I saw Lori for a couple of weeks, maybe five dates, tops. I knew before the last date that there wasn't anything there, nothing substantial enough to keep up a relationship."

Megan heard confessions all the time in her profession, but had never had the sensation of literally being able to see into someone's soul, the way she did now. The expression in Cade's eyes was direct, almost neutral, but she could sense what it had taken him to tell her all of this. "What happened?"

"A month after I saw Lori for the last time, she showed up on the set of a movie I was working on. They let her on, because they thought she was with me. She was waiting in my trailer when I finished the stunt. I can remember thinking, how on earth can I get her out of here without a scene?" His gaze dropped to the floor. "I didn't have to worry. She was unusually calm while she told me she was pregnant, that the child was mine, and that she wanted us to be together."

Megan looked down at the sleeping toddler, speaking what she thought. "Adam looks a lot like you."

"I know. He's mine, all right," Cade said. "Oh, I tried to deny it at first, using the usual arguments, like how did she know I was the only one? None of them worked."

She looked back at Cade, at his broad shoulders and the way his hands were clasped tightly behind his back. "How did she get pregnant?" she asked.

"I asked myself that a lot. In this day and age, with contraceptives on every store shelf, it seems crazy. But I forgot protection and Lori assured me she was on the pill. Later she told me the pill had made her feel fat and gave her headaches. So she skipped a few. Enough to get pregnant."

He ran both hands over his face, then looked at Megan. "I married her a week later." He came nearer the crib, stopping just a few feet from the railing. "What I'm trying to tell you, Doc, what I'm admitting to, is that I was a terrible husband. I was never meant for it. I know the buzzwords you would use—inability to bond, dysfunctional. I should have never even tried marriage, but, despite my lifestyle, I found out that I actually have a core of traditionalism in me. I found out that I believed that a child should be born into a family, with a father and a mother together under the same roof, and raised that way."

"So, you made a family," she murmured.

"A poor facsimile of one. I was away on location when Adam was born. I didn't even see him until he was four days old. By that time I knew the marriage was a joke."

"Did your wife know you only married her because of the pregnancy?"

"Yes, she knew."

"Why did she agree to it? She had everything here, and surely, having a child without marriage isn't the same stigma it used to be?"

"Lori didn't worry about what people thought." He smiled, a tight, humorless expression. "She only thought about Lori. She thought she was going to get included in the *real* Hollywood if she married me, that we'd be at parties all the time, mingling with stars." The chuckle was harsh and abrupt. "All I mingle with is other stuntmen, and Lori hated every one of them."

Megan tried to keep some distance from the man, to maintain a semblance of professional balance, but the more Cade talked, the more she could tell he was a man torn. He was a traditionalist who wanted to be a rebel. He had married to do the right thing. Now he had a child.

"How do you think you'll bring Adam up?"

"The best way I can."

"And what's your best?"

He stared at her hard. "I love him. He's mine. I'll go the whole nine yards for him."

"He's not a possession," she countered, remembering the way she had been one for Frank, something to get him what he wanted, a means to an end. Never a daughter. "He's a human being, who deserves to have a good life."

"And you don't think I can give it to him?"

"I don't know. That's what this is all about."

"I can't give him all of this," he said, sweeping his hand at the room around them. "But I make damned good money at what I do."

"It's a hard way to make a living," she said bluntly.

He sucked in air, needing to steady himself against her words. "There are harder ways, believe me," he said. "I know what you think about my work. What I'm hoping you don't think is, if I washed out at marriage, I'll wash out at fatherhood."

"I don't have any absolutes yet. All I have to go on is what I can see and hear and observe. That's why I agreed to go to Texas with you. I want to be impartial, to do what's best for the child."

"Listen, Doc—" When Adam stirred, Cade came around the crib, so close that Megan could see a pulse beat just under his ear. He lowered his voice and asked, "Do you think this is right for the child? Is being spoiled and indulged and pampered right? Is having a parent who's sane and safe and stuck in a dead-end job the right thing?''

"The right thing for whom?" she asked softly.

Cade exhaled harshly. "For anyone."

"I don't deal in abstracts. I deal in reality."

He reached out suddenly, without warning, cupping her chin in a callused hand. "Let's get one thing straight between us, Doc."

She stared up at him, stunned by the sudden contact and the heat of his touch on her skin. She could barely focus on what he was saying. "What?"

His hold tightened just a fraction as he spoke in a rough, tight voice. "Reality is that I will do *anything*, whatever it takes to have my child with me permanently."

She moved her head back, shocked that a simple touch from this man could send waves of sensation through her whole body. She gripped the brass of the bed so tightly that her hand began to tingle. She turned from Cade and looked down at the child sleeping so peacefully.

She envied Adam that peace, his sureness that life would go on, no matter what. She knew that she didn't want to do anything to snatch that away from him until he was old enough to totally understand. She'd had it taken from her when she was six. Completely. Totally. No, she wouldn't let that happen to Adam Daniels.

She held tightly to the side of the crib, then made herself look at the boy's father. "You should understand something, too."

"What's that?" he asked in a low voice.

"The only thing that matters to me is what's best for Adam. Period."

He studied her silently, then unexpectedly spoke out of context. "We leave for Texas, Friday afternoon at one o'clock, from Burbank Airport. Go to the information center when you get there. They'll tell you what gate we fly out of."

Megan watched Cade reach down and touch Adam on the hand. "See you later, buddy," he whispered, then straightened and looked at Megan. "I'll see you in three days, Doc," he said, then walked away and out of the room.

Adam stirred fitfully in his sleep, and Megan reached out, patting the child gently on his back, crooning softly to him until he settled again. Yes, she would do whatever was right for this tiny human being. She stood straight when she heard a door in the distance shut with an echoing crack and turned toward the empty entrance.

Go to Texas, see Cade do whatever he did for a living, then get back here and make her decision. Megan had never felt God-like, doing what she did, but right now she wished she had a modicum of the wisdom of Solomon.

Cade spent three days and three nights alone at his house. He talked on the phone to Ross Barnette in Texas, outlining what he needed for the gag and going over possibilities for variations on what Walters wanted.

He worked out in the gym he'd had built behind his garage and used the trampoline on the lawn overlooking the bluffs. By the time he stepped out of the sauna Thursday night, he felt reasonably sure that he'd figured out how to do the gag and that he was in good enough physical condition to see it through.

He grabbed a towel from the cupboard, then briskly rubbed at his skin as he stepped into the silent bedroom. Cade felt inordinately aware of the fact that this room, this house and his life were very empty. He was alone. He'd never sensed this before and had no idea where it came from now. He'd missed people—his parents and Ethan—but he'd never felt lonely.

God, the loneliness ate at him. It made him feel as if the world was gone and he was the last survivor. He'd meant it when he told Megan that he needed Adam. Needed him badly. Needed him here.

He crossed to the bed and tossed the towel onto the side table, then dropped onto the bed and fell into the coolness of the sheets. Megan. He could need her, in an entirely different way, if he let himself. Stupid, foolish ideas were still in his mind, ideas that had grown since he'd first heard her on the phone.

"Dumb," he muttered and closed his eyes.

What he needed was a woman here and now, someone to hold on to, to hold him, to share warmth, to stop the loneliness.

He threw a forearm over his eyes. No, that wouldn't work. He knew that a warm body was far from what he really needed. He needed intelligence and humor and sensuality, all rolled up into one person. And he'd never found that. In all his life he'd never found it.

God knows, he'd tried often enough.

"A real failure," he muttered and sighed, his voice echoing strangely in the total silence around him.

His body ached, his muscles were sore and tested, but he felt as if he'd done something right. He'd got the job with Walters at a good rate—for the complicated gag and for helping with a few other, minor stunts. He'd made the decision to fight for Adam. And he would make Megan see that he might not be perfect, but that he'd do his level best to be what Adam needed.

There she was again, intruding on his thoughts, and his body involuntarily responded to the image that flashed through his mind. With a groan he rolled onto his side, pushing the images away and making himself relax. He

needed sleep, a night of uninterrupted rest, because tomorrow the work would begin in earnest.

For several minutes he went over in his mind some of the
information Ross had given him, on what Walters expected
and the way he planned on making the effect a reality.
Gradually he slipped into an exhausted sleep.

One minute he was relaxed and totally aware that he was
sleeping, then the next he was in a storm, a bone-chilling,
drenching hurricane that ripped at him. He was alone,
somewhere dark, standing, facing the onslaught, knowing
he couldn't survive it.

The pain and cold were everywhere; his soul hurt, that
particle deep in his being that made him what he was. And
he cried out, a muffled sound of pain that died when he felt
hands on his bare shoulders, warm, gentle, healing hands;
the hurt inside began to fade.

He turned slowly in the dream, seeing shadows and uniformed images in the darkness, then he was being held
tightly, protected from the storm all around. As the pain
diminished, something else took its place. Something akin
to the pain in its intensity, yet at the opposite end of the
spectrum.

The fire of passion ripped through him, and he became
intently aware of the woman holding him, the pressure of
her breasts against his bare chest, her hips fitted to his, her
legs tangling with his. He fell backward with her, farther,
farther until they lay on softness, suspended above reality,
and his passion was matched by hers.

Chapter 5

Her hands were touching, caressing, knowing him in a way Cade had never experienced before. Fingers played across the small of his back, the breadth of his shoulders, the span of his chest. And everywhere they touched they left fire, a healing fire that seemed to burn away every bit of agony Cade had harbored for what seemed forever.

He knew it couldn't be, that one person's touch couldn't make right all the wrongs in the world, that one person's touch couldn't make his soul feel whole again. Yet this woman he didn't know, this woman he couldn't see, was doing just that.

Then she spoke, saying words that flowed around him in a voice that was achingly gentle in his ears. The heat of her breath feathered across his naked skin, making his whole body begin to respond in the most basic way. The pleasure gave way to need, and that need drove him to draw back and look down at the woman under him.

Megan. There was no shock when he recognized her, just acceptance. He took in the sight of her, the burnished halo of her silky hair on the pure white of the bed where they lay; her eyes, heavy with desire, shaded by impossibly long lashes. The sweep of her throat, the fullness of breasts that were small, but perfect, their rosy peaks hard nubs, showing her own need for him.

His body ached for hers, it throbbed and came to life with needing and wanting. It demanded a knowledge of her in the most intimate way, yet the more that need grew, the more distant she seemed from him. The sense of her beneath him began to diminish at the same rate his desire grew. And frustration all but choked him.

He reached out to touch her, just to trace the line of her jaw, feel the sleek heat of her skin, cup her breasts or taste the essence on his lips, but there was nothing. Nothing.

Consciousness came with a sickening jolt as agony flooded back to fill his soul, and he knew he was awake and alone. His rapid breathing echoed in the stillness all around him, and as he opened his eyes to a room in complete darkness, he felt a cold breeze from the open doors drift across his naked body. The currents of chilly air robbed him of any lingering sensation of Megan's touch in his dream.

Muttering a curse of total frustration, he rolled to his side and stumbled off the bed. After freeing himself from the tangle of sheets around his legs, he crossed to close out the cold and the night. With the doors shut, the cold began to dissipate, but Cade, as he stood in the shadows of his empty room, couldn't deny the remaining physical evidence of what the dream had done to him. And he knew he wouldn't be able to easily shut Megan Lewis out of his thoughts tonight.

When Megan went to Burbank Airport on Friday to meet Cade, she checked in at the information desk just before one o'clock. The uniformed clerk looked down at her notes, then gave her a gate number at the farthest end of the terminal and said, "Someone will meet you there."

Megan thanked the middle-aged woman, picked up her garment bag and headed down the busy corridor. As the low heels of her leather pumps clicked on the hard floor, she caught sight of herself in the sheets of glass that fronted the souvenir and magazine shops along the way. She'd skimmed her hair back from her face into a low knot and chosen an ivory linen suit to wear with an ice-blue blouse. The look had seemed sensible when she'd dressed earlier, but now she wondered if she'd overdressed.

Texas. It conjured up images of jeans and boots and plaid shirts. At least she'd thought to pack some casual clothes, she reflected, as she shifted the bag to her other hand, looked ahead and kept walking. What she wore or didn't wear wasn't at all important. It was getting this case finished, one way or another.

When she got to the departure gate and set her bag by her feet, leaning it against her leg, she saw a short, heavyset man in a plain, black suit coming toward her.

"Dr. Lewis?" he asked as he approached her.

"Yes," she said, readjusting the strap of her leather purse on her shoulder. "I'm supposed to meet—"

"I know. I'm Sanders. Mr. Daniels told me to be on the lookout for you and get you on board the plane as soon as you showed." He reached for her garment bag. "Is this all you have?"

"Yes."

Sanders motioned to a uniformed man near the doors and as he came closer, said, "Take Dr. Lewis's bag and secure it in the cargo hold."

The uniformed man nodded, took the garment bag and went through the doors to the gate. Then Sanders looked at Megan. "Now I'll see you on board." He turned from her and spoke over his shoulder as he started toward the gate. "Follow me, Dr. Lewis."

Megan hurried after him, through the doors and down an enclosed ramp, but instead of going left to board the plane there, Sanders pushed open a side door marked Employees Only and stepped outside. Megan followed him into the sun of the December day and down a flight of stairs onto the runway. As he hurried across the blacktop, Megan looked past him and saw where he was heading. A white and blue smaller jet stood about fifty feet ahead of them on the runway, its engines emitting a dull roar. Megan stopped, narrowing her eyes at the glare of the sun glinting off its polished finish. She had expected to go with Cade on a commercial flight, but she knew this had to be a private jet.

"Excuse me, sir?" she called to the man in front of her.

He turned and squinted at her. "Yes?" he shouted over the engine noise.

"Where are we going?"

He motioned with his head to the jet. "They're waiting."

That was what Megan had been afraid of. Flying had never been easy for her, but she'd learned to cope with commercial flights, to subdue the grip of anxiety when she was flying with two hundred other passengers. Now that anxiety came at her in a rush. The man watched her, then took a few steps back in her direction. "This is Mr. Walters's plane. They're holding it for you. Is there a problem?" he called, his expression indicating that he hoped there wasn't.

"I just didn't...I..." Megan shook her head. "No, there isn't."

"Good," he said and turned back, walking once more toward the jet. When he stopped at side steps that led up to an open door near the front, Megan made herself cross to him. He motioned to the steps. "Go on in, Dr. Lewis. I'll make sure your bag is secured."

When he went around to the other side of the plane, Megan looked up the steps at the open door. *It's a plane, a mechanical device to fly through the air, and it's completely safe.* She repeated that over and over again to herself as she touched the handrail and took the steps one at a time.

But when she got to the top, she wasn't able to kill the jolting memory of her first flight, from Tulsa, Oklahoma, to Tucson, Arizona. She could only have been nine or ten. She didn't remember now exactly, but it had been one of their hasty moves. What she did recall clearly was boarding an old propeller plane with faded, red paint and engines that seemed to vibrate the air all around her.

In the cabin with its dozen or so seats and tiny windows, not more than half an hour after takeoff, they had flown through the fringe turbulence of a tornado. The sharp jarring and shudders of the plane's frame had driven Megan to curl into a tight ball in her seat by the window and press her hands to her eyes.

But Frank hadn't been afraid. Now she really wondered if anything frightened him, besides not being able to gamble. He'd thought the storm was funny and had seemed excited by the danger. Talking nonstop, he'd joked about their chances of making it, and had even offered to give odds to any one of the passengers. They had thought he was kidding, trying to make the best of a terrible situation. They hadn't known how deadly serious he had been. The fact that they'd physically all been in one piece when they landed hadn't meant a great deal to him. Getting to a phone to talk with one of his connections had been all-important.

It was the first time she'd looked at her father and felt something akin to hate. But not the last.

Now she had to force herself to go through the door and step inside the jet, into the luxury of leather and brass that would have been right at home in a man's club. The cabin, she saw, was about thirty feet from the front to a wall with a door in it that cut across the middle of the plane, dividing it more or less in half.

Four high-backed leather chairs were arranged in a conversation circle in the center of the space and anchored by bolts to a floor covered with thick carpet. Built-in couches with matching throw pillows ran the length of the far wall, an intricate stereo system lined the near wall, with a bar set into it by the door and an oversize television screen near the front. Four smaller television screens were set into the corners, giving every passenger a good view.

This was nothing like the other plane, and Frank would have loved it. "One day we'll own something like this," he would have said. Megan exhaled harshly. All he'd ever owned was a mountain of debts.

She took a steadying breath, pushing the memories into the past, where they belonged. Today was what counted, not Frank. Just her life. People flew every day and didn't plummet to the earth. She knew that, yet it didn't stop her heart from racing a mile a minute as she took another step inside.

"So, you made it."

She turned and saw Cade stepping into the cabin through a door at the front of the plane, making the space seem even smaller, the air closer. Over the past three days she had begun to think that her reaction to this man had been an aberration, a quirk, but now, face-to-face, she knew better.

Her awareness of Cade Daniels not only hadn't diminished, it felt as if it had intensified. And it made her heart rate increase still more.

He came to stand not more than five feet from her, lean, dark, intense, and casually dressed in a chambray shirt, faded jeans and well-used, brown boots. She had certainly overdressed. But that didn't bother her as much as the fact that she was incredibly aware of everything about this man—his thick hair, curling stubbornly at his ears and the collar of his shirt, the slight cleft in his chin, the strength of his shoulders. He seemed less gaunt to her, maybe less tense, too, but his eyes were the same—dark as night and just as unreadable.

She felt her anxiety increasing instead of diminishing, and the reaction made her wish she could walk away, get off the plane, call the court and tell them to find another psychologist for this case. One who wouldn't sense this raw male sexuality that sent shards of heat through her. No man had ever affected her like this before on such a blatantly physical level, and her mind began to wander; in any other place, at any other time... She stared at him and added unerringly—if she'd been in any other profession...

Objectivity meant everything to her and to her decision. Yet she was anything but objective about this man in front of her.

Her professionalism was being sorely tested, but she knew she couldn't back out now. The hearing was too close for another psychologist to deal effectively with everyone involved, and a continuance would only prolong the pain for the adults.

"Where's your luggage?" he asked, looking at her leather shoulder bag.

"Sanders, the man who met me, had it put in the cargo hold." She looked away from Cade to the luxurious cabin. "I didn't realize we were flying out on a private plane."

"It's Rick Walters's plane. He had it here to get equipment and thought it would save us time, money and get us there quicker."

She looked back at Cade and asked, "Who's we?"

"You and me, Doc."

"But—?"

"Everyone else is already on location."

The thought of three hours in these tight quarters with this man seemed overwhelming. Especially right now. "But Mr. Walters—?"

"Is in Texas. Now, why don't you take a chair and get comfortable? I'll check with the pilot, then be right back."

Megan watched Cade walk away, through the door into the cockpit. She caught a glimpse of instrument panels and two men before Cade closed the door after him.

Slowly she sank into the nearest chair. A private plane with Cade. Three hours in this tiny space. Her stomach felt decidedly nauseous. She'd make the best of it, get through it, and walk away when it was done.

Holding that thought firmly in her mind, she rested her hands on the arms of the chair, leaned back against the support and closed her eyes. She began a relaxation technique she'd learned when she was going to college—tensing, then relaxing each part of her body from her toes to her head.

But when she ended, she was holding tightly to the arms of the chair and could feel the ache of tension in her shoulders. "Relax, relax," she muttered to herself, her jaw clenching with each word. She exhaled, inhaled, exhaled, then gave up. She'd get through this flight the way she did everything else in life, by doing what she had to and surviving.

When Cade came back into the cabin, he closed the cockpit door and stopped. Megan was sitting in her chair, her head resting against the leather cushion, eyes closed. Her long lashes swept dark half moons against her flawless skin, and her pale pink mouth looked appealingly soft. Her burnished copper hair added a rich accent to the paleness of her suit and the cool color of her blouse.

The memory of how she appeared in the dream suddenly burst into his mind, and he felt his body begin to react. Damn it, he couldn't afford this, not now, not here with her. *She's a doctor,* he wanted to scream at himself, a head doctor, whose job is to analyze you, to see what makes you tick and decide what your life is going to be.

That reality brought Cade up short, and he moved quickly to take the chair opposite Megan. He looked directly at her, an action he allowed himself, since she still had her eyes closed and wouldn't know. But it was a mistake. As he noticed the way her breasts rose and fell with each breath she took, saw the delicate translucency of her eyelids and inhaled the lingering scent of a soft perfume, he knew the only way not to be affected by her was not to be around her.

But he didn't have a choice. He had to be here. He had to make sure she came with him to Texas and saw him work. He knew it might be the only thing he could do to persuade her that he wasn't crazy, that he was a professional and he could take good care of Adam.

Then he saw her hands, clutching the arms of the seat so tightly that the knuckles were bloodless. She was scared to death. A psychologist afraid of flying? "A white-knuckle flier?" he asked as he made himself settle back into the seat.

Her eyes flew open, and a blush touched her cheeks with color. "Oh." She blinked at him, as if she had forgotten he was even on board. "I'm sorry. Does it show?"

He motioned to her hands. "The chair isn't going anywhere, not while you've got it so firmly in hand."

She sat straighter and shook her head sharply, freeing tiny curls from the braid, so they feathered at her temples and cheeks. "I can rationally figure out that flying is the best way to get from one place to another, but that doesn't stop me from feeling as if I'm a stone, waiting to fall, when I'm in the air."

Cade studied her from under his lashes. "I would have thought a psychologist wouldn't be fighting wars with phobias."

"I never thought of it as a war," she muttered, flinching slightly when the engines seemed to grow louder all of a sudden. "But it is human nature to have some phobias."

"Mr. Daniels?"

The pilot, a slender man dressed casually in cords and a polo shirt along with a Dodgers baseball cap, looked through the door. "We've got clearance. We'll be taking off after we do our final check."

Cade nodded to the man. "Good, George. Just let us know when we get there."

With a touch of one finger to his cap, the pilot went out and closed the door. Cade found his seat belt and as he snapped it together, he looked back at Megan. A tinge of paleness in her cheeks made her eyes seem incredibly large and an almost iridescent blue. *She's scared to death of flying,* he thought. He wasn't the only one on edge around here.

For three days and three nights he'd done little but talk to Ross on the phone, work out at his home gym and think about the doctor. Then he'd had the dream last night. In the dream he had been overwhelmed by her sensuality, something that still held true when she was here in person, yet it was tempered by a mixture of control. But seeing her so obviously apprehensive about flying made him feel as if she didn't have complete control after all. Strange. Instead of feeling superior, he found that he wanted to reassure her in some way.

For a fleeting moment he wondered where the impulse had come from, where the Cade had gone who shot through life without making contact any more than he had to. Then he looked into her eyes and pushed aside the questions when he saw the edge of panic she was fighting to control.

"Can I tell you my secret of how I get through anything that's frightening?"

"You get frightened?" Megan asked, wondering why she had assumed that nothing in this world would frighten him.

"Every human being with an ounce of sense is afraid at one time or another."

Megan was uncomfortably aware that the plane's engines were revving higher and higher. "What's your secret?" she asked, needing an answer, or maybe just a diversion from being so conscious of every new sound on board.

"While you're doing it, don't do it."

"Don't do what?" she asked, looking right at Cade, but feeling the first bumps as the wheels began to turn for the plane to taxi down the runway.

"Don't jump out a window, or run through fire, or fly. Use your mind, the ability to visualize. Think about something you'd love to do, something that you've only dreamed of doing and never got a chance." He rested his head on the high leather back, his hooded eyes narrowed even more by dark lashes. "What do you like to do, Doc?" he asked.

"What would you be doing right now, if you could be doing anything at all?"

"Not flying, that's for sure," she breathed, the bumps of the tires on the blacktop getting closer together as the world outside began to move past the windows.

"Not fair," he said, claiming her attention again by sitting forward and touching her hand where it clutched the arm of the chair.

Megan looked at Cade when she felt the tips of his fingers tap the back of her hand and saw him settle back in his seat. "What's not fair?" she asked, fighting the urge to brush at her skin where he'd touched her, to banish the lingering sensation of the contact.

"That's not fair," he said. "You have to take this seriously, or it doesn't work. What would you be doing, if you could do anything at all?"

Megan spoke quickly, just to get the words out. "I'd be on a deserted island, soaking up the sun and listening to the sounds of the ocean."

"That's it?" he asked, both brows rising in question. "Nothing more original than that?"

She frowned at him. "You didn't ask for something original. You asked for what I would want to do. Originality wasn't a prerequisite."

"Obviously," he murmured.

"All right," she said with exasperation. "What would *you* be doing?"

"That isn't what this is all about—"

"Fair's fair. I told you, now you tell me. When you're jumping off a building, what do you visualize yourself doing?"

He shrugged. "Hang gliding over the Grand Canyon at night during a tornado."

"What?" she asked, sitting forward.

"That got your attention, didn't it?" he said, a suggestion of a smile tugging at the corners of his mouth. "Isn't that what you expected a stuntman to say?"

She hadn't really considered what a stuntman would want to do in his fantasies, but for some reason she'd thought Cade Daniels would want to be riding a horse in the mountains, all by himself. "No, it's what you *think* I expected you to say."

That brought a burst of laughter from Cade, a pleasant sound that seemed to surround Megan. "Touché. So, what did you really think I'd say?"

She spoke the truth, vaguely aware of the speed building for takeoff. "I thought you'd want to be riding a horse in the mountains."

He sobered. "Really?"

"Just an impression," she said quickly. "I don't know why I thought it, but it just came to me. Maybe it's because you're wearing Western boots."

He drew up one booted foot to rest it on the other knee, then rubbed the well-worn leather with the tips of his fingers. "It sounds good."

"But?"

"I don't ride horses unless I have to. The smell of manure and hay makes me slightly sick."

"Then what would you do?" she asked.

His hand on the boot stilled, and his lashes lowered slightly on his dark eyes. "I think I'd like to be on an island in the sun, listening to the ocean sounds."

Megan laughed at that. "That's really not original. Besides, it was my idea first."

Cade didn't laugh the way she thought he would. Instead, his eyes seemed more intense, unblinking. "No," he said, "but it sounded good to you. It sounds good to me."

Megan felt her expression falter when an image of Cade came to her, his body, strong and defined by clear sunlight, sleek with water, his hair clinging to his head. An image of herself, with him on the sands. She could feel the heat rising into her face and silently cursed the way her imagination could conjure up things that were patently impossible.

Quickly she pushed that thought away. "It sounds good, but I'll never get there, and you'll probably end up jumping off a building."

"So much for make-believe," he said. "And so much for taking off."

Megan looked out the window at sky and clouds. They were in the air, and she hadn't even noticed that moment when the wheels left the ground. She sank back in her chair and met Cade's amused gaze. "That's your secret? Distract someone until the deed is done?"

He shrugged. "Pretty good one, eh?"

The plane seemed to purr, the sense of movement all but nonexistent. "Yes, pretty good," she echoed.

"You know, I never doubted it would work on you."

"Why?"

"Because you apparently have a curiosity that would kill a cat."

"I what?"

"You're interested in life and what makes it work. I imagine that's why you're so good at what you do. People fascinate you, don't they, Doc?"

She almost said, "You do," but didn't. Instead, she nodded. "Most of the time."

"Do you get that from your parents?"

Megan felt her good humor begin to evaporate. "I don't remember too much about my mother, so I don't know what I got from her, except my height and hair color. And as far as my father goes, I don't think I inherited anything from him.''

''Do you remember much about him?''

She closed her eyes for a moment, then looked at Cade. ''Everything.''

''He was that special?''

''He *is* memorable,'' she said with more tightness than she intended. Then she felt the plane lurch, and her hands closed like vises over the arms of the chair. ''What was that?''

''Turbulence of some sort,'' Cade said, never moving.

She took a breath, trying to ease the tightening in her. ''God, I hate this.''

''Why?'' he asked.

''Pardon me?''

''Why does flying scare you so much? Did you have a bad experience?''

He'd hit the nail right on the head, but she simply shook her head. ''I'm just not a good flyer.'' When the plane leveled out and the ride became smooth again, Megan took an unsteady breath. ''Does Mr. Walters always lend his plane to people who work on his pictures?''

Cade shrugged. ''I don't know. He just knew that I had to get to Texas, he had to get equipment to Texas and he offered to combine the two trips on this plane.''

''You've worked with him before?''

''No, but I always wanted to.'' Cade undid his seat belt and stood, stretching his arms over his head, then he looked down at Megan. ''Drink?''

Megan didn't think she could keep anything in her stomach right now. ''No, thanks. I don't think so.''

Cade crossed to the built-in bar by the large-screen television and opened the doors. ''He's stocked everything from champagne to soda.'' He glanced at her over his shoulder. ''You sure you don't want something cold?''

"No, I'm fine. But you go ahead."

She saw him hesitate and thought about the interview she'd had with Doris and Leo Sinclair yesterday. The older lady and her husband, a large, quiet man, had been models of calm and determination. "The man's a drinker and a fool," Doris had said. "I don't think he's had two sober days to string together in the past six months."

Leo had nodded, simply adding, "Yes, that's right."

If Megan hadn't known how bad Cade's marriage had been, she would have passed off his excessive drinking as an expression of grief, but not now. There had to be another reason. He didn't act or look like an alcoholic. Then Doris's other words came back to her. "He killed my daughter."

Megan heard ice cubes clink in a glass, then Cade turned and came to his seat. He held up a glass with clear liquid in it. "Club soda. He's even got lemonade in there. Can you beat that?"

Megan shook her head. "Money gets what money wants, I guess." She looked at Cade as he settled, sitting low in the seat, his legs out in front of him, almost touching the toes of her shoes. He rested the glass on his middle, both hands clasped around it.

The plane lurched slightly, and Megan held on to the arms of the chair again. Cade didn't seem to have noticed the lurch. He sipped his drink, then looked at her over the rim of the glass. "What do you want to do during the flight? I can tell you what's going to happen when we get to Texas, or I can give you a bit of background on stunt work, or—"

She cut him off. "I'll see all that firsthand when we get there. Why don't we just talk? Maybe you can give me background on yourself, about your childhood."

Cade groaned and rolled his eyes ceilingward. "Oh, no, the old, 'tell me about your childhood,' approach." He reached to his right and set his glass in a holder built into a side table. "How about, I was born very young?"

"We all were."

"And I grew up during my growing-up years?"

Megan tilted her head to one side. "And you were a smart aleck, weren't you?"

He feigned shock and pressed one hand to his chest. "Me?"

"You."

"Would you hold it against me?"

"It all depends."

"On what?" he asked, but the humor in his eyes was beginning to fade.

"On—" She stopped dead when the plane lurched again, as if it were dropping in the air, then it settled. "Is there a problem, do you think?"

Cade shook his head. "No. I think it's just an air pocket. Now, answer the question."

"What question?"

"Will you hold my childhood against me?"

"Tell me about it, and I'll let you know."

"Is that fair to make a decision after the fact?"

"That's exactly the way this works. How do I know until I hear what you did?"

He looked at her for a moment, then drank almost half of his drink before resting the glass on his middle. "All right, Doc. Where should I start?"

"Anywhere you want to."

He ran a hand over his face. "Why do I feel like I'm on a couch, ready to spill my guts?"

"You aren't." She looked at the built-in couch under the windows. "But if you'd rather...?"

"No. This is fine." He lifted one brow as he gave her a considering look. "I'll make you a deal, Doc. I'll tell you about my childhood, if you tell me about yours."

"No deal." She shook her head. "You don't want to hear about my childhood."

"How do you know until you tell me?"

"Just tell me about yours. We'll figure out the rest later," she said, and knew one thing for sure—Cade Daniels was a charmer.

She could see how he could get through life without commitments, doing what he wanted, when he wanted, with whom he wanted to do it. Some women wouldn't look any farther than the chiseled cheekbones and the glint in his dark eyes. Her mother had never gotten beyond Frank's charm and good looks.

She didn't want to think about Frank anymore, or about the parole hearing. For the next few days she would be far out of his reach and she had a job to do. "What was your childhood like?" she asked.

Cade took a breath, then began to speak quickly, skimming over most of his past. But Megan saw a pattern. Cade was the outsider, the one who didn't quite fit the family mold. He was the son of intellectuals, with a brother who had become an archaeologist and fulfilled all of his parents' dreams. Cade apparently felt he hadn't fulfilled anyone's dreams.

In some strange way, Cade was like she had always been. He'd chosen a diametrically opposite direction for his life than the one taken by the rest of his family—deliberately.

She fingered the arm of the chair and watched Cade talk, his eyes on the now empty glass he'd propped on the worn leather of the boot that rested on his other knee. He told her about teenage years, when the chasm between himself and his parents had grown. "They're great people, wonderful people, but they never understood what I wanted."

"Did they care what you wanted?" she asked, the first words she'd spoken since Cade had begun talking.

He looked at her, his gaze slightly unfocused, then it sharpened. "Yes, very much. They just couldn't understand, that's all."

"What's your relationship now?"

He shrugged. "Loving and distant. They saw Adam when he was a month old, then just before Lori died."

"Did they come to see you after the accident?"

"They wanted to, but I wasn't in any condition to be around them then. They probably talked to Doris and Leo. But they knew Adam was being taken care of and I was doing what I had to do." He looked away from her, out the windows. "That's what life is all about, I guess. Doing what you have to do."

She knew that better than most. "Yes, it is."

He looked back at her. "How about you?"

"What about me?"

"What sort of childhood does a psychologist have?"

She wanted to lie and say "normal," or just tell him it wasn't interesting, but something about Cade made that evasion impossible. "Not an ideal one," she admitted.

Cade sat forward, his elbows resting on both knees, the empty glass caught loosely in his hand. "I'm sorry. I shouldn't have asked. You already told me that your mother died."

She passed that off with a hand gesture. "It's all right. I was six." The memory didn't seem as strong as usual. "It was a long time ago."

Cade knew he had never been particularly sensitive to other people's emotions, but he could clearly sense pain in Megan, a deep, abiding pain that he could almost feel himself. And he wanted to ask her what had caused it. Her mother's death? Or something else? Someone else? He realized he knew very little about her, but wasn't in a position to ask any more. Instead he just watched her and saw the undisguised sadness in her eyes. "So, psychologists aren't immune to life's whims, are they?" he murmured.

She shrugged. "We're human beings. If we're cut, we bleed. If there's pain, we cry."

Her words moved him on a level he couldn't begin to comprehend. He didn't know where her pain came from, but he hated its source. That was very plain. And with the same intensity, he wished he could rid her world of the pain. A silly notion, especially when he didn't even know her very well, and he had his own pain.

Yet the dream... He closed his eyes for a moment and remembered that she had been the healer in the dream. He could almost feel the way she had touched him and the sensations that contact had generated. Cutting off the memory, he made his voice sound abrupt when he said, "Remember that applies to all people, when you give your final decision."

He saw her blink, as if the case had been the last thing on her mind, then she looked down at her hands clutching the chair arms. Slowly she let go of the chair, then shifted her hands to her lap, spreading her slender fingers on the paleness of her skirt. Those hands... He stood quickly as the dream's images washed over him. "Sure you won't have a drink?"

Her tongue touched her lips, an action that immediately tightened Cade's middle. "No...no, thanks," she said softly.

He sure as hell needed another drink, but not club soda. He got up, crossed to the bar and pulled a bottle of brandy out of its holder. Before he began to think about his actions, he had splashed the brown liquid into a glass and turned as Megan stood. He saw the way she looked at the glass, then at the brandy bottle in the holder, and knew what she was thinking. Doris had obviously given her every bit of ammunition she had.

He wasn't going to make it any easier for Doris to undermine him, and he wasn't going to do it to himself. But before he could turn and pour the brandy back into the bottle, the plane lurched and dropped in the air. It threw Cade off balance, propelling him forward, and as if in slow motion, he saw the brandy leave his glass and wash all over Megan. He had an impression of a dark stain spreading on the light linen of her clothes, then in the next beat of his heart he was stumbling against her, his body tangled with hers as they fell to the floor.

Chapter 6

It was as if he was in the dream again, her body under his, so small, so soft, so sexy. Every curve of her fitted neatly against him, and her scent seemed to fill his being. Then the cutting odor of brandy assailed Cade's nostrils and blotted out the delicate perfume.

He let the glass roll out of his hand, then pressed both palms flat on the carpet and pushed himself up and off Megan. For an instant he was looking down at her, her hair freed from the knot, a tangle of amber curls spread on the pale carpet. Her eyes were wide with shock, and her mouth, pale and free of lipstick, formed an expression of complete surprise.

Before he could do something like tasting her lips, to see if the experience would duplicate the one in his dreams, he forced himself to move to one side, away from her.

"What . . . what happened?" she gasped, struggling to sit up.

"Another air pocket," Cade said as he got to his feet, then crouched by her and reached out a hand, meaning to help her up. But as she twisted to her left, his fingers touched her cheek. She froze at the contact, staring at him with wide, blue eyes; the heat of her skin under his touch was as potent as any aphrodisiac. The invitation of her softly parted lips brought back the urge to kiss her, something that could destroy any chance he had of getting Adam. He wanted to kiss her. He wanted to taste her and explore her softness. His needs in the dream were as nothing, compared to this reality.

Worse yet, he could imagine her responding, arching to him, needing him the way he needed her. And when he took her... He drew back abruptly, standing up and turning from her on the pretense of reaching for the all but forgotten glass. Anything to hide the evidence of what his imagination could do to him and to avoid having to look into her eyes again.

He straightened. Distance. God, he needed space, but there was no way to get it. Right then the captain came into the cabin, his Dodgers hat gone, his face lined with worry.

"Everything all right back here?" George asked.

Cade looked at Megan, who was on her feet, brushing ineffectively at the brandy stain on her jacket and skirt.

"Ma'am, I'm really sorry," the pilot said. "I had no idea or I would have warned you." He looked at the front of her clothes. "Wow, that's really a mess."

Megan felt the dampness under her hands and sensed that her emotional balance was as out of kilter as her footing had been. For a moment when Cade was over her, she'd felt such a need for the man, she'd been rendered immobile. Then he'd moved back, and when she'd turned, his hand had touched her cheek.

She took an unsteady breath; the smell of the brandy seemed to permeate the whole cabin. "I need to change."

"No, your luggage is in the cargo hold," George said.

Cade motioned to the back of the plane. "Does Mr. Walters have some clothes in the sleeping area?"

"Oh, sure," the man said, his face clearing. "I'll bet he does, at that."

Cade looked at Megan and pointed to the back door. "Go on in, find whatever you can and get out of those clothes. When we land, I'll get your bags and you can change before we head out to Dedrick."

Anything would be better than her brandy-soaked suit and blouse. She hurried toward the door, opened it and stepped into a bedroom area that held a round bed, covered with a beige suede throw. On the right wall was another large-screen television set, and along the left wall was a series of folding doors. She drew them back and found a closet, filled with shelves and racks of men's clothing.

She looked through the folded clothes, an assortment of tie-dyed T-shirts, jeans and shorts in outrageous colors. Then she came upon a black velour bathrobe. She took it off the shelf, shook it out and saw gold initials on the pocket, an intertwined *R* and *W*.

It would do fine for now, she thought, but before she could start taking off her own clothes, she heard Cade call from the other side of the door.

"Is there a shirt in there I could use?"

Megan looked back into the closet, found a blue and white striped, cotton shirt and tugged it off its hanger. She went back to the door, opened it and saw Cade. His shirt had been discarded, and the sight of him bare-chested made her mouth dry. While they'd been tangled together, she'd been overwhelmed by the hard strength she'd felt in his body, the all-male scent of him and the sensation of his weight.

Now she could see the expanse of his chest, the smooth, tanned skin, and a scar—a pale rope line that looped over his shoulder and down toward his breastbone. She could hardly breathe. A souvenir of one of his "safe, well thought-out stunts," she'd bet, and a sight that made her tremble inside. She couldn't begin to comprehend what it had taken for that damage to be done to Cade.

And she wouldn't ask. She wouldn't stand here, this close to him, listening to a story about the injury that had caused the scar. Instead she thrust the shirt at him. "Is this okay?" she asked.

Cade took it, shook it out to look at it, then nodded. "Sure. Thanks."

Megan quickly closed the door, then leaned against the cool wood while she took several breaths. Finding the liquid had even gotten into her shoes, she stepped out of her pumps and slipped off her panty hose, then began to strip the damp clothes off her body. She put on the robe over her bra and panties and tied the belt at her waist. Pushing at her loose hair to get it off her face, she caught sight of herself in a mirror by the television as she turned. Her face was pale, her hair tangled and her expression tight.

This wasn't going well. She'd never wanted to be thousands of feet in the air with a man who addled her thinking. She wasn't a celibate, but knew her sex life had been extremely limited. There had never been a man who put her mind into a jumble and produced this heat in her body... until she met Cade. A sorry state of things, she conceded, and looked away from the sight.

She tugged the robe more tightly around her, then went back into the cabin. Cade turned from locking the bar as she entered, and she saw the shirt he had on was so small that he

Child of Mine

hadn't even attempted to button the front. As he rolled up the sleeves, exposing strong forearms dusted with black hair, he stared at her so intently that she felt heat rush into her face.

She pushed at the carpet pile with her toes, but made herself keep eye contact. "This robe is all he has, except T-shirts and some horrible Hawaiian shorts." Awkwardly she pushed her hands into the pockets of the robe. "How soon can I get my own clothes?"

"As soon as we land," Cade said.

The pilot looked back into the cabin. "Sit down and buckle up, and in three minutes we'll be ready for our approach to Love Field in Dallas."

Megan crossed to her chair, settled down and buckled her belt. Then she watched Cade sit down, shifting low in his chair and had a hard time not looking at his tanned chest where the shirt parted, or at the tiny part of the scar she could still see.

"I'm really sorry for all of this," Cade said. "I intended to impress you on this trip, explaining my profession and telling you how much I wanted Adam with me. Instead I tell you about my childhood and spill brandy on you."

She tried to smile, but the expression on her lips felt tight and artificial. "It's not what I planned, either."

"What had you planned?" he asked.

Megan felt the plane begin to lose altitude and gripped the arms of the chair once again. "Talking, and getting the information I need to know."

"Well, we've got a few minutes. Ask me whatever you want to know."

She concentrated on ignoring the hollowness in her ears as they descended. "I want to know why Doris Sinclair accused you of killing her daughter."

Cade laced his hands together in his lap and let his head rest against the back support of the chair. "I thought I explained that before."

"No, you explained everything except that."

He closed his eyes for a moment before looking back at her from under his dark lashes. "Didn't Doris tell you?"

"No. When I saw her and Mr. Sinclair yesterday, I didn't bring it up."

He exhaled harshly, then shrugged. "Doris thinks that just being married to me was the ruination of her daughter, and she was probably right. I didn't want to be married. I don't suppose I ever loved Lori, and when she took off from my friend's house that last night, I didn't go after her."

"Why?" she asked.

"Why didn't I go after her?"

She nodded without speaking, her hands all but numb from gripping the chair arms as the plane began to slow and descend.

"Truthfully, I guess I was relieved to have her gone. I could finally admit that the marriage was a mistake, and I had to deal with it. So I let her go. And when she didn't come home, I thought she was playing one of her games. She'd done it before, leaving, not coming back, then showing up a few days later. I guess she wanted me to go after her, to beg her to come back." He ran a hand roughly over his face. "The first time she did it, it drove me crazy with worry, then I got used to it. The last time I realized that I didn't want her to come back." He raised one brow in her direction. "Sounds cold, doesn't it?"

She shrugged, realizing that that was exactly how she'd felt about Frank so many times. When she was young, she'd actually wished him dead. Death she could have dealt with. "It sounds as if you were at the end of your rope."

He sat up straighter, his eyes narrowed on her. "You understand?"

"That you aren't necessarily a bad person for wanting an end to a problem, to a mistake? No, you're human."

He sank back with a release of air. "Thank God. I thought you'd brand me as an emotionless bastard."

The longer Cade talked, the more Megan realized how deeply he felt things. As he shifted forward and the shirt parted, showing more of the scar, she saw real evidence that he just made bad decisions. "No. I can tell you didn't walk away from your marriage without remorse."

He put his head into his hands, elbows propped on his knees. Silent for so long that Megan thought he hadn't heard her, he finally looked up. "I think a better word is guilt."

She knew about that. "You blame yourself for Lori's death, don't you?"

His expression became bleak. "With just cause."

"Were you driving the car when it crashed?"

"You know I wasn't."

"Did you force her to leave by herself?"

"No, but—"

"Did you rejoice when she died?"

That made him blanch. "Of course not."

"Then why do you feel so responsible?" She hadn't rejoiced when Frank was arrested and sent to jail. But she had grieved, been filled with pain and blamed herself for everything.

"Why not?" he muttered.

"Why? You aren't responsible. You never were. You did what you could. Maybe it wasn't always the right thing, but you tried. You did your best, didn't you?"

He sank back in the chair. "Maybe that's it. My best was lousy. I've got a God-given gift for fouling up relationships."

"I doubt it's God-given," she said, finding it easy to smile at Cade. "But I can assure you, it's not fatal, either."

He stared at her, then seemed to relax just a bit. "Is this your rapid-learning seminar? Get yourself straight in ten minutes of intense questions and answers?"

"I wish fixing lives was that simple," she said, her smile dying.

"Are you speaking from personal experience?"

That stunned her. She had thought she was being so impartial, so analytical and professional, yet he'd seen right through her. "A bit," she said in what she knew was a monumental understatement.

"A bad marriage," he asked.

He couldn't have been farther off the mark. "No, I've never been married, good or bad."

"Why not?"

"Pardon me?"

"Doc, in case you haven't looked in the mirror lately, you're a very attractive woman. I can't believe that you've never had a man want to marry you."

Megan could feel the heat in her face and cursed it. There'd been a few men she'd let get close to her, but never anyone she trusted and loved. There wasn't a man on earth who could make up for the damage Frank had done to her life. That last thought brought her up short. Why should any man have to make up to her for what Frank had done?

But was she truly looking for that in a man? Was that why she'd always picked "safe men," men who were the diametrical opposites of Frank? She certainly didn't want to invest a lifetime in a man like her father. The very idea chilled her. "I never found anyone I wanted to marry," she said honestly.

She'd always felt she'd be just as happy alone, yet now the notion made her feel incredibly sad. She looked at Cade. Never to know what it was like to be with one person, to wake with and fall asleep with that person. To have that person's touch be the last thing she felt at night, the first thing she felt in the morning.

To be vulnerable to that man, to make him the most important part of her world... No. That put everything into perspective. She never wanted that. She knew the pain that came with that sort of commitment.

As she opened her mouth to say something mundane, anything to change the subject, the plane bounced slightly, and Megan saw they were on the runway, the jet engines roaring while the plane slowed to a stop. She looked out the windows at the buildings of the airport terminal. "We're down."

"You sound surprised," Cade murmured.

She was. Talking with Cade had taken all of her attention again, even though it had been vaguely upsetting. "I...I am," she admitted.

As the plane came to a full stop, Megan undid her seat belt, then stood at the same time Cade did. Not more than two feet from him, she stared up at the man, intent on not looking at his bare chest. "Did you do that on purpose?"

"Do what?"

"Keep me distracted, so we could land without me thinking about it?"

He shrugged, the action separating the shirt even more. "I wish I could say I did, but it wasn't intentional this time."

Megan heard a heavy thud on the outside of the plane, then the door to the cabin slid back and a man stepped inside. In a bright turquoise shirt and jeans, his black boots studded with silver, he looked like a fluorescent cowboy. With bowed legs, a bristly, gray haircut and the darkness of a beard at his square chin, the man appeared to be about fifty or so and clearly surprised at the scene before him.

"Well, I'll be damned, Cade," the man said as the pilot walked through the cabin and past him, out the door. "And here I thought you were in a bad way. But you look like you're back in rare form, boy." He squinted at Megan. "And she's a real beauty." His eyes skimmed over her short robe and bare legs. "A real beauty. I got to admit your taste's improving."

Megan clutched the lapels of her robe more tightly at her throat as Cade moved forward. "Leon—" he started, only to be cut off.

"Hell, it smells like you're being unkind to good liquor in here," the newcomer said on a chuckle. "Smells like you've been playing in it." He laughed harshly. "Reminds me of that time in Vegas when we had the woman up to the room and filled the tub with —"

"Leon," Cade said again, stepping toe-to-toe with him, "shut up."

Megan watched the other man blink. "What in the—?"

"Leon, this lady is *Dr.* Lewis. She's a psychologist with the Los Angeles Family Court, and she's with me to see me work and decide if I get custody of my son, Adam. She's here as an observer in a professional capacity. We had an accident and brandy spilled, so we used Rick Walters's clothes. Do you understand?"

"Yeah, I sure do," the man breathed and shook his head. "I'm real sorry, ma'am...er...Doc. I'm just running off at the mouth, and I'm real sorry."

"And so am I," Cade said. "This man is Leon McCann, a friend and someone who talks before thinking."

"Boy, I sure do," the man agreed readily. "Always putting my foot in my mouth." He smiled at Megan. "You being a head doctor, you should know about people just running off at the mouth like that."

Megan had never felt more embarrassed in her life than she did then for Cade. "That's all right, Mr. McCann."

"I didn't mean nothing I was saying. I was joking. Cade knows how I joke. And I was talking about before he got married. Back in his bachelor days."

Megan looked at Cade, at the tightness at his mouth and eyes. But before she could do or say anything, the pilot stepped back into the cabin with her garment bag in his hand, along with a small, leather tote.

"Here you go," he said, handing her bag to her and putting the other one on the floor. "Now you can get changed."

She took them without a word to anyone, went back into the bedroom area and closed the door.

"Damn it, Leon," Cade said in a harsh whisper as soon as the door clicked shut and the pilot had left. "What in the hell were you doing?"

Leon scratched his head. "I'm damned sorry, boy. I just thought . . . I mean, you here, with a looker like that. And her in a robe and you all undone. Shoot, it'd be just like you to get a woman alone at twenty thousand feet, just to see what it was like."

Cade had to smile at that idea, but kept his voice low. "Did Walters send you?"

"Hell, yeah, with a limo and everything. He's really giving you the royal treatment. We're to take you right out to Dedrick. They've ordered everything, and the setup's about in place." He glanced at the door to the bedroom area and leaned closer. "Is she really a doctor?"

"She sure is."

"It's not right for a doctor to look like that."

Cade could agree with that completely. "She is a doctor, and it's important that she sees that stuntmen are just like everyone else in the world, not reckless idiots."

"She's giving you a hard time?" Leon asked, his face sober now.

"Not intentionally, but things haven't been going real well between us."

Once again Leon leaned close and said in a low voice, "Take care of her. Turn on the old charm and get her to do whatever you want."

Cade grimaced. "That's the last thing I need to do. Hell, if she thinks I'd do that, she'll give Adam to my in-laws, for sure."

"I'll talk to the guys when we get back. Let them know what's going on. Anything I can do, boy, you know I'm good for it."

"Thanks," Cade said with feeling. He needed all the help he could get.

Leon looked at Cade. "You going out like that?"

Cade tugged at the blue and white cotton shirt. "Looks bad, doesn't it? I got brandy all over my own shirt, and Walters and I aren't exactly the same size."

"Not even close," Leon said. "And you're going to freeze. It's about twenty degrees out there, and heaven knows what the windchill factor makes it."

"I'll change here," Cade replied, picking up his leather tote.

Right then Megan came out of the bedroom, dressed in snug jeans, a white shirt and running shoes. A corduroy jacket in deep brown was over her arm. She'd caught her hair back from her face into a high ponytail and looked as if she didn't have a speck of makeup on. Even so, she couldn't hide her beauty or kill the response Cade felt, just at the sight of her.

He looked away from her to Leon and said, "As soon as I get changed, we'll head out."

He went to the door of the sleeping area and stepped into the space which seemed to be saturated with Megan's essence. As he closed the door, he heard Leon say, "So, you're really a doctor...?"

The ride to Dedrick took over an hour, and while Megan stared out the windows at the Texas landscape, drenched in the colors of twilight, she listened to Cade and Leon talking about the stunt that Rick Walters wanted.

She didn't understand too much of what they said beyond the facts that there were "setups" to be made, and that Cade would have input on a few other stunts to get a bonus. She finally let their voices become a background drone and stared out at the flat land with its scattering of ranches and lines of low, black-green cedar trees.

Cade was a charmer. He could make her think about things that she hadn't considered for a very long time. Maybe things she'd never considered. Things that disturbed and unbalanced her. And that went beyond the sheer sense of masculinity that emanated from him. Beyond hard thighs, midnight-dark eyes and the sharp lines of his face. They went deeper, to the core of her being, which seemed to respond to him on a level she didn't want to even think about.

"...and the car rolls at least twice before righting to its wheels and making impact."

She glanced at the two men, little more than blurred shadows as the evening advanced, Cade on the seat beside her, Leon in a smaller seat facing Cade. It was easier to look at Cade this way, easier to consider the man himself. She had no doubt that he and Leon had been in Las Vegas and had filled a bathtub with... With what? Champagne? Beer? Milk?

She could almost smile at the idea, almost. Then she realized that Cade was looking at her, his expression a dark blur. "Excuse me?" she asked, her voice muffled in the plush interior.

"I was just asking how you want to do this."

"Do what?"

"I'm here to work. You're here to see how I work. How do you want to do it?"

"Just do whatever you'd normally do, and I'll follow. I'm here to observe, just as you told Mr. McCann."

"That's Leon," the other man said. "No one calls me mister. I won't answer to it."

"All right, you and Leon do whatever it is that you do, and I'll watch. I'll ask questions if I don't understand what you're doing."

"Fair enough," Cade said, settling back.

Megan could feel the seat move as his weight shifted.

"What's the setup at Dedrick?" he asked.

"We've sort of taken over the town. They love it. They're getting money, and we're getting use of just about everything there. Most of the crew's being put up in motor homes at the site, but the others that aren't there all the time are at the hotel and a couple of small motels on the north end of the town, about five miles from the prison."

"It's a real prison?" Megan asked.

Leon looked at her. "Used to be, years back. It looks damned depressing, all bricks and stones and bars. And it stinks, really musty and stale. I'm glad they aren't doing more than just a few interior shots in it. Everything else is being done outside. If it was up to me, I'd dump it full of potting soil and make it one huge planter. It ain't good for nothing else."

"Except to be a movie set," Cade said.

"Yeah, that's for sure. It's going to look just right on film. They've fixed up a few bits of it inside, and made it look just like it used to look. There's a spot north of it, about a mile, and that's where they've put another set, built it from scratch. That's where your gag's going to be done."

"How long an approach?"

"As long as you need. Pure, flat, hard dirt. A few trees, but not in the way. We've already got the wall set up, so it's going to be easy to finish up when the machine gets there."

Megan saw lights ahead, then the car slowed. "Well, here we are," Leon said. "Dedrick, Texas. One main street, a population of fifteen hundred, including the dogs and cats, and a wind that would like to suck the life right out of you."

Megan sat back, watching the colored, neon signs coming into sight—Lavery's Feed and Grain, Delloe's General Store, Hall's Hotel, and Bill's Gas Station, with a huge yellow ball rotating slowly above two pumps, and a building that looked more like a shed.

"This is it?" she asked.

"In all its glory," Leon said as the limo pulled up in front of the hotel.

Cade moved first as the door opened, getting out into the night. Then he looked back into the limo at Megan, the colors from the lighted signs playing strange shadows over his face. "Let's find out where our rooms are, then get something to eat."

Quickly she scrambled out of the car and went toward the hotel, a large, sprawling three-story building done all in brick, with wood trim reminiscent of Victorian times. A porch sprawled all the way across the front, with wide, wooden stairs leading to double, frosted-glass doors.

Megan followed Cade up the steps, across the porch and into the lobby. The high-ceilinged interior had the same flavor as the exterior, with a massive, half-circle desk to the right, backed by a wall covered in faded cabbage-rose paper. Hardwood floors were covered by Turkish throw rugs, and a large marble fireplace to the left had a fire blazing in it. The heat swept out to meet Megan, touching her cold skin in the most pleasant way.

A man with thick glasses and a completely bald head sat behind the desk, smiling and nodding at Cade and Megan. "Good evening to you. I'm Horace Hall, proprietor of this hotel. Would you be Mr. Daniels?" he asked.

Cade crossed to the desk. "Yes, I'm Cade Daniels. Someone from Mr. Walters's office called for a reservation for me."

"Yes, sir. You're lucky you got a room, space is tight. Most have to stay out there at the prison in those recreational vehicles. They came through town two weeks ago, real big ones, all looking like a parade."

Cade looked around the reception area. "I'm happy to be in the hotel."

"Good, good, and I have your room all ready for you." He rose and came round from behind the desk, and didn't stand more than five feet tall. "Your luggage?" he asked.

"Our driver will bring it up later."

"Fine. Then follow me, sir," Mr. Hall said as he headed for an old-fashioned, cage elevator at the back of the lobby.

Leon called to Cade from the doors. "I'll be talking to you tomorrow," he said.

Cade nodded and went with Megan. The ride up in the old elevator took so long that it would have been faster to take the stairs, but not as interesting. Mr. Hall told them the background of the hotel, which had been built in 1910 by his grandfather. "It was the only hotel in Dedrick then. It's the only one now. Those motels don't count," he said as they stopped at the top floor and got out.

Mr. Hall led the way down the corridor to the last door. "Here you go," he said, putting an old-fashioned passkey into the lock. Then he opened the door and went inside, followed by Cade.

Light flashed on inside, then Megan went into what looked like a sitting room, done in plain, but sturdy furniture. An overstuffed couch in a green and blue floral print sat to one side, faced by two armchairs in royal blue. A braided rug covered the thin hardwood flooring, and delicate panels of lace draped the series of high, multipaned windows on the far wall.

"Here's your sitting room, and—" he crossed to open a door to the left "—here's the bedroom."

Megan stayed by the door, but could see into the bedroom when Mr. Hall snapped on an old-fashioned tulip-shaded ceiling fixture. A huge poster bed with a gauzy canopy seemed to fill most of the space. Windows covered by cream-colored drapes flanked the bed.

Cade looked into the room, then down at Mr. Hall. "And where's my room?"

"Your room? This is it, and you're lucky you got it. I had to ask one of our regulars to vacate it for a while. They weren't happy, I can tell you that."

"And Dr. Lewis's room?"

"Whose?"

Cade motioned to Megan. "Dr. Lewis. I told them to tell you, when they called, that she would be here for a few days, too."

"Oh, sure, of course. They said about the lady, but I just figured you'd be wanting to share quarters." He colored slightly. "Being as how you're from Hollywood and all, I didn't think you'd be wanting separate rooms."

"Well, we do," Cade said without looking at Megan.

"I'm really sorry, sir," the little man said, "but there isn't any other room in the hotel. Heck, there aren't any empty rooms in the whole town."

Megan stared at the little man. "Surely you've got—?"

"Nope, nothing," Mr. Hall said. "Nothing at all. This is it. Take it or leave it."

Chapter 7

Megan waited for Cade to say something, to come up with an alternative, but instead he looked at her and shrugged. "I guess this is it."

"You can't mean that."

"I mean that there 'isn't any room at the inn.' We have to take what's offered. When movie crews come to town, especially one this size, they take over everything." He turned back to Mr. Hall. "Thanks. Would you mind telling our driver where to bring our luggage?" He reached into his pocket for a tip, but the little man shook his head.

"No, sir, I don't need that. That's all taken care of by Mr. Walters's people. You just enjoy your stay here," he said, then hurried out the door and closed it after him.

Megan stood rooted to the spot. Sharing the plane ride with Cade had been bad enough, but she couldn't do this. Even being in here just a few minutes, she was totally aware of his presence, of the way he seemed to fill the air with his own scent and the room with his heat. No way could she survive two days with him. Or, the thought continued, two nights.

Cade didn't say a word. Instead he went to the windows and touched the delicate lace curtains. "I feel like Wyatt Earp, looking down at Main Street, waiting for the big gunfight to start. A step back in time," he murmured as he let the lace drop and turned back to Megan.

"You're sure there isn't some place—"

"If Mr. Hall says there isn't, I'd trust him. I told you the supporting group is huge for a movie, and I'm sure the town's accommodations are stretched to the limit."

"What about the RV's that the man was talking—?"

"Recreational vehicle is an understatement. The portables are self-contained motor homes for the actors and the technical crew. The support groups and temporaries get to use motels and hotels or their own campers. It's easier on the budget." He shrugged, holding out both hands, palms up. "I'm sorry about this, Doc. I thought Walters's people understood." He looked at the couch. "Listen, you'll only be here a few days. You take the bedroom, I'll take the couch." He looked back at her, and a crooked smile lifted one corner of his mouth. "I can survive a few days. Can't you?"

She wasn't too sure, but she lied. "Sure, of course, that'll . . . be fine."

"Good. If you want to freshen up, go ahead. I've got a few calls to make."

"Then what?"

"Food. I'm starved."

Food was something she could deal with. Her stomach had been threatening to rumble for the past hour. "I am, too."

There was a knock on the door, and Cade crossed to open it for their driver, a slender Mexican in an immaculate uniform, who had their luggage. "Will you be needing me anymore tonight, Mr. Daniels?" the man asked as he stepped in and put the luggage on the hardwood floor.

"Where's the best place to eat around here?"

"Just down the street. The Homestyle Inn. Nothing fancy, but the food's good."

"Then I won't be needing you. We'll walk when we get ready."

"Mr. McCann said to tell you someone will be by for you at seven tomorrow morning."

"All right," Cade said, then closed the door.

He picked up Megan's bag and carried it toward the bedroom. "Can you be ready in ten minutes?"

"No problem." She watched him set the bag down, then turn to her. "What would you be doing if I wasn't here?" she asked.

He shrugged. "If you weren't here?" His eyes narrowed. "About the same thing, I guess, except I'd probably be thinking that room service, if there is such a thing here, could bring me up a dry sandwich. Honestly, I'd rather get a real meal. How about you?"

"Yes, a real meal," she murmured and hurried into the bedroom, brushing past Cade. Before she could fully absorb his male scent and body heat, he was out of the room and Megan was staring at the closing door. Yes, going out for food was definitely better than spending the rest of the evening in this suite, trying to behave as if everything was just fine.

By the time Megan had splashed her face with water in the pedestal sink of the old-fashioned bathroom off the bedroom and recombed her hair into a ponytail, she was starving. She left her garment bag hanging on the back of the bedroom door, grabbed her brown corduroy jacket and hurried into the sitting room.

Cade was talking on the phone, but glanced up when she came into the room, and smiled. He motioned to the phone, held up one finger, then without taking his eyes off her, continued. "We'll work it out when the car gets here. We'll time it and pace it off. See you tomorrow," he said, then hung up. "One last call," he told Megan as he punched the numbers again.

She crossed to the windows and looked out at the night. Cars were cruising slowly down the main drag of Dedrick, people were walking and the glow of neon lights was playing off the glass storefronts. Like a step back in time, but back to the fifties, she thought, not to Wyatt Earp's and Buffalo Bill's time.

"Doris?" she heard Cade say. "I'm just checking to make sure everything is all right with Adam." He paused, then inquired, "How bad is it?" Another pause. "Because I'm concerned, damn it." He inhaled harshly, then lowered his voice. "All right. All right." Apparently answering a question, he added, "Room 315. I'll be in touch tomorrow evening."

Megan heard the receiver clank back in the cradle, then turned and saw Cade staring at the phone. "Is something wrong?" she asked.

He shook his head. "I don't know. Doris said Adam has a cold. He didn't look sick a few days ago, but he's running a low fever and he's congested."

"Children get colds all the time," she said.

"Sure, I know," he said and stood as he ran his fingers through his hair. "I just hate being all the way in Texas, if he's sick."

"I'm sure Mrs. Sinclair is giving him the best of care."

Wrong thing to say, she thought, when she saw him glare at her. "I know," he muttered, "are you ready to go?"

"I sure am," she said, reaching for her purse on the side table.

Cade picked up his denim jacket and put it on while he crossed to the door. "Let's go."

They rode in silence down to the lobby, then stepped out of the elevator cage to find the space deserted, except for Horace Hill behind the desk. He looked up and asked, "Going out for the evening?"

She had the idea that the hotel owner was expecting them to take off for some wild party. "We're going out to eat. I heard the Homestyle Inn is pretty good."

The man looked vaguely disappointed. "Oh, sure. It's a pretty good place to eat," he said with a grin, "and it's about the only place to eat in this town, except for the fast-food place on the south end."

"How do I get there?" Cade asked.

"Out the door, go right and it's about a block and a half down. You can't miss it."

"Thanks," Cade said, then started for the door. Megan followed.

They stepped out into the street and into the cold night air, then headed north. Megan looked around at Dedrick, the main street now all but deserted, the glow of the neon lights the only illumination, except for the brightness of the occasional car's headlights. Businesses were mostly closed, but Megan could see the sign for The Homestyle Inn in the distance, a flashing red glow with yellow lettering.

She took some running skips to keep up with Cade's long stride, and when he looked at her, he almost stopped. "Sorry. I forgot. I'll take it slower. This isn't the hundred-yard dash, is it?"

"No, it's not," she said, easily able to match his slower pace.

They turned into the restaurant's blacktop parking lot, passed the cars and trucks that stood there and went to the entrance of the sprawling, flat-roofed building. Cade pushed back the wooden doors and let Megan go ahead of him inside out of the growing cold.

She found herself in a room with a heavily beamed ceiling, filled with warmth, a halo of smoke, small tables and booths, a bar to the right and a dance area in the middle by a huge jukebox. Country music wailed in the background.

Most of the tables and booths were occupied, and a few people were standing in the entry area. A hostess in tight jeans, silver silk shirt and cowboy boots came over and smiled at Megan and Cade.

"Howdy," she said with a toothy grin. "I'm LaVerle. You all here for dinner or the bar?"

"Dinner," Cade said.

"All right. You just follow me, and I'll take real good care of you."

She led the way by the tables and headed for the booths along the back wall. They passed some couples, dancing to plaintive lyrics about a man who loved a woman, then was haunted by her after she left him. When they got to an empty booth, Megan slipped off her jacket, laid it on the vinyl seat, then slid opposite Cade.

"You two with the movie people?" LaVerle asked as she chewed gum and smiled at them.

Cade nodded. "Yes. How about some coffee?"

"Sure thing," the girl said, then pointed to folded, blue paper stuck in the back of the napkin holder against the wall. "There's your menus. See what you want. I'll be back in a sec with your coffee and I'll take your orders."

As LaVerle left, Megan glanced up at the neon signs decorating the walls with advertisements for every brand of beer imaginable. Finally she looked at Cade and found him looking at her with an openly assessing gaze. "Is something wrong?" she asked.

"No, not at all. I was just thinking that no one would mistake you for a doctor right now."

She reached for a menu, then sank back in the seat and fiddled with the edges of the blue paper. "Well, you look right at home," she said honestly.

He grinned at her, the expression startling in its boyishness. "Yeah, I guess this fits the image—a stuntman in a honky-tonk."

Megan found herself smiling back at him. "This isn't exactly a honky-tonk saloon, but I wouldn't be surprised to see a fight break out anytime now, with breakaway chairs and fake bottles."

He reached for a menu, opened it, but didn't look at it. His eyes were on Megan. "So, you know all our secrets?"

"No, just something I've seen . . ."

"On television," he finished for her. "But you're right. Nothing is as it seems in the movies. Special wood, special glass, special equipment."

And, she suspected, a special kind of man to do the work. "You really like doing it, don't you?"

He shrugged. "I like it when it all works, when all the planning and ideas come together to make something special for a film."

"Like the stunt you're doing for Walters?"

"Yeah, that'll be great. We've also got a few minor stunts that I'm going to help with. They're scheduled for tomorrow. Then the big one. That's the one I'm here to make work." Megan could see a glint of excitement in his eyes while he spoke. "I've got it all planned, but making it go the way I want it to go..." He shrugged again as his voice trailed off. "It's going to make one hell of a shot for Walters's picture."

LaVerle returned and set two mugs of coffee in front of them, then took out an order pad. "What'll it be tonight, folks?"

"What's good?" Cade asked.

"Well, there's ribs and there's hamburgers. We've got plenty of both."

Cade raised an eyebrow in Megan's direction. "Hamburger or ribs?"

"A hamburger with extra tomatoes."

Cade ordered the same, and when LaVerle left, Megan slipped her menu back behind the napkin holder, then cradled her coffee mug between both hands. "Can I ask you something?" she inquired.

Cade sipped some of the hot liquid, then put his mug down and nodded. "Shoot."

"What is the big stunt?"

"It's part cannon roll, and part—"

She cut him off. "No, I want to know *what* it is in lay terms."

"Simply put, it's a car hitting a ramp at a certain speed, enough speed to make it airborne. Then, with the help of explosives, the car flips a certain number of times, then stops where you want it to. Stunts like that are really big in some sorts of movies."

"What sort of movie is this?" she asked, rubbing her hands back and forth on the warmth of the mug.

"An action-adventure, buddy movie. It's going to have a lot of hard physical stunts in it, and Walters wants a spectacular ending. That's why I'm here." He took a drink of his coffee. "Any gags in a Walters movie are first-rate."

"Any what?"

"Gags. That's what stuntmen call a stunt that's hard. They pass it off as nothing, as easy, as a gag."

"Have you done this gag before?"

"Not exactly. But I've done all the parts of it before. Just not the sum total."

"How dangerous is it?"

"On a scale of one to ten?" he asked.

"Realistically," she said.

"It's dangerous. I can't deny that. In this gag, the car's going to fly over a brick wall, flip, land on its tires and crash into a parked car." He grimaced. "I know how that sounds, but that's why you're here. To see it firsthand, to see all the planning that goes into it, the time and preparation. That takes a lot of the gamble out of it."

She frowned at his choice of words. "So, you see what you do as a gamble."

"Life's a gamble, Doc. What was it Benjamin Franklin said? 'But in this world nothing can be said to be certain, except death and taxes.'" He picked up his mug, took another drink of coffee, then looked at her over the rim. "Don't you think you gamble every day in this world?"

She shrugged to cover a sudden shudder that ran through her body. "There's gambling and there's gambling."

"Oh? What's the difference?"

She started to say the difference was between sanity and insanity, in not tempting fate, not doing things to hurt other people, but she never got the chance. LaVerle came back then with their dinner, and the next ten minutes were spent eating a hamburger that was delicious. When Megan was finished with everything except a huge, dill pickle spear, she sat back with a sigh. "That was really good."

"Not bad," Cade said, tossing his napkin over his completely empty plate. "You've got a good appetite, for such a little thing."

She shrugged. "Hunger is hunger."

"Cade," a man said as he approached the table. He was tall, thin, about fifty and dressed all in denim. "The little guy at the hotel said you were checked in and came down here. Good to have you finally with us."

Cade shook hands with him. "Good to be here, and thanks for the recommendation."

"Hey, I wanted the best, and you're the only one I knew who could possibly pull off the gag." He glanced at Megan. "The hotel clerk said that Cade had a pretty lady with him. I'm Ross Barnette, stunt coordinator for this project."

"Megan Lewis," she said. "And what's a stunt coordinator?"

"That means I'm Cade's boss." He held out a hand to her. "So I can assert my power and ask you to dance. That'll give me a chance to explain the rest of my job to you."

Megan looked at Cade, who shrugged and spread his hands, palms up. "I'm outranked here. But you dance with him at your own risk, Doc."

Megan smiled back at Ross. "I'll take the risk." She put her hand into Ross's and went with him to the dance floor. She caught a glimpse of Cade watching her, then looked up at Ross as he began to move to a ballad about lost love and tears. "So, what is a stunt coordinator?"

"A used-up stuntman, who still wants to be in the business, so he gets a crew together and coordinates the gags."

"You don't do the stunts yourself?" she asked, easily able to follow the man's simple dancing style.

"From time to time, the easy stuff. Nothing like the gag Cade's doing."

"You requested him?"

"Yeah, and I'm glad he took the job. He's one of the best. A real professional." He neatly executed a tricky step, then drew Megan back to him. "He's one hell of a guy. A real friend. Someone you can count on for anything."

Megan caught a glimpse of Cade at the table, talking to a young, dark-haired man, then the other dancers blocked her view. She looked back at Ross, who was still talking about Cade.

"I'd trust Cade with my life, any day. Actually I have, when I was active, every time we did a gag together or when he planned one for me. No one better in this industry."

By the time the music stopped, Megan was beginning to realize that Ross had done nothing but list all the virtues of Cade Daniels. When she thanked him and turned to go back to the table, another man approached her, the one who had been talking to Cade before.

He introduced himself as Bobby Slate and asked her to dance as another song started. She agreed, and while they moved to the music, he spoke in general about stunt work, then proceeded to tell Megan even more about Cade. If Ross's version had made Cade seem too good to be true, Bobby's version all but canonized the man.

After two more friends of Cade's, who "just happened to be stopping in for a drink," cut in and danced with Megan, she knew she was the target of one of the world's biggest and most pleasant snow jobs. The word must have gotten around, probably through Leon, about why she was here, and these men had come to make sure she saw Cade in a very favorable light.

When she caught sight of another man approaching her out of the corner of her eye, she turned to tell him she was too tired to dance. Then she saw the man was Cade.

"I'll take over now, Gus," he said to her partner, who was telling her all about how Cade rigged one of the best gags anyone ever did. As Gus moved to one side, Cade took Megan's hand, neatly slipped his other hand around her waist and in the next second, she was against him, moving easily to the slow ballad on the jukebox.

She used the excuse of looking up at Cade for moving back just a bit. "Was any of this your idea?"

"No. I thought they had come in for a drink, but I finally figured out what was up. I could see that you needed rescuing."

"I'm not sure rescue is the right word. Actually I've been treated to a thorough assessment of your character, and according to one and all, you could walk on water, if you tried."

That brought a burst of laughter from Cade, and he held her closer as he twirled her around. "I was afraid of that. Did this do permanent damage to me?"

"No," she said with her own smile. "They were trying to help, I think."

He shook his head, moving easily to the music and carrying her along with him. "They're friends, well-intentioned friends. Leon must have been in touch with them since we got here."

"I figured that out, when Mr. Larson said that you were as close to a saint as any man who ever walked this earth."

One dark eyebrow lifted sardonically. "You didn't buy it, did you?"

She shook her head. "Not when I know about those women in Las Vegas, taking baths in heaven knows what."

"It was champagne and it was Leon's idea," he said as he pulled her closer.

"A waste of good champagne," Megan murmured, trying to ignore the way she could feel every angle of the man against her. When she realized that not only could she not ignore the sensations of hip to hip and of her breasts against his chest, but had an impulse to just melt into his embrace, she forced herself to keep a modicum of distance between them. As long as she didn't lean against him and let herself use his strength as her support, she'd be all right.

What she couldn't handle was the way he moved his hand to the small of her back, neatly stopping any retreat on her part, or the way he moved seductively to a song about falling in love with the wrong person.

She inhaled the clean scent of after-shave and maleness and closed her eyes. But she opened them immediately when she realized that the action only sharpened her other senses, sensitizing her to every spot where his body touched hers. It focused all her attention on a sweet burst of longing for closeness and even more that flooded through her body. Reason was within reach, and she tried to keep herself from moving even closer, from letting herself become one in movement with the man and the music.

"Sad, isn't it?" Cade asked, the rumble of his words vibrating against her breasts.

"Pardon me?" she asked.

"This song, it's so sad. Falling in love with someone who can only hurt you."

"Yes, it is," she said, thinking that anyone who fell in love with Cade Daniels would be setting themselves up for hurt. And it would be so easy for him to charm a heart, to get someone to love him. That brought her up short and she all but stopped dancing.

"Is something wrong?" Cade asked as she looked up at him.

The deep brown of his eyes seemed almost liquid, and she knew a woman would be in danger of getting lost in that gaze. She knew she could—if she let herself. She'd been told once that no one fell in love without letting themselves fall in love with that person. Free will. It sounded simple, too simple. She hadn't had an option about being Frank's daughter, but she did have the choice of whom she'd be with now. A man like Cade Daniels didn't even make the list, despite the way he could scramble her reason and make her feel a fire that she could have sworn had never existed in her.

Cade was looking down at her questioningly and she realized she'd stopped dancing. It was her chance to move back, to break the contact, and she did, covering her tangle of thoughts with a mundane apology. "I'm sorry. It's been a long day."

"Yes, it certainly has been," he murmured, reaching out to cup her elbow with his hand and walk back with her to the table. "I think it's time to go. You look exhausted, and we have to be on the set by seven."

"Yes, let's go," she said quickly, breaking the contact by reaching for her jacket when they got to the booth. She slipped it on quickly, picked up her purse, then went with Cade through the restaurant to the front doors.

When they returned to the hotel, the lobby lights were turned down. A sleepy-looking teenager in a brilliant turquoise T-shirt that read Hell's Bargain in bright red letters across the chest looked at Cade and Megan and nodded. "Help ya?"

"We're staying here," Cade said as they approached the desk.

"Name?"

"Cade Daniels and Megan Lewis."

"Would that be Dr. Lewis?" he asked Megan.

"Yes, that's me."

"You've got a message," the boy said, shuffling through papers on the desk, then picking up a pink slip. He passed it across the desk to Megan. "Came in before I got on duty."

Megan looked down at the scribbled writing. "Call Rose at home as soon as possible," she read.

"Important?" Cade asked.

She folded the paper in half. Rose wouldn't have left a message like this, if it wasn't something really important. And that thought made Megan very uneasy. "I'm not sure. It's from my assistant." She looked around the lobby and spotted a pay phone near the elevator. Whatever Rose had to tell her, she didn't want Cade to be standing there when she heard it. "I'll call Rose from down here."

"You can use the phone—"

"No, this is fine. You go on up, and I'll be up in a while." Without giving him a chance to say anything else, she turned and walked quickly to the pay phone.

She put in a call on her credit card, heard the phone ring just twice, then Rose picked it up.

"Hello?"

"Rose? What's going on?"

"I hated to call, but I thought you should know this as soon as possible. Frank called the office today."

Megan closed her eyes for a moment. "Collect?"

"Yes, and I accepted the charges, so I could tell him you were gone for an indefinite period of time." She hesitated. "I don't think he believed me."

"What did he say?"

"That I was to get in touch with you and tell you about his hearing coming up, that he's really changed, that he wants out of that place and he loves you."

Megan held the phone so tightly, it felt as if the plastic would snap. He was still manipulating her emotions, very deliberately. She hated it.

"Are you still there?" Rose asked.

"Yes. I was just trying to think." She took an unsteady breath. "Listen, if he calls again, don't accept the charges. Hang up."

"That's it?"

"That's it," she said. "And thanks for everything, Rose. I'll be in touch tomorrow or the next day, at the latest."

"How's it going there?"

Just about as well as it was there, Megan wanted to say, but held her peace. "Fine, just fine," she lied, then said her goodbyes and hung up.

After crushing the slip of paper in her hand, she tossed it into an ashtray by the phone and pressed the button for the elevator. So Frank had called and tried to make contact. She'd expected it, yet hadn't wanted to believe he would. She swallowed hard as the cage door opened and she stepped into the elevator.

When she got to the room, Cade was nowhere in sight, but she could hear the shower running. Two sidelights by the couch were on, and she saw that someone had brought up sheets and blankets and left them on the coffee table. Megan stepped out of her shoes, dropped her purse and jacket by the door, and then, just to keep busy, began to make a bed for Cade on the couch.

When she'd finished, she crossed to the windows and stared out at the night. Massaging her temples with the tips of her fingers, she wondered why she had let herself think that Texas was far enough away to keep Frank out of her life. Stupid, stupid, she thought, and felt an ache starting behind her eyes.

"You didn't have to do that," Cade said from behind her.

She turned, then knew what she shouldn't have done—come with Cade Daniels to this place. She saw him crossing the room, with nothing on except a towel wrapped around his lean hips. His hair lay damply on his neck, curling at his temples and forehead, and she could see scars she'd only guessed were there before.

The imperfections weren't recent and had healed to a paleness that stood out against his naturally dark skin.

There was one on his upper right arm, long and straight, following the line of the muscle. Another was on the side of his left calf, a jagged mark about six inches long. Then there was the one on his chest. He looked pieced together.

"Excuse me? What did you say?"

"The bed. I could have done it," he said, then smiled at her. "But I appreciate it."

"No problem," she said, and started across the room to go into the bedroom, so she could be alone.

But Cade stopped her with a question, halfway between the couch and the escape hatch of the open bedroom door. "Bad news?"

She hesitated, then looked at Cade. "In a way. But it's taken care of." She was so close, she couldn't avoid the sight of the scars.

Cade wasn't oblivious to her reaction. "I've got a few battle scars. I'm sorry if they upset you."

Upset her? How could she tell him that she was feeling sick, realizing how much pain he must have endured because of the injuries? Yet he'd chosen this way of life. It didn't make any sense to her, no more than what Frank's choices did. "I . . . I just . . ."

He kept his gaze on her, his expression almost neutral, like a disinterested third party, giving a rundown on something. "The collarbone and shoulder were broken in Memphis ten years ago, the arm in Toronto, Canada, last year, and the leg is from good old Hollywood, almost fifteen years ago. I have various and sundry aches and pains, pulled muscles and torn ligaments. But nothing serious."

"Nothing serious," Megan echoed, not knowing what to say. She turned from Cade and headed for the safety of the bedroom. "Good night," she said over her shoulder as she stepped into the room and quickly closed the door after her.

She went right to the bathroom, stripping off her clothes on the way, then stepped inside, into a room still full of steamy heat from Cade's shower. A razor, toothbrush and brush lay on the ledge of the pedestal sink. She ignored the signs of his occupancy, and bent down to turn on the water in the claw-footed bathtub.

While the tub filled, Megan leaned back against the sink and buried her face in her hands. There was no way for her to erase the image of Cade, standing in front of her in the towel, from her memory, no way for her to forget Rose's words on the phone.

She stepped into the tub, sank low into the hot water and stared at the high ceiling. She wasn't going to let this happen to her. She was going to keep control, keep Frank out of her life, and give an impartial recommendation for Adam's custody. Then she'd walk away from Cade. Simple, she told herself. But in her soul she wondered if any woman had ever been able to simply walk away from a man.

Megan's first glimpse of the movie set the next morning was with the sun rising behind the gray walls of the abandoned prison complex, as the limousine drove along the road that led to the massive, metal security gates.

Barren land spread out in both directions, but about two hundred feet from the solid, brick walls that soared twenty feet into the sky, was a cluster of large motor homes. She thought in passing that it looked as if they had formed a circle, the way covered wagons used to before an Indian attack.

As the limo got closer to the gates, Megan could see that production was in full swing. Banks of lights were trained on an area along the security fence, a man sat in a basket on the end of a crane over twenty feet above the action on the ground, and three vans stood with their back doors open, filled with banks of equipment.

She couldn't see the main action because a crowd of people, dressed in bright orange jumpsuits with State Prison stenciled across the backs, was milling around. But the cameras—there looked to be four of them in all—were trained on the center of the crowd. Cade explained that the extras, people who filled in for the prisoners that were supposed to be the inmates of the prison, were mostly townspeople, making extra money.

The limo pulled up by the nearest motor home, just as the scene by the wall came to an end. The people began to move away, the basket on the crane was lowered, and the lights were turned off. With the loss of the bright artificial glow, the day took on an edge of gray.

"Here we are," Cade said as the car stopped. He opened the door to get out.

Megan followed him out and onto the packed earth, thankful that she'd worn a pullover along with her jacket, jeans and suede walking shoes. The smell of evergreens was in the air, and the wind that came from the north played havoc with her hair, which was already freeing tendrils from its ponytail.

She tucked her chin into the collar of her jacket and followed Cade toward the motor home. When they got within ten feet of it, a small man in a brilliant turquoise satin jacket, with Hell's Bargain emblazoned on the chest, hurried toward them. Flame-red hair was pulled back into a single braid, and a scruffy beard only partially hid a full, round face.

"Daniels. All right! Your timing's terrific." He hurried up to Cade, his hands out. Not more than five and a half feet tall, he looked small and plump next to Cade, and when he caught Cade in a bear hug, he ended up wrapping his arms around Cade, somewhere near his waist.

Megan watched the two and heard the red-haired man say softly as he drew away, "I know the pain, man, it's miserable." Then he stood back. "But life goes on. That's not cruel, just a fact."

Cade looked uneasy, muttered something like, "I appreciate that," then pushed his hands into his pockets.

The red-haired man patted Cade on the shoulder and looked at Megan. "And this is the good doctor?"

"Dr. Megan Lewis," Cade said. "This is Rick Walters."

"Good to meet you, Megan," Walters said, then grinned at her. "Another redhead. What a treat."

The man wasn't at all what Megan had expected, not after seeing his plane and the luxurious accommodations. She felt strange to think that she'd worn his robe, that Cade had had on his shirt, although now she understood why it hadn't come close to fitting Cade. "Thank you for the plane, I mean, for letting us use it."

Walters flicked away her thanks with a wave of his hand. "Glad to do it. It would have just been flying out equipment, if you hadn't been on board."

Megan glanced around at the activity, which seemed to be gaining momentum. "This looks like an alien land to me," she said. "I never knew so much went into making a movie."

Walters came closer to her, his blue eyes sparkling the way a child's would—a child who was into mischief. "Tell me you're a big fan of my movies."

She was taken back. "I would, but . . . I mean, I'm sure I would be, but I hardly ever go to the movies."

"Not what I wanted to hear," he muttered, then winked at her. "But you do know who Peter Shaw and Lincoln Steele are, don't you?"

"I've heard of them," she admitted.

"Don't say that to them," he said. "You'll ruin the day, and we won't get anything done. Look duly adoring when you meet them." He tugged at his jacket, trying to keep it zipped up over his stomach. "Actually, Shaw looks a hell of a lot like Cade. He's the one who recommended Cade for the project. Likes his work. Likes what he can do."

Another glowing recommendation, Megan thought, but she couldn't sense any of the earnest patronization she'd heard the night before from the others. "Do stars do that, ask for certain stuntmen?"

"Sure, if they fit the type and do a good job. A lot of actors have a favorite fall guy and keep him working for years, doubling for them in stunts." He looked back at Cade, who had been silently watching the exchange. "Ready to rock and roll, Cade?"

"Whenever you are."

"I'm ready and able right now. Let's get this show on the road. You know about the lineup today?"

"Ross and Gus filled me in."

"Good. We're doing an upper-story fall, then staging a fight in an exercise yard. The sets are already in place. Speaking of sets, we've finished the one for your gag." He motioned to the north. "We gave you a lot of distance before the fence, as much as we could." He looked intently at Cade. "Any doubts?"

"No, I've plotted and laid it out on paper. All I have to do is see the setup, and when it gets here, try the car."

"That's all here tomorrow morning, first thing. Until then . . ." He slapped Cade on the back. "We've got work to do."

"Show me the way," Cade said.

Walters turned and yelled at the top of his lungs. "Scene twenty-four. Now!" He motioned with a sweep of his hand away from the vehicles. "Get me a Jeep! We're going inside!"

Chapter 8

As soon as Megan drove through the open security gates in Rick Walters's Jeep, she felt a smothering sensation in the pit of her stomach. The inner yard, the buffer between the sprawling complex of brick that formed Dedrick Federal Prison and the massive outer wall, was dusty; browned weeds stretched along both sides of the cracked concrete driveway that went to the main building.

The dull red brick structure was over three stories high, with narrow windows covered by metal mesh. The touch of the movie company was seen clearly here in the form of new, green paint on the steel doors, and an inlaid, brass sign that read Dedrick Federal Prison high over the entry.

When the Jeep stopped by the doors, Walters helped Megan out, then led the way inside. As Megan stepped through, she felt as if she'd entered another world, an ugly, colorless world—one she didn't want any part of.

But, almost the way people are drawn to look at a horror movie they know they don't want to see, she took in the disquieting details. Paths were worn in the stone floors, all the locks had been taken off the doors, leaving holes in the metal, and the air was heavy with musty age, disuse and the pungency of fresh paint.

They went through a reception area, through a rusty, steel door that looked to be almost six inches thick, along an echoing hallway and into the main cell block. Row upon row of empty cells lined all three levels. The walls were a chalky gray, chipped and scarred with graffiti, and the bars were rusted. Some were even falling out of their bed in the thick, concrete walls.

On the ground floor, Megan saw equipment, banks of lights on massive roller platforms, cameras and heavy cables crisscrossing the area. People hurried back and forth, a few stopping to say a couple of words before rushing off to take care of something.

Walters led the way to the metal staircase and Megan followed him and Cade up to the second level. Here, for the benefit of the cameras, the walls had been painted a deep gray over the chipping and graffiti. The bars had been painted flat black, and the metal doors a dull green.

When Megan stopped by the closest cell, Cade went ahead, calling out to a man farther down the balcony. She leaned against the wall to keep out of the way of the cameramen setting up their equipment and adjusting the lights. She looked across the way at the cells on the far side. For an instant she didn't see all the equipment crowded onto the gallery, the space heaters that vainly tried to heat the cavernous area or the ever growing number of people milling around. All she could think of was Frank. That he was living in something like this, that he had no freedom, no sense of himself, and no way to walk away from it except for parole.

Walters jarred her out of her thoughts by calling to her in a booming voice. "Doctor! Over here." He motioned her to the metal railing, so that she could overlook the lower floor. "Come on and meet the stars of this little venture."

She picked her way carefully over the heavy cables, lying helter-skelter on the cracked, concrete floor, and crossed to where Walters stood.

"Peter Shaw," Walters said, "Dr. Megan Lewis."

Megan hoped she looked duly impressed as she shook hands with Peter, a dark-haired man with compelling, green eyes and a crooked grin. She could see that Cade bore a slight resemblance to this man, with his solid build, medium height and broad shoulders. If the camera was at a distance and both men wore the same clothes, they could pass for each other.

"And this is Lincoln Steele." Walters rested a hand on the shoulder of a startlingly handsome, dark-skinned man. Lincoln stood well over six feet and had a remarkably cocky smile that was strangely endearing, instead of being annoying. "Boys, this doctor is a shrink, so be careful what you say around her. She's apt to figure out we're all dead nuts."

Everyone laughed, then Walters's mood changed abruptly, the humor gone. "All right!" he yelled. "Let's get this show on the road." He turned to Cade and Ross, who had just shown up. "What's going down?"

"The fall first," Ross said. "No pun intended."

Walters laughed, then nodded. "Then let's do it." When he moved farther down the balcony past a mobile camera, Megan moved back to the wall and watched Cade from a distance. For what seemed a very long time, he and Ross went over every detail of the stunt, where Lincoln Steele was supposed to be hit, then shoved backward over the railing.

She saw Cade coaching a young, black stuntman, who was doubling for Lincoln, showing him how to hit the rail, how to hesitate, then plunge over it. Cade hit the railing with the small of his back over and over again, showing the man how to spread his arms just right at the moment of impact.

Megan flinched when Cade suddenly vaulted to the top of the safety rail that overlooked the floor far below and stood there, balanced, looking down for what seemed an eternity.

All the while she held her breath, unable to make her chest expand to take in air. Then Cade turned, jumped down to the balcony floor again and said something to Ross.

"Cade?" Walters called from the other side of the second level. "How's it look?"

"It's a go," he shouted back, then as he swung around, his gaze met Megan's.

He must have read the shock there, because he gave the thumbs-up sign and called out, "There's an air bag down there, Doc." Then he turned to speak to a cameraman who'd come up beside him.

Megan closed her eyes for a moment, trying to settle her nerves. God, she felt sick. An air bag. Had she really thought he'd stand like that, if the possibility of accidents hadn't been provided for? She really didn't know. For all the years she'd lived with a person who took horrible risks, she still couldn't figure out what they did or why they did it.

"Sorry about that," Cade said by her ear, and she spun toward him, her elbow thudding against his middle.

"What were you doing?" she demanded in a whisper.

He rubbed at his stomach, where her arm had hit him. "Not thinking. I promised to tell you what I was doing and I didn't. I should have explained."

She felt vaguely mollified by his apology, but that didn't stop the lingering fear she felt, just thinking about him on the railing. "Yes, you should have."

"I forget that people don't understand. I was watching the bag setup, making sure it was lined up the way it should be.'' He frowned at her. "I wouldn't let Jack go over the side without making sure everything was all right.''

It sounded so rational, and she knew that her reaction was anything but that. She could only nod and would have turned from Cade, hoping she could get herself under control, separate her personal problems from her questions about this man, who didn't blink an eye when facing death. But Cade stopped her by touching her shoulder.

She looked back at him, but jerked free of his touch. "What?" she asked.

"Are you going to give me a break on this?"

"For what?"

"For not explaining it. It's so basic, something I do without thinking, that I—"

"Without thinking," she echoed. "Like an addiction."

"No, like a job. Like something that goes on every day. I don't have any fear of heights, so I can do that."

"I'll make a note of it."

He stared at her hard, then moved away abruptly and headed back to the place where he'd climbed onto the railing.

As Megan watched him go, she could almost see Frank walking away, heading off to the casinos, angry that she didn't want him to leave her alone one more time. But this was different. This was a job, a case, and nothing to do with Frank, beyond the fact that he was in a place like this.

She hugged her arms around her chest. She had never allowed herself to think about what his prison would look like, how he would live. That was part of the bargain she had made with herself—to cut him out of her life and get on with living. But now she couldn't ignore it. She was in the middle of it here, in a hole. That was what this place was, a hellhole.

She heard Cade's voice again and focused on it. He was talking to another stuntman. "All right. After Linc takes the blow to the jaw, we'll block and you take over."

Walters was still across the way on the same level, looking through one of the three cameras set up for the shot. He swept his hands in large gestures, looked over the camera and called out to Cade, "Whenever you're ready, boy."

"Now's as good a time as any."

"Then let's go for it," Walters replied. Banks of lights flashed on everywhere, radiating a warmth that the heaters couldn't begin to match. They drenched the cell block in a clarity that only made the prison look more depressing.

Megan watched as Lincoln took his place, standing very still while they checked light meters around him, then Walters yelled for action.

A big man, an extra Megan had noticed before, because of his size and the bright orange coverall, ran up behind Lincoln, grabbed him by the shoulder, spun him around and aimed a blow at his jaw. The actor's head snapped back, but from Megan's angle, she could see that the blow had touched nothing but air.

Then Walters called, "Block," and the stuntman, Jack, was there, easing Lincoln out and with Cade's help, getting himself into the actor's position. When everyone was satisfied with the match, the scene continued. The stuntman swung his head back as if he'd been hit, then staggered against the rail, pitched backward over the metal barrier and disappeared from view.

Megan didn't go to the edge to look, but knew he'd made it safely when everyone cheered and Walters yelled, "It's a wrap!"

"Nothing to it, Doc," she heard Cade say, his lips so close to her ear that she could feel his breath ruffle her hair.

When she turned to look at Cade, he'd moved back a bit, enough to give her some breathing room. "He did it well, didn't he?"

"Perfect. The kid's got potential. That's the reason he graduated the head of his class."

"What class?"

"There's a stuntman school in California. The best there is. And the kid made it through at the top of his class."

"They actually teach men to do this?"

"And women. Sure. That's what takes a lot of the risk out, an educated person doing the stunt."

"I thought—"

"That all stuntmen fly by the seat of their pants, taking whatever risks they need to take?"

She felt embarrassed that she hadn't had time to do any research into stunt work. "I guess so."

"That's how I got started. I couldn't afford the school, so I teamed up with an older fall guy and earned as I learned, as the saying goes."

"What's next?" she asked.

"We can't do much on the big stunt until the car and equipment are here. We'll tackle that tomorrow. But we've got another one I agreed to help on."

"A stunt like this?" she asked, aware of the extras heading towards the exits in long lines. It was all too real for Megan, the men in line, all looking alike, confined in this place.

"No, it's a riot scene—lots of shots, reshooting and different camera angles to fill in for the scene in the movie."

"How about the stunt you're going to do, the big one? Do you get to do it until you get it right?"

"No, that's a stunt where you go for it just once." He frowned. "And I don't mean do or die."

"I just thought . . ."

"I know what you thought. Didn't anyone tell you that your face is an open book?" Cade touched her chin unexpectedly and the action made her freeze. She couldn't look away from his gaze, even though she felt as if his fingers were branding her with fire. "You're easy to read, Doc, real easy."

She was afraid of what he could see there now. Closing her eyes to shut in her emotions and shut Cade out, she turned away from him. She opened her eyes to an almost empty cell block. Even the equipment was being rolled out. "Where do you go for the next stunt?"

"Down below and out into an exercise yard. Are you coming with me?"

"Yes," she said as she faced Cade once more. Their eyes met, and she quickly walked past him to head for the stairs.

The next stunt depicted a riot, taking more than two dozen stuntmen and forty extras and staged in a huge exercise yard that was surrounded by the prison building on all four sides. The noise and confusion bounced off the brick walls in the one-hundred-yard-square space, and Megan stayed off to one side, standing behind the main camera crew near the security doors.

By the time lunch break was called, it was two o'clock. Noon back home, Megan thought, and felt her stomach rumble. Her breakfast of toast and juice, delivered by room service, hadn't kept her going for long. But the effects of a horribly restless night had stayed with her. She knew her lack of sleep was partly the cause of her emotional sensitivity today.

She went with Cade and the others into what had once been the prison mess hall, a cavernous space that had a catwalk, a narrow gallery about six feet above the floor, going all the way around it, and an observation booth overlooking the entire room.

It hadn't been refurbished at all, just cleaned, though extra lights had been brought in to lessen the innate gloom that seemed to hang over everything in the prison. The lunch—sandwiches, fruit and cookies boxed and delivered by the Homestyle Inn in town, was served on long, picnic tables covered incongruously with white linen and bright red, plastic tableware.

Megan sat at the table with Cade and the four other stuntmen, Ross, Leon, Bobby and Jack. The men seemed at ease with each other, talking about the stunt, speaking in a shorthand that Megan didn't bother trying to follow. She picked at her food and tried not to stare at the room around her.

But she couldn't help wondering if this was the way Frank ate every meal. Was he in some prison jumpsuit, eating packaged food? She tried to swallow and had to reach for coffee to wash down the bite.

Damn it, why was she thinking these things? Why should she care, after everything Frank had done to her? She'd cut him off, but obviously that physical separation hadn't cut him out of her thoughts. She pushed the barely touched sandwich back into the box and finished her coffee, letting the heat trickle down her throat. But it didn't touch the chill deep inside her.

With all of her professional training, she couldn't deal with her own life. That upset her the most. She'd been trained to help people, but couldn't help herself. She stood and without looking at anyone in particular, muttered, "I'm...I'm going outside to get some fresh air. I'll be back in a bit."

She didn't wait for Cade to say anything before she headed for the door and left the room. When she got into the empty hallway, she hurried down the stone-floored corridor, and by the time she came to the first open door, where sunlight streamed inside, she was almost out of breath.

She stepped into the sun, hating the way it shone so brightly, yet gave such little heat. The cold air cut through her jacket, and she pushed her hands into her pockets as she leaned against the brick wall. Then she realized she was in another exercise yard, a smaller one, but just as contained by the four walls.

The dusty ground was choked by weeds and when she looked up at the sky to a patch of clear blue, she saw the ever-present frame of the thick walls of the prison on all sides. There was no freedom out here, just an illusion of it.

She jerked to her left when she heard footsteps and saw Cade step into the doorway and look at her. The harsh clarity of the sunlight cut deep shadows at his chin and cheeks, and he shaded his eyes with his hand as he gazed out at her.

"Doc?" he asked, lowering his hand and coming toward her. "Are you all right?"

She touched her tongue to her lips, trying to form words. How could she tell him? How could she explain why she was standing out here? Her own thoughts stopped her. Why would she even consider telling him? That was an even better question. She hardly knew this man.

"You look white as a ghost," he said as he stood right in front of her. "Are you sick?"

Sick and tired, she wanted to say, but only shook her head. "No, but this place. It...it's really frightening to think of human beings locked up here."

"There hasn't been a prisoner here for twenty years. Walters was telling me the first thing they did when they got here was to remove all the locks, just in case."

She licked her lips and moved her hand in a futile gesture. "It's cold and ugly and..." She closed her eyes. "I never thought about what a prison would look like, what it would feel like to be inside it, to sense the thickness of walls separating you from the rest of the world."

"Why would you? I certainly hadn't, until I went to see Alcatraz a few years back. You get a tour, and they let you go in a solitary confinement cell, and close the door, so you can feel what it's like to be locked up." He frowned. "It's awful. That loss of freedom, of choice. I suspect it could kill a person, but very slowly." He looked up at the sky. "To see the sky, but know you can't walk away..." His voice trailed off as he looked back at Megan. "It really bothers you, doesn't it?"

"Yes, it does," she whispered. "I didn't know it would until I got here." She took a shaky breath. "Why don't I just look around on my own, while you finish that riot scene?"

"Is the noise getting to you?"

She felt the throbbing at the back of her eyes trying to become a headache. "Yes, it is. Everything echoes around here."

"Go ahead and wander around. Just be careful. They've got some riggings for different scenes already set up, and parts of this place aren't fit for human occupancy."

"I'll be careful," she said, and turned to go back inside, hoping to find the real exit.

Cade watched her until she was through the door and out of sight. He wished he understood Megan Lewis. He understood completely how she could touch him with such potency on a physical level. All he had to do was look at her, to see her move, to hear her talk in that soft, low voice. But he didn't understand why she touched him on another level, one he'd seldom felt before.

For no reason he could fathom, he had an overwhelming need to protect her. When he'd seen her looking at him after he'd jumped off the rail, he had seen stark terror on her face. And he'd experienced the need to reassure her. When he'd touched her later, it had been all he could do to fight the urge to pull her to him and hug her tightly. To protect her.

What a concept. He'd seldom thought about others, about their needs and fears. He'd gone through life doing what he wanted to, not deliberately trying to hurt anyone, but answering to no one. Then he'd found that he really wanted his son, that he wanted to be the one to help him grow up, to be the one with him, day in and day out.

That had shocked him, but he'd accepted it. Adam was his son. It was a blood connection, a joining that went beyond wants and needs. But he didn't understand his feelings toward Megan. In the week that he'd known her, he'd realized that he not only thought about her and dreamed about her, but that she could rob him of sleep, just by being in the next room, the way she had last night. And she could make him feel her pain.

But he didn't know where the pain came from. And he couldn't do anything about it. He sensed something was wrong, but was at a loss to help. The idea of a lover somewhere was definitely unsettling. But it didn't dampen that need to protect.

Right then, Cade wished that Megan trusted him enough to talk to him, to let him understand what was going on with her. Then he stopped himself. Egotist, he thought. How could he help her, when he was having such a hard time getting his own life in order?

He walked slowly back inside, into an empty corridor. For an instant he had the impression he could catch Megan's scent in the air, a sweetness overlaying the odors of neglect and age, of cold stone and steel. Then it was gone.

An illusion, he told himself, just like everything else he was doing at this place. He turned and headed back to the others. As he stepped into the mess hall, he hesitated, then crossed to where some of the men were still sitting together. They looked up as he took his seat again. "Everything all right?" Ross asked.

"Sure, why not?" he murmured, fingering the empty box his lunch had come in.

"When I saw the doctor leave like that . . ."

"She's having a hard time being in this place."

"Oh, claustrophobia?"

"Something like that." Cade exhaled, then reached for the notebook Ross took everywhere with him. "Let's go over things again. We've got a lot of work ahead of us."

Ross nodded and pointed to the top of the page, where Cade had opened the book. "That's the measurements, right there," he said and began to explain his figures.

But try as he would, Cade couldn't concentrate. All he could think about was Megan and the look on her face in the exercise yard. He had to literally force himself to listen to Ross's words, to focus on what was coming up. And that bothered him, it bothered him a lot. One thing he needed above all else with this job was concentration. Maybe asking the doctor to come with him had been a mistake, after all.

Cade didn't see Megan for most of the afternoon, and when he caught glimpses of her, she was talking to cast members. Then he realized around four o'clock that he hadn't seen her in over an hour. When he asked about her, Walters told him she'd left with some cameramen, who were going back to Dedrick. She'd left a message for Cade that she'd see him later at the hotel.

As soon as Cade knew Megan wasn't close by, he found he could focus entirely on the stunt. With a sense of relief he buried himself in the work, and was shocked when he realized they had lost the sun and it was almost six o'clock.

After driving back into town with Leon and grabbing a quick dinner together, he left Leon and headed back to the hotel. As he unlocked the door of their room and walked inside, he was met by shadows and silence. He experienced a gripping sensation of being totally alone, and instead of the usual thankfulness for solitude, he felt isolated, as if he'd been set adrift in a world where he was the only resident. He hated the feeling.

He had no idea where Megan was, but he had a real need to make a connection, to hear another person's voice. Even if that person was someone who hated him. Without turning on the lights, he tossed his jacket onto the couch and dropped into the chair closest to the phone. He put through a call to Los Angeles, waited, then heard the maid at the Sinclairs' answer.

"Sinclair residence."

"This is Cade Daniels. I need to talk to Mrs. Sinclair."

"Just a moment." He heard the clatter of a phone being put down, then waited in the shadows.

When he finally heard Doris come on the line, his whole being tensed.

"Cade, is that you?"

He closed his eyes. "Yes, it's me."

"What do you want? I'm very busy, and I—"

"Doris, I want to . . . to know how Adam's doing."

"Why?" she asked, a single clipped word.

He exhaled in a rush and muttered, "Give it a rest, Doris. I don't have the energy to do battle right now. I just want to know how he is."

She was silent for a long moment, then finally said, "He's got a cold. He's stuffy and miserable, but he's being taken care of by the best doctor, and I'm with him as much as I can be. Does that answer your question?"

"Yes, it does. Thank you."

"I heard Dr. Lewis is going down there to observe you at your job."

It didn't surprise Cade that Doris knew. She made it her business to never be taken by surprise. "Yes, she is. As a matter of fact, she's here now."

"I'm thankful she's so conscientious. She knows I want to get this over and done with as soon as possible."

Doris saw Megan as her ally. The thought was very disturbing to Cade. It didn't feel right in any way. "Don't you have any doubts at all about the outcome of the case?"

"None, Cade, none at all," she said firmly, then hung up.

When the line buzzed in his ear, Cade slowly returned the phone to the cradle. She sounded as sure of herself as he was uncertain of himself. What if they got Adam? What if he didn't even get visitation rights? His stomach clenched. What if Adam never really knew his father? Cade closed his eyes, and the image that came to him was Megan.

She could change everything.

Megan had come back to the room around five, checked in with Rose, and found out that Frank had tried to place two collect calls to her. When she'd hung up, she'd ordered a light dinner in the room, and after it had come and she'd nibbled on the salad, she'd soaked in a hot tub.

Even though it had barely been seven o'clock, Megan had emerged from the bath so sleepy, she could hardly keep her eyes open. After dressing in an oversize T-shirt, she'd crawled into bed and been asleep, almost before her head hit the pillow.

She slept for what seemed forever, relishing the deep softness of forgetfulness. She snuggled into it, wrapping it around her, and didn't know she was in a dream until she realized that everything was changing. She knew it was a dream, but when she found herself in a house alone, she wondered if dreams were the past, and the past nothing more than dreams.

She couldn't see the house or really define it, yet knew with certainty that it was a place she and Frank had rented on the outskirts of Las Vegas, when she had been about ten years old. A tiny, one-bedroom cottage at the back of a lot, with cracked tile on the floor and barely enough room for the two of them.

But Megan had pretended that the house would be the one she'd live in forever. "Forever" had lasted a little over three months. Then there had been the inevitable move, the school left behind, the friends barely made.

But in the dream, as Megan made out her surroundings, that house was larger, the walls clean and bright, the floor covered in soft carpet. It was the way she had always dreamed it would be, her fantasy of the home she'd have some day.

She spun around on her toes, around and around like a ballerina, the sun pouring in through lace drapes in a diffused dappled glow. Music was everywhere, soft and gentle. Warmth surrounded Megan, mingled with the fragrance of baking cookies that drifted from the kitchen.

It's perfect, she thought, then felt it slipping away at a frightening rate. The sun dimmed. The music became discordant; the warmth was turning to a bone-deep chill. Frank was suddenly there, but not the man she remembered, not the tall man with the wide smile and the glad hand for anyone he met who looked as though they had money.

Frank stood in the doorway, a dark man, with pale skin and sad eyes. Lines of what looked like grief were cut deeply in his face, and his shoulders sagged. "I'm dying, girl, I'm dying," he whispered and held out a hand to her. But she couldn't touch him. She wouldn't.

He was lying, the way he always did, she told herself, while she huddled back in the corner of the room, which was now every bit as drab as it had been in reality. "No, go away, leave me alone," she whispered.

He took a step toward her. "But, Meggie, you have to save me. You have to make things right. Don't let me die."

"You're not dying," she managed. "You're lying, you're just doing this so...so..." She couldn't get any more words out, when she saw the way Frank began to shimmer, then shrink in size.

"I'm dying, Meggie, I'm dying," he whispered over and over again, "and you won't help. You won't save me. My own little girl... Child of mine. You won't help. You... won't...help...."

As he began to fade more and more, she knew she had to do whatever it took to save him and ran toward him. But she couldn't reach him. She ran harder, faster, yet she didn't move. The distance stayed undiminished, and her outstretched hands closed on air. "Frank! Frank!" she called out. "Please, don't go! Don't go!"

But his image was gone, dissolved, as if it had never been. "No!" she screamed. "No, Frank, no!"

Cade heard the scream tear through the dark hotel suite, and was on his feet, running for the door to the bedroom, before he even thought about what was happening. He jerked the door open, and in the dim light that filtered through the drapes from the street, he could see Megan in some sort of oversize T-shirt, sitting bolt upright on a bed that looked as if it had been torn to shreds.

"No," she sobbed, "Frank, no." Her hands were stretched out in front of her.

Her pain tore at him, and he was overwhelmed by his need to stop her hurting. He hurried to the bed, climbing onto it on his knees to pull her to him. For a moment she was stiff and unyielding, then she let out a soft sob and all but collapsed against his chest.

"It's all right," he said over and over again, holding her tightly to him while he stroked her loose hair. He felt shuddering sobs rack her body, and she buried her face in his chest.

Megan came out of the dream in fragmented stages, first knowing that Frank wasn't there, that he wasn't dying, then realizing that she was being comforted in a way no one in her life had ever comforted her. She snuggled into heat and support and the dream dissolved even more, though her sobs increased. The relief of leaning on someone was overwhelming, and she gave in to it. She couldn't remember anyone holding her like this, anyone making her feel safe and protected, even after the nightmare she'd had.

She spread her hands on silky heat and inhaled on a shudder. Heat and male essence surrounded her, and the dream was fading, being replaced by another fantasy—of Cade, holding her to him and whispering to her through the shadows. "It's all right. It's all right. I'm here."

And the world shifted, spinning precariously close to being out of control. She would have drawn back right then. She knew she should have, yet hesitated, the need of Cade's comfort and support far outweighing any alarm at being in Cade's embrace.

And that was her mistake, she realized a fraction of a second later, when she felt his lips press against her bent head. The gentleness of the contact took her breath away, and when she moved back far enough to look up at Cade, he seemed to fill the entire world. His scent, his heat, his eyes on her. She froze. She had no idea what to do and no ability to do it.

"I...I..." she stammered, then touched her tongue to her lips, tasting the saltiness of tears. But that wasn't what she wanted. Suddenly she wanted to taste Cade with her lips and tongue, to feel him under her hands, to drink in his gentleness.

Cade had told her her face was an open book, and it must have been truer than she'd known, because no sooner had she thought of her want of him, than she heard Cade take a soft, jerky breath. Knee to knee he faced her on the bed, shifting his hands to cup her face. He brushed at her clinging tears with the balls of his thumbs, then his lips found hers.

Chapter 9

Cade felt Megan sway into him, and when she looked up, her tongue touching her lips, he felt a surge of desire that was all encompassing. His need for this woman, here and now, was past imagining. And there was nothing to stop him from doing what he desperately wanted—to kiss her.

The instant he touched his lips to hers, a flood of desire washed over him and threatened to drown him. He didn't think it could ever be any more intense, yet it grew as he tasted her softness, as his tongue skimmed her teeth and invaded her warmth. It seemed to consume him, to wrench at his soul, and the dream was reality.

He could sense a healing in him, a lessening of all the pains of the world in this woman's kiss. And when she touched his bare shoulders with her spread hands, when she began to respond with an abandon that stunned him, he knew he was the one who needed comfort. He needed to know her, be one with her.

He tasted her essence—sweetness and heat and incredible softness. His body almost trembled with the fire inside. Her body was against his in that ridiculous excuse for a shirt, molding to him, almost absorbing him. Yet he felt as if he could be burned where her breasts pressed yearningly to his chest. With a muffled groan, Cade fell with Megan back onto the bed, tumbling into the tangle of sheets and blanket.

Then she was alongside him, and he pressed his face into the heat of her neck while his hands explored her, trailing down the line of her throat, over the soft cotton of her top to the swelling of her breast. She moaned, arching her head back at his contact. And he pushed aside the thin fabric, needing a direct, skin-to-skin connection.

What he found was beyond the dream, bare skin, so incredibly smooth, and her breast, full and soft in his hand. His tongue moved higher to her ear, while his hand found the firm peak of her nipple as it tightened with sensation. Her gentle whimperings were a primal sound that he felt deep in his soul.

Then he lowered his head and his lips found the heat of her throat, skimmed over the material of the top bunched above her breasts, before his mouth took the place of his hand. He had to have her, to lie with her until this need was satiated. His body knew that unerringly, his fullness almost painful in the confines of his jeans.

He drew on her breast, taking the nipple into his mouth, and Megan cried out, her hips lifting instinctively, invitingly. He drew back and shifted, looking at her in the lights from the street that filtered in through the lacy fabric on the windows.

With her hair spread in wild disarray, her eyes large and shadowed and her lips slightly parted and swollen, she was the most beautiful woman he had ever seen in his life.

Nothing with any other woman had prepared him for what he felt at that moment, not for the intensity, the rightness of it all, nor the driving force in him to know her and possess her.

His gaze fell to her breasts, now swollen with desire, and he found them again with his hand. Then he lowered his head to taste her lips and trailed his hand down to her stomach, spanning the rapidly rising and falling diaphragm with his fingers. His touch moved lower to the elastic of her panties, hesitated, then gently worked its way under the flimsy material.

He felt her tense, then suddenly roll away from him. "No," she whispered in an unsteady voice. "No, please, no."

Megan couldn't look at Cade over her or feel his touch on her any longer. She knew that if she let herself go, she wouldn't turn back. She could block reality and let herself get lost in the heady passion that had replaced comfort, give herself up to a need that made her ache. But she wouldn't.

Cold reality was there, exposing the reason she was here, why she had first met Cade, and who this man was, who could set her blood on fire with a look, a touch. She closed her eyes and tugged at her T-shirt to cover her naked breasts. "I don't know why..." She bit her lip hard and awkwardly sat up. She knew why. She didn't have any illusions about why she'd let him touch her and kiss her like that. She pressed her bare feet to the braided rug and kept her back to Cade. "I'm sorry."

"You're sorry?" He spoke from behind her; she was grateful that he did not touch her again. "I heard you cry out. I didn't know you were even here." The bed shifted and his voice was farther away. "I came to see what was wrong."

She hugged her arms around herself, trying to stop a trembling that was growing from the inside out. He'd helped

more than he could know . . . at least, at first. He'd brought
her comfort. Recognizing that brought tears to her eyes and
almost killed the frustration she felt physically from turning away from Cade.

"I had a . . . a nightmare," she breathed. "But this . . . this
is wrong, a violation of everything, every reason I'm here.
I'm supposed to be objective."

In that instant she remembered his words in Adam's
nursery at the Sinclairs'. *"I will do whatever it takes to get
my son."* That brought sickness to her throat, and she had
a horrible thought. Did that include seducing her? Making
her want him with a hunger that defied reason? Cade could
charm and manipulate. She didn't have any doubt about
that. But he probably hadn't counted on her being so easy
to sway, so desperate for the contact.

She bit her lip so hard, she tasted the metallic sharpness
of blood on her tongue. Oh, yes, she'd been easy, so easy.
Desperate was the word. She gathered what control she
could muster and stood. Crossing to the bathroom, she
spoke without looking back. "I had a nightmare, and it's
over. Let's just forget about this, all right?"

"Sure, Doc, whatever you say," she heard Cade mur-
mur, just before she closed the bathroom door.

In the total darkness of the small room, she leaned back
against the door and tears came. Hot, silent tears. When she
heard the bedroom door shut, she slid to the floor, pulled
her legs to her breasts and pressed her forehead to her knees.

She hadn't felt like this since she was a child, this uncertain about what was going on and what she had to do. Focus on the job, she told herself. Just focus, and block out the
memory of Cade's touch and his kiss. Lord, she'd never felt
that alive before, never. Yet if he'd been counting on sway-
ing her decision . . .

She raked her fingers through her loose hair and exhaled shakily. No, this wouldn't make a difference. It couldn't. And she couldn't walk away from this case, either. She knew that if she did, she'd always wonder what she could have done, what she should have done for Adam Daniels.

She'd done enough walking away lately. She wouldn't do it this time. She was a professional and could get through it. In the light of day things would seem better. The dreams about Frank wouldn't be there, and she wouldn't wake to find Cade holding her in his arms. That last thought brought a sense of sorrow that was bone deep, a sorrow she couldn't assuage.

Cade lay on the couch in the darkness, heard water run in the bathroom, then a door close. Silence fell. But sleep wouldn't come to him. He'd gotten past the physical loss, but couldn't forget the sound of her scream or the name she'd called out—Frank. A man. Someone she cared enough about to have dreams of, someone whose memory could make her so vulnerable, she'd turn to anyone for comfort.

She'd never been married, but he would be a fool to think that she'd never had a lover. Frank. Whoever the man was, he'd touched Megan in a way that had branded her soul. He twisted on the couch, then, with a sigh of exasperation, sat up. For just an instant he considered knocking on the door and asking what was wrong. Who was Frank? And what had he done to hurt her so deeply? But he immediately rejected that idea. He didn't want to see Megan in the bed again, her hair tousled, her eyes heavy with sleep. And he didn't want to hear about another man who had known her.

He stared into the shadows at the illuminated hands of the clock on the television set in the corner. 2:00 a.m. The wanting was still with him—right or wrong. And he needed distance to make it go away. That would never happen if he stayed here, hearing each creak of her bed, every sound.

He stood abruptly, grabbed clothes and slipped them on in the darkness. Quietly he left the hotel room and walked away into the night.

When Megan woke in the morning, with gritty eyes and a weariness she knew came from hours of fitful sleep, she lay on her back, not moving, memories of Cade coming to comfort her, so real that she could feel a heat beginning to flicker to life in her. She had to face him today, in the cold light of morning, and make some sense out of what had happened last night.

She threw back the tangle of covers, anxious to get it over with, to put it behind her. Then she heard Cade's voice coming from behind the closed bedroom door. "I can do it. That's why you brought me here, and that's why you're paying me the big bucks."

She heard laughter and recognized Walters's voice. "Yeah, a big chunk out of the budget. But you're worth it. Just give me a time frame to have it on film."

"Three, maybe four days, tops, if everything is the way it looks right now."

Walters was an answer to a prayer. If the man was here, surely she could face Cade, get past the last night and get on with this job. Megan quickly dressed in jeans, a heavy sweater and casual shoes, hoping that Walters wouldn't leave before she got into the sitting room. She skimmed her hair back from her face and caught it with a large barrette while Walters asked, "And the danger factor?"

"It's bigger than usual, I won't deny that, but it's under control."

Megan was at the bedroom door. She braced herself, took several deep breaths, then opened the barrier.

Cade had his back to the windows across the room, and for a heartbeat seemed to be the center of the universe. Dressed in faded jeans, the familiar boots and a chambray shirt loose and open, he filled every inch of space in her awareness. His hair was mussed, and the shadow of a beard darkened his jaw. Leaning toward Walters, he spoke in a low voice. "And that's between you and me, all right?"

Walters nodded, the man's braid dancing from the motion. "Absolutely, boy. I just came to check with you. I don't want any problems with it. That's why I talked to Ross about bringing you in on it." Walters looked toward the bedroom door and saw Megan. His face broke into a smile as he stepped back from Cade. "Good morning, Dr. Lewis. It's a great day in Texas!"

The man never seemed to be down or have a bad day, and today that grated on Megan, especially now, when she felt as if she had slept on a bed of nails. She stepped into the room, saw a tray of coffee and rolls on the table by the couch and headed for it. "I'll take your word for it," she said, thankful that Cade had called room service.

Without looking at Cade, she dropped onto a chair and reached for the coffeepot. She poured a cup and sank back into the cushions, cradling the warmth between her hands, then looked up at Walters. "What's going on today?" she asked.

"Cade's going to start work on the main gag for the film. I just came to double-check a few things."

Cade spoke up. "I'm going to start the setup. It's boring work, so maybe you'd want to go with Walters and see some of the other filming."

She didn't want to be around Cade, but knew she didn't have a choice. That was why she was here, to see how he did what he did. "I'll go with you," she said, without making eye contact with him. "When do we leave?"

"You don't have—"

"I want to," she said in her coolest professional voice and finally made herself meet his dark gaze. For a second she saw the awareness there, the memory of what had happened last night. Her thinking blurred, and all she could focus on was the way Cade was fingering the belt buckle at his waist. That's not the place to be looking, she told herself, dragging her eyes back to the coffee in her cup. "I think it's important. It's the biggest stunt, isn't it?"

"That's why I'm here."

"And the most dangerous?" she asked, concentrating on the overhead lights shimmering in the dark, steamy liquid.

Walters cleared his throat. "Doctor..."

She could handle looking at Walters. "Megan. Call me Megan," she said with a smile she knew was tight.

"Well, this stunt, it's hard. Damned hard, but Cade here knows what he's doing with it. That's why his name came up, and that's why I agreed to call him in on it. He's the best in the industry."

It wasn't so hard facing Cade now, since he was acting as if nothing had happened last night. She wanted it to stay that way. She concentrated on the job at hand while she sipped some coffee and let the heat slip down her throat. "If you were a stuntman, would you do it?" she asked Walters.

He colored slightly. "I'm not a stuntman. I get to pay others to do it."

"But if you were trained at it, would you take the chance? Would you gamble that you could make it work?"

"He's not a stuntman, so the question isn't valid," Cade interjected. When Megan turned to him, she was finally able to really look at him. She could see the shadows around his eyes, the weariness in his face; it gave her a degree of satisfaction to see proof that he hadn't slept any better than she had. "I was just asking for an opinion," she said.

"His opinion is that I can do it. That's why he's paying me to do it. He doesn't want film of a man dying, if that's what you're getting at."

Megan felt the heat in her face, but wasn't about to let it drop. She put her coffee cup back onto the tray, then stood and made herself hold eye contact with Cade. "I never said that. But it's happened, hasn't it?"

Cade shook his head with obvious exasperation. "I don't have time for this. We'll talk on the way out to the site, but right now I need to shave and shower." With that he crossed the room, went into the bedroom and closed the door behind him.

Walters waited until the sound of running water came from the other area before he spoke to Megan. "Doctor, there's been accidents in this business. Hell, there's always a chance of the wrong thing happening, but I can tell you right now, I take every precaution. I do it the safest, most effective way. Cade knows that if there's a problem, he can walk away at any time. Screw the money."

She hadn't even thought about the money Cade would be making on this project. "Is it top secret, or can I ask how much Cade is making for doing this stunt for you?"

"You can ask, but I won't say. It's between me and him. He's being paid very well, and I suspect that he needs it, too. He's been on the short end of the business since his wife's death. And life goes on, expenses and all, no matter what happens."

She thought about Cade's house, the expensive area it sat in. The idea that he'd risk everything for money to keep that life-style was repugnant to Megan. She made a mental note to check and see what his financial situation was right now.

"I'm sorry. I was just asking. But I need to figure out why Cade does what he does."

"I understand that, but you have to understand that Cade's motives are his own. He hasn't confided in me about them. All I know is he's as good as or better than anyone in this business."

"I know that. He's the best. That's all I've heard since I've been here."

"And that's the truth."

"Then why didn't you get him to be stunt coordinator on this project instead of Ross Barnette?"

He pushed his hands in the pockets of his slacks. "Honestly?"

"Yes."

"He was suggested to me, and I wanted him. I'd seen the way he did a film for Zucker a year or two back, and I was impressed. Damned impressed. But when I was starting this project, his life fell apart. And I understood. He did what I did about ten years ago."

"You?"

"Yeah, me. My wife died from a stroke. Just like that. Never sick a day in her life, and she turned around to say something to me and dropped dead." His voice was flat, but Megan could see the pain that still lived in him in his eyes. "I walked away. I left everything. It took me two years to get sober and back to work. Cade took six months. I think he did pretty damned good."

Walters thought Cade's breakdown was from grief, just what she'd thought at first. Now she knew better. It was the guilt that had all but destroyed him. "Yes, he did well to start again."

Walters came even closer and lowered his voice as the water sounds stopped. "Then give him a break, give him another chance. He needs that boy. I didn't have children. I had nothing, but he's got his son.''

''But what does his son have?'' she countered.

''A father who loves him like hell.''

Megan knew that was true, but love didn't always make up for the rest of what a parent could bring to a child. Before she could say a thing, Cade came back into the room. Freshly shaved and with his shirt done up and tucked in, he seemed to have shed the weariness like a second skin.

Walters walked over to Cade and touched him on the shoulder. ''Get back to me on the time when you've had a chance to really work it out,'' he said, then looked at Megan. ''See you all later, and I'm glad we had this talk.'' With that he left, pulling the door shut after him.

''What was that all about?'' Cade asked as he crossed to reach for the denim jacket he'd tossed over the back of the couch.

Megan ignored the question and hurried into the bedroom to get her jacket and purse. When she came back into the room, Cade hadn't moved. ''Well?'' he asked. ''What was that all about?''

''He was just like the men the first night, telling me what a wonderful stuntman you are, talking to me about the business.''

Cade looked almost embarrassed. ''He's exaggerating.''

''Not the way he sees it,'' she said, barely suppressing a sudden yawn.

Cade came closer until he was no more than two feet from her, and his dark eyes met hers. ''Didn't you sleep well?''

She wasn't about to lie, but looked away as she put on her jacket. ''No, I didn't,'' she admitted, a flicker of fire threatening to ignite again. Out of self-defense she concentrated on doing up her jacket before glancing back at Cade. She couldn't resist asking, ''How about you?''

"I managed to get some sleep."

"Before you left, or after you came back from your walk?"

He lifted one dark eyebrow at her, but spoke in an even voice. "After." Then he turned away to head for the door.

"Cade?"

He stopped with his hand on the knob and looked back at her, his eyes hooded and unreadable. "Can I meet you downstairs in five minutes?" she asked. "I need to make a phone call."

"Sure. I'll be waiting out in front."

When he was gone, Megan turned and put her purse on the couch before reaching for the phone. Rose's answering machine kicked in, making Megan glance at the clock in the room and realize the time difference. It wasn't even six in Los Angeles.

"Rose, it's me. I'm sorry to call so early, but I was just wondering—"

"Hello there," Rose said as the machine clicked off.

"I didn't mean to wake you. I forgot about the time difference."

"I was up and just stepping out of the shower when I heard you start to talk."

"I called to find out—"

"No, Frank didn't call again," Rose cut in, once again clearly reading Megan's mind. "Yes, I found out the parole board will probably hear his case in a week. No, I don't know who'll be testifying for Frank. Yes, I'll find out."

"Thanks, Rose," Megan said, "and take care," then hung up and went to find Cade.

Megan stepped out into the cold air of morning and squinted at the clear sunlight that bounced off the pavement and the glass fronts of the businesses on the street. She took sunglasses out of her shoulder bag, slipped them on, then looked in front of the hotel. Cade was there, waiting, leaning against the fender of a large blue pickup.

Cade looked at his watch, then back at Megan as he flipped up the collar of his jacket. "Five minutes. Right on time."

Megan walked toward him. "No limousine?" she asked.

"No, Walters is using it, but he arranged for us to use this for now." He opened the passenger side door. "Climb in and we'll get going."

While Cade circled around the front of the truck and climbed into the cab, Megan settled on the hard bench seat. Resting her purse on her lap, she pushed her hands into her pockets for warmth and watched Cade start the truck, shift it into gear and pull out onto the main street.

"We'll get a little heat," he said, flicking on the heater.

Megan felt the rush of warmth around her ankles and turned away from the sight of Cade, from the awareness of every little thing about the man—from the fine lines that fanned out at the corners of his eyes, from the strength of his jaw and the way his hands held the steering wheel. It was too easy to remember the way those hands had felt on her skin. Too easy by far.

She looked at the countryside passing by, but didn't really see any of it. Images of Cade over her on the bed filtered through, tormenting her in a way she couldn't deny, yet couldn't control. And the question she'd had last night, the one that had tormented her in the darkness, came back to her. Had his actions been premeditated? Had he thought that if they were closer, she'd recommend in his favor at the hearing?

She nibbled on her bottom lip, knowing that she had to have an answer. And the only way she could think to get it was to ask. "There's something I want to ask you," she said to Cade, long after they'd left Dedrick far behind.

"Go ahead, Doc. I'm sort of getting used to being psychoanalyzed," Cade said. "Besides, I'm a captive audience."

"It's about last night, about what happened."

"What *almost* happened," he said in a low voice.

"That's just it. No matter what did or didn't happen, it wouldn't make a difference in the case. I mean, no matter what you thought, I'd have to do what I thought was best for Adam. You understand that, don't you?"

Cade stared straight ahead and was silent for so long that Megan thought he must not have heard her or was ignoring her. Then she was shocked as he actually laughed out loud. But before she could make head or tail of his reaction, he drove the truck off the road, onto the gravel shoulder, and came to a stop.

He twisted in the seat, one hand resting on the top of the steering wheel, and his dark eyes were on her. She could see the humor lingering in their depths. "All right, let me get this straight. You think I went in the bedroom to seduce you, to try and work on you, to make you find in my favor in the custody hearing?"

She didn't know what to say, when he laid out her fears so neatly and clearly. "I was just—"

He cut her off. "I know what you've been told about me. I've admitted to a lot of things myself, and I've never been accused of being a saint, but this takes the cake. You believe that I'd do something like that?"

"Well, I . . ."

"I don't believe this. I did one of the most unselfish things I've ever done by going in there, at least at first, and you think . . ." He shook his head. "I understand where you're coming from on this, but you're way off the mark. Way off.''

She clenched her hands into fists in her pockets, horribly embarrassed; she didn't know what to say. "What was I supposed to think? You were in there, and we...you and I..."

"That's it exactly, you and I. Not me. I didn't force anything on you."

That struck a nerve, and Megan could feel the heat in her face. He hadn't forced a thing. "No, of course not, but you can't blame me for thinking that you might have thought that it would be worth a shot to see if I..." She let her voice trail off as she saw the humor in Cade slipping away.

He held up one hand, palm toward her. "Stop right there. I cut my hair, got a shave, had my house cleaned, dressed in a damned suit, and sat and talked to you like a civilized human. I was as nice to Doris as I could manage, and I offered to let you come here with me to see me work, so you could understand what I do. This, believe it or not, was not an elaborate scheme to seduce you and get you to let me have my son." His eyes narrowed, their depths filled with something Megan didn't want to identify. "Not that seduction would be so horrible a price to pay," he said, his voice dropping to a rough whisper. "It wasn't that way at all, Doc. I give you my word on it."

Megan felt her stomach clench. She would admit how much she could want Cade, if she let herself. How much she might need him. But now all she wanted was to be far, far away from him. Being in the cab of the truck, this close, was making everything worse. Especially because she could remember her ridiculously stupid reaction last night after he'd left her, the sense of disappointment that she hadn't taken what he'd wanted to give. A stupid reaction, she repeated, and turned from Cade to look out the windows.

She had never responded to any man that way, and it embarrassed her to imagine what he must have thought. "I apologize," she said in a tight voice. "I misread everything."

"Don't be so hard on yourself. You were wrong, but honestly wrong."

She'd been honestly wrong a lot in her life. "I'm sorry."

The truck started to move again, and Megan looked ahead as they drove back onto the road and headed out. Cade was silent. And Megan stared at the countryside slipping past.

Then he said her name. "Megan?"

"Yes?"

"Who's Frank?"

She turned to Cade, shocked by his question. "Pardon me?"

"You said a name last night when you had the nightmare. I thought it was Frank. I could be wrong."

Oh, God, it had been worse than she thought. "No, you're right. It's Frank."

"Someone close to you?"

Cade watched the road, but could feel Megan shift on the seat, as if she were trying to get farther away from him. "Yes," she said softly.

The single word cut Cade to the quick. He gripped the steering wheel so tightly, his fingers tingled. A lover. A man who loved Megan, who knew Megan and had lain with her. "I see," he said, but didn't understand his reaction at all.

Chapter 10

"No, you don't understand," Megan said softly.

Suddenly Cade didn't want to. He didn't want her to tell him anything about Frank. Not when his own memories of her were so fresh, so cutting. Not when he could almost feel her under his hands, the way she'd arched to his touch, the silky heat. No, he didn't want to hear anything about another man. But he couldn't tell her that. Instead he heard himself saying, "You're right. I probably don't."

"Frank's my father."

Cade felt shock rocket through him at the blunt statement, then a tremendous rush of relief that had no place in this conversation. "Your father?" he asked, just so she could confirm it for him.

"Yes," she whispered, tucking her chin low into the collar of her jacket, while she stared at the road ahead of them.

"The dream must have been terrible for you," he said softly.

Megan didn't want to hear that tone of understanding in his voice, maybe even a touch of pity. She'd heard that before from social workers and so-called friends of Frank's. "It was a nightmare," she said flatly.

"Do you want to talk about it?"

"I don't think so. It's just something I have to deal with."

"What is?"

"My father, the way he is, what he does to people...to me."

"What has he done to you?" Cade asked.

"Everything. Nothing. He's a compulsive gambler, and I've been unlucky enough in this life to live in the fallout from his habit."

He slowed the truck and looked at Megan. "He's a gambler, as in 'Hello, my name is John Doe and I'm a compulsive gambler'?"

"Yes, except his name is Frank Lewis. And he's in prison because of his gambling."

"So, that's why you were so spooked yesterday, wasn't it?"

"I'd never thought about what he lived like, or what prison could do to him."

"When you visited him, you must have—"

She cut off the words before he finished. "I haven't seen him since he was arrested, over two years ago. I had to break with him completely."

"You must hate him a lot," he said.

He hadn't looked at her since she'd told him about Frank, and it made it easier for her to keep talking. "Among a lot of other emotions."

"What other emotions?"

"Frustration, anger, sadness. I can't do a thing about what my father is. All my professional training doesn't do one iota of good."

"Is that why you're doing what you do now?"

"Probably." She turned from him and watched the road. "No, it *is* why. I thought if I could help others, that in some way I could help myself."

"And?"

"And it doesn't work that way. What I do with others doesn't change what my father is or where he is."

"How long is he in prison for?"

Not long enough she almost said, but stopped the words before they were uttered. "He's coming up for parole pretty soon and they'll probably let him out. He's good at playing games, letting people see and hear what he wants them to see and hear."

"And the dreams?"

She made her hands relax and took them out of her pockets to rest them on her purse in her lap. Then she looked at Cade, thankful for the dark glasses she was wearing. "I dreamed he was dying in prison. I've always felt responsible for what Frank did, even when I was just a kid. I tried to make things right, to protect him from men who came to collect from him, and even from social workers who came to check on me. I'd lie and say I was happy, that I just wanted to be with my father. That he took good care of me and we had a great home."

"And the reality?" he prodded.

She moved closer to the door and rested her head against the cold glass. "The reality was shabby houses, days when I didn't know where Frank was, and hating him for what he was doing." The words tumbled out, coming before Megan even knew she was going to say them. "I kept thinking I could make things right, that if I wished hard enough or was good enough, Frank would stop gambling and I'd have a home."

She fingered the leather of her purse. "The thing is, I could never make things right. I could never change Frank, and I blamed myself for that."

"And you didn't have a thing to do with it, did you?"

"No, but I thought I did."

"But you know you didn't, don't you?"

"Now I do. And I finally let go. I cut him off completely."

"Is it that simple?"

She closed her eyes. "No, it's not, but I'm doing my best."

"You're still fighting the war, aren't you?"

She opened her eyes, saw the prison in the distance, then turned to Cade. "What?"

"Did you make your father a gambler?"

"Of course not."

"Then you don't have any responsibility for him, not any more than I had for Lori's death. But I fought that war for six months, and I almost lost. Then Adam was there and I knew I wanted him, and that I had to get my life in order, to do the best for him."

"Your wars are over?" she asked.

"No, but they're new wars, not ones I've pulled along with me for years."

She sat straighter and watched the prison coming closer. This talk about wars made little sense to her, and she didn't want to be thinking about it right now. She just wanted to get on with things, then leave and go back to Los Angeles. "I don't want to talk about this anymore."

Cade let go of it easily, and Megan felt very relieved when he glanced at her and asked, "How about letting me explain just what I'm going to do today?"

That was definitely something safe to discuss. "All right."

Cade didn't turn onto the road that led to the front of the prison. Instead he drove past it and headed north. "I'm going to the site of the stunt." He pointed ahead of them into the distance. "That's where we're going."

Megan looked ahead and saw a blurred shape coming closer and becoming more defined, until she could see a large estate, with a brick wall all around and a huge house beyond it. "I had no idea this was here."

"It wasn't until about two months ago."

"What?"

"It's a set. Walters thought it would be just as cheap to do that here and make it part of the whole layout as to do it in the back lot at the studio." They drove along the paved road that headed toward high, iron gates that stood open and were supported by the brick wall on both sides, and he explained. "The house is a front, just enough to look real. The rest was built around it."

Megan could hardly believe it. "You mean the house—?"

"It's like the old, false-front towns you've seen in cartoons, but a lot more expensive."

He drove through the gate, onto a blacktopped circular driveway that led up to the front of the house. It looked real to Megan, a neocolonial, two-story structure in red brick and white wood trim, with massive columns along the front. At the entry he stopped the truck. "This is it."

Megan and Cade got out and stood at the foot of brick stairs that led up to a sweeping porch. It looked so real with drapes in the windows, furniture on the front porch and plants lining the brick walls. Megan stepped onto the first stair. "There's nothing behind it?"

"Just a lot of beams that support the facade. A false front, that's it."

Cade led the way up the steps, onto the porch and to the entry. He twisted the knob, then eased back the wood and glass door. He moved to one side for Megan to see past him, and she stared at the skyline in the distance, the rough brush and scrub cedars that surrounded the prison all seen through a crisscross of raw lumber. False. All a beautiful, convincing illusion.

Megan turned to Cade as he closed the door. Just like people. Like Frank. Maybe like Cade Daniels. Was the sense of comfort last night an illusion? Or the passion that had all but consumed her, when he kissed her? Were they real or just a facade, a facade carefully constructed by a man determined to get his child?

Cade turned to Megan right then, his gaze locking with hers, and she quickly averted her eyes. She didn't want Cade to read her thoughts—he was too intuitive about her, as it was.

She turned and went back to the top of the stairs and saw two vans pull through the gate, followed by a huge semi diesel with a double trailer. The vans came up behind the blue pickup, and when several men got out, Cade said, "This is what I've been waiting for."

He walked past Megan and down the steps, said a few words to the men from the van, then waved at the driver of the semi, pointing to a side area, where he could park and unload. The driver expertly steered the truck into the parking area, while Megan came down to Cade and stood beside him. "What's in the truck?" she asked.

"Supplies for the stunt."

"In that size truck? What do you need?"

He looked down at her, his eyes narrowed by the clear, morning light. "I think I need to explain about the basic concept of the gag. This house is supposed to be the warden's, part of federal property around the prison, and when there's a prison break at the end of the movie, Peter Shaw's character manages to get a hold of one of the guard's cars.

He's coming after the warden, but has to get in past armed guards, security gates and an eight-foot, brick wall. So he's going to hit a rise outside the fence, using it as a projectile ramp to sail over the wall. If everything goes right, the car flips at least twice, lands on its wheels and crashes into the governor's car, parked right there.''

He pointed to a spot about twenty feet from where the pickup stood. ''There's an explosion, but Shaw gets out just in time and confronts the warden.''

Megan could almost see it in her mind's eye; couldn't think how anyone could do it and walk away from it in one piece. ''And you can do that?''

''Yes, I think I can. Ross and I have the plans done. Now it's up to me to make it work. Today I'll get the ramp started, lay out the route, do a walk-through, and see how the distance works up to the ramp.'' He shaded his eyes and looked out at the wall. ''It's simple, really. Get the ramp just right, then make impact, take the roll, the crash and get out.''

''Simple,'' she echoed.

''I need to check on the delivery,'' he said, ''then get the carpenters started on the ramp construction. If you want to sit in the truck to keep warm, feel free, and I'll be back in a while.''

''No, I'm here to observe,'' she said, falling into step beside him as he started toward the truck. Cade cast her a slanting look, then nodded and kept walking.

Megan stayed by Cade as he went over the invoice the driver gave him, and when he went around to the back of the second trailer. He waited for the driver to undo the security lock, then helped the man open the doors. Megan didn't know what she had expected to be in the trailer, but it wasn't a blue sedan that looked totally ordinary. The driver pulled out two drive-off ramps, snugged them into the ground, then Cade swung himself up into the trailer.

He climbed in through the driver's open window, got behind the wheel, and turned on the engine. Slowly he inched the car down the ramp to the driveway. He motioned to Megan through the window. "If you want to observe, get in. Let's take it for a walk-through."

She hurried around to the passenger side and tried the door, but it didn't budge. "You have to get in the window," Cade said. "The doors are sealed shut for safety."

Megan did what she'd seen Cade do. She grabbed the top of the door, scooted her feet in through the window first, then slipped down and into the bucket seat. She settled and looked at the inside. It was a shell, all metal braces and emptiness except for the two seats.

"This is it?" she asked, feeling the heavy throbbing of the idling engine.

"It's all I need. And the less inside, the less to break and cause problems. That's why there's no window glass in the sides, and the front is molded Plexiglas." He tapped the inside of the heavy, metal roof. "This is reinforced with three roll bars, double strength, lengthwise, and the undercarriage is one solid piece of steel. It weighs twice what the normal car does, and it can go over a hundred and fifty miles an hour . . . if it has to."

"That fast?"

"I have to be able to get up speed, to do what I need to do." Cade motioned to crash helmets that were lying in the back. "Grab one for yourself and give me one," he said.

Megan twisted to reach for them and handed one to Cade. "Just what is a walk-through?" she asked, as she tugged the helmet over her hair.

Cade looked at her as he fastened the chin strap of his helmet, and she could have sworn there was a glint of mischievousness in his eyes. "I'll show you." He tugged a harness restraining strap over his shoulders and buckled it at his lap. "Put on your restraint and I'll give you a demonstration."

"Of what?"

"What I need to do with the car."

She fumbled with the straps and got them snapped together as Cade began to drive slowly toward the gates. Megan watched Cade shift as they went through, then press the accelerator; the car began to build speed. Once on the clear road, Cade speeded up even more as he drove back in the direction of the prison.

"A walk-through," Cade said, raising his voice to be heard over the rushing of the wind through the open windows and the engine noise, "is when you test equipment. You have to know what it can do, how much you can trust it." He gave the motor more gas. "You have to know your limits in this business—and the limits of your equipment."

Megan felt the car shake, then just before they got to the back fence area of the prison, Cade hit the brakes. Tires screeched on pavement and the car's back end began to come around. But instead of letting it fishtail and go out of control, in one fluid motion, Cade neatly reversed the car's direction. It came to rest, facing the set for the warden's house in the distance.

"Now we see what we need to see," he said, hitting the gas once more. With a squeal of tires he took off again, building speed with breathtaking rapidity. The wind tugged at Megan's hair, almost burning the skin on her face. She clutched the sides of the seat, felt her heart rate speed up, and watched with fascination as distance became irrelevant.

She felt something she could only call a rush, a sensation of almost flying in this car, where there was no roughness, no sense of the road under the tires. Strangely she felt no fear until the open gates were no more than fifty yards ahead of them. She braced herself as Cade stepped on the brakes, and the world became a mixture of burning rubber filling the air, of tires keening on concrete and distance diminishing.

Just when the car felt as if it would stand on its nose, it settled, then came to a shuddering stop just inside the gates. "Nice, very nice," Cade said, then looked at Megan. He studied her for a long moment before saying, "It's a rush, isn't it, going that fast?"

Megan sucked in a deep breath, shocked by the fact that she hadn't felt real fear during the ride. She closed her eyes for a fleeting moment, horrified that there must be a part of Frank in her, the part that found excitement in living on the edge. To admit that really undid her, upset her more than anything. She didn't know what to do about it.

"It . . . it's different," she mumbled as she took off the helmet and tossed it into the back. Then she tried—and failed—to make her hands work to undo the seat belt.

Cade reached over and with one motion unlocked the buckle, releasing Megan from the harness. Then he touched the hand on her thigh, and she stared at the point of contact without pulling free. "Speed with control can be very exciting."

He patted her hand, then regripped the steering wheel and drove toward the front of the house. Leon was there now with the other men, and he came ambling up to the car. He bent down and peered inside. "Nice shot, Cade. Saw it all. How'd she handle?"

Cade tossed his helmet into the back, grabbed the top of the door and slid out. "Great touch, Leon. They did it right." As Megan scrambled out her side, she felt the cold against the heat in her face.

The huge truck was slowly backing up, leaving stacks of boxes and lumber on the blacktop. It came forward toward the gates and as the cab came even with the car, the driver rolled down the window and spoke to Cade. "Looked damned good."

"Thanks," Cade called over the engine noise. "Do me a favor, and when you get back up to the offices, tell Margo, Walters's assistant, that I need the carpenters down here."

"Sure thing," the other man said, then drove off toward the prison.

Cade turned to look at Megan over the roof of the car. "I'm trying to show and tell you everything I'm doing. If I miss anything or you don't understand something, just ask."

She nodded, touching the cold metal of the car with the flat of her hand and making herself ask, "What if this whole thing doesn't work?"

"It'll work."

"But—?"

"I'll *make* it work. Now, I'll be measuring and plotting with Leon, getting exact impact points and figuring the speed needed at each point." He turned to Leon. "Got the paint and tape?"

"Yeah," he said, pointing toward the porch. He and Cade started toward the house, and Megan followed. While Leon and Cade measured and paced off an area between the middle of the circular driveway and the lawn, spray-painting yellow circles on the ground at each spot, she moved to the porch and sat on the top step.

She never took her eyes off Cade. Her heartbeat was normal now, but she couldn't forget that moment of speed with Cade, something almost akin to the excitement she'd felt last night when he'd touched her and kissed her. Wrong, so wrong. How could she have allowed a client to touch her emotionally this way?

Then she admitted that every client touched her in one way or another. Adam Daniels certainly had from the first, and now she wondered if it was because he was so like his father. No, she knew the child's vulnerability, a feeling she remembered herself so much from when she was younger. But she hadn't thought she was vulnerable anymore. She'd thought she'd dealt with Frank and gone on with her life.

Now she wondered if she'd simply turned away, so she wouldn't have to deal with Frank. Maybe that was why Cade could make her feel exposed, could make her feel emotionally fragile, because she couldn't turn from him. But she had to do her job.

She closed her eyes, but only succeeded in conjuring up more shadowy images from the night before. He'd exposed a side of her that she'd given little thought to for so long, she'd almost forgotten it existed. The men in her life had drifted in and out, never becoming substantial enough to stay, or substantial enough for her to even want them to stay. She'd found safe men, nice men. Not one of them had reached her on the level Cade did without even trying. Yet Cade was everything she didn't want in a man. And he was a client.

What she had to do was make sure she maintained a professional image around him and a professional distance. She wouldn't let herself melt when she thought of the way he looked at his son, or of the pain in his eyes when Doris had accused him of killing her daughter. Or let herself remember his touch, his kiss.

She would stay with the facts, with the reality that was Cade Daniels. He was gambling with his life. And indirectly gambling with his son's life. There was no way she would allow him to come any closer, certainly not close enough for her to let him gamble with her heart.

She opened her eyes when she heard Cade shouting at Leon. He was almost at the fence and turned to look at Leon, who stood halfway between the fence and the house. "Two flips before impact," he called.

She heard a tone in his voice, an edge of excitement, and remembered her own rush at the speed. Was she closer to that sort of personality than she could admit to? Maybe, but there was a huge difference between knowing it and letting it rule her life. It was obvious he liked to live on the edge, no matter what he said. Just the way Frank had always needed that excitement.

A red van coming in the gates drew her attention, and she watched it come up to park by Cade's stunt car. Gus, one of the men she'd danced with the first night, got out and crossed directly to Cade. Megan walked over to where the two men stood, deep in talk.

"...and they thought, since you've done it before, you could go up front and see what's going on."

Cade swiped at grass, clinging to his pants from kneeling on the lawn. "Sure. I guess I could. The carpenters aren't here yet and—" he motioned to Leon "—he knows what has to be done when they get here."

Gus smiled past Cade when he saw Megan. "Hello there again. Hope you're getting along fine with everyone."

"Just fine, thanks," she lied, pleased that she sounded so controlled.

Cade turned to Megan. "I'm needed to help back at the prison for a while, probably for a few hours, at least. You can come, if your like, or—"

The other man interrupted. "Why don't you let me take the doctor down to the food van they set up inside the wall and get some coffee?" He rubbed his hands together. "I know that *this* California boy is freezing his...er... It's colder than a... Well, a good, hot cup of coffee would hit the spot for me right now.'' He grinned sheepishly at her. ''How about you?''

Megan took the offer; it would put some distance between Cade and herself for a while. She could regroup and get her thoughts in order. ''That sounds great,'' she said.

She could have sworn Cade almost looked relieved when he nodded and said, ''I'll see you around later on. All right?''

''Fine.''

Gus motioned Megan to his van. ''Climb on in, and let's get that coffee.''

Cade stood where he was, watching the van drive off until he could barely make it out down the road. Then he got back into the stunt car, parked it where the semi had been before, got out and crossed to his pickup. Leaving Leon to oversee the work, he drove slowly out the gates and toward the prison. He couldn't see the van anymore, and took his time driving back.

If Megan wasn't there, he could concentrate, something he was having a horrible time doing, with her anywhere close by, especially after last night. He couldn't understand his reactions to her. Sure, she was beautiful and sexy, even in those jeans and with her hair brushed back from her face and wearing little makeup. And she'd been so stunning last night that just the thought started an uncomfortable tightening in his groin.

He could deal with that. He understood it. What he didn't understand was why he felt sympathy for her, why he felt intense anger toward her father for all the pain he'd put her through, and why he had a ridiculous impulse to try and help her. Especially when he couldn't help at all.

He'd been on his own too long, doing what he wanted, when he wanted. Even when he'd been with Lori, he hadn't felt a connection where he could almost experience what the other person felt. It didn't make sense.

He turned at the front of the prison, glad to see that Gus's van was parked inside the gates and Megan wasn't anywhere in sight. No woman had never distracted him this way. No other woman's image had kept coming to him, edging into his consciousness, when he knew he had to focus entirely on his job. Kisses that were a mistake hadn't come back to haunt him far into the night, and just touching a woman hadn't set his world on end.

Making a real effort to close his mind to all the distractions, Cade parked past the gates by one of the equipment vans and got out. He spotted Ross, standing by a power pole the crew had set in the ground about a hundred yards from the front of the prison wall, and headed for him. Weaving his way through cables and camera stands, he stepped into the clearing by the pole.

"All right, Ross," he said. "What do you need me to do?"

Megan hadn't deliberately set out to avoid Cade for the next two hours, but that was exactly what she'd ended up doing, she realized. She stayed inside the prison walls, had her coffee, watched the wardrobe mistress adjust the clothes of the man who was playing the warden, a character actor whom Megan knew she'd seen before, and she talked to Peter Shaw for a while.

The man was funny, good-looking, totally self-absorbed and a relief after her time with Cade. There was nothing complicated about him at all, and nothing in his eyes that could make her thinking turn to mush and her bones to water. The man might ooze sex appeal on the screen, but in person he was just a man who seemed as friendly and open as an overgrown puppy.

After Peter left to read lines with Lincoln, Megan glanced at her watch and saw it was almost two o'clock. About that time her stomach began to rumble, but the idea of eating in the mess hall again wasn't at all appetizing.

She spotted Gus in a group of extras near the gates and headed toward him, calling, "Gus?"

He turned and came toward her. "How's it going?"

"Fine. I was just wondering if I could use your van to eat lunch in."

"Well, sure you can, but they're setting stuff out in the mess hall. That'd be—"

She cut him off with a shake of her head. "No, I'd rather not."

"Go ahead, the van's unlocked. I need to get back. I'm teaching the local yahoos how to look like a milling crowd on cue." He smiled at her. "See you later."

Megan thanked him, then turned to go back inside and get her lunch box, but one of the extras rushed past, bumping her on the shoulder.

He stopped and apologized. "Sorry, ma'am. I was in a hurry."

"What's so interesting out there?" she asked.

"There's going to be a stunt done. I wanted to see it."

"A stunt?"

"Yeah, one of the other guys tried it, but it didn't work. Now Cade Daniels is going to do it." He started off toward the gates. "Sorry again." He loped away.

Megan thought of going back inside, but stopped herself. She needed to see this. She needed to put this into perspective. Most of all, she needed to give Cade an honest chance to convince her that if Adam was depending on him, the boy would be all right.

Slowly she headed for the gates, then stepped through and stopped. She'd expected the large half circle of onlookers near a huge power pole, and she'd expected the cameras, portable lights and the director's boom, but she hadn't expected to see an ambulance on the sidelines and two attendants leaning nonchalantly against the white and red vehicle.

She looked around and spotted Leon coming toward a van near the gates. "Leon!" she called and hurried over to him. "I need to ask you something." She motioned to the ambulance. "What's that there for?"

"Oh, just a precaution. Walters always has a crew ready, if he's trying anything the least bit chancy."

"Cade was called up here to help with a stunt. Is it that one?"

"Yes, ma'am," he said, then seemed to understand where she was coming from. "But it's fine. It's just a precaution, like I said. A stuntman was hurt a few years back, and there wasn't medical help real close. It's been a policy of the better directors to make sure medical help is there, even if it's never needed." He touched Megan on the shoulder, and she jumped slightly. "Sorry. I was wondering if you're going to watch this one."

Although she knew she needed to watch, to observe, she almost said no. She almost headed for the van to shut herself in. But she didn't. She nodded instead. "Yes, I am."

"Then come with me." He turned and headed off and she followed him toward the crowd, then circled around behind it to the director's basket. "Walters!" he called to the red-haired man, deep in conversation with a nearby cameraman.

The director looked up. "Yeah?"

"The doctor here wants to watch the gag. How about a spot for her where she can see?"

"Yeah, sure." He motioned to a huge motor home back behind everything. "There's stairs on the side, so you can climb on the roof. Go ahead. It's the best seat in town next to my crow's nest."

"Thanks," Megan said, then turned to Leon. "When's Cade doing it?"

He glanced at his watch. "Soon. The first guy that messed it up set everything back about two hours. And there's only so much daylight left."

He walked back with her to the motor home and pointed to a steel ladder on the side. "Come on up. I'll watch with you."

"You aren't in it?"

"No, this is a one-man show," Leon said and grabbed the side rails to pull himself up.

Cade stood on the roof of the prison, looking down upon the scene below, at the cable, where it went over the wall and ran to the power pole, where the mats had been stacked. The cold wind whipped around him, cutting through the orange, prison jumpsuit that hid his heavy knee and elbow pads. Flesh-colored gloves covered his hands, and the heavy, black prison boots felt as if they weighed five pounds each.

Concentrate. Concentrate, he told himself. Focus on the gag. He closed his eyes and rotated his head slowly from side to side. But try as he would, he couldn't put Megan out of his mind. He couldn't shut out the memory of her under him in the shadows of night, the lingering memory of her taste on his tongue and lips. Silky skin under his hands, swelling breasts.

Quickly he opened his eyes and reached above him for the heavy cable, closing his hand over it so tightly that he could feel the twist of metal on metal. He tugged at it, absent-mindedly testing the tension. Focus. Focus, he told himself as he stared at the power pole. But it began to shimmer in the distance, overlaid by an image of Megan looking at him, the blueness of her eyes deep and pure, the pain in them raw and cutting.

How could she have a father in prison? How could she have endured a life with a compulsive gambler? What she must have gone through, dealing with that! His parents had never stopped telling him what he'd put them through, but he had never come close to anything like prison.

He knew he'd hurt them, though never intentionally, that he'd worried them and caused them lots of sleepless nights. For the first time he wasn't just sorry about it; he genuinely regretted it. He'd felt bad about it before, but never like this. He'd slid through life only thinking of himself, worrying about his freedom, his need to do what he wanted to do.

It had been worst when he found out Lori was pregnant. He'd felt strangled, suffocated, yet things had worked out for the very best. He had Adam. A little life that was becoming more and more precious to him. Damn, he'd meant to call Doris and check on the boy, but he'd been so distracted by Megan.

The thought of putting in the call had been there while he talked to Walters, but once Megan had stepped out of the bedroom, all thoughts had been centered on her. Now he almost didn't recognize himself, worrying about the child having a cold, about something happening to him. Was being a parent the only way people understood what their parents had gone through? Did it take caring about someone else to realize how those who cared about him felt?

And now Megan.

Beyond the physical reaction, he couldn't begin to label what her presence did to him or how he felt about her. He couldn't sort it out and define it with any accuracy or any satisfaction. He only knew that now, when he should be concentrating on the gag, he was thinking about her. He was having foolish fantasies about what could have happened last night. About what she would be like driven by passion, giving herself to him, letting him know her in the most intimate way.

He shook his head sharply, then took the specially treated strip of leather from his pocket and flipped it over the cable, grabbing the ends with both hands and wrapping them around and around for a tight grip. He took a deep breath.

"We're set!" Ross shouted from the far side of the wall. "How about you, Cade?"

Cade closed his eyes, flexed his hands, then shouted back, "Ready!"

Chapter 11

Up in the basket, Walters called, "Cameras. Action!"

Cade hesitated for a split second, then pushed off the platform and started his slide down the cable. His target, strategically placed mats that would break his fall, were ten feet this side of the pole. Just get over the wall, clear it, then head for the mats, he told himself. But after just a few seconds with the wind roaring in his ears, he knew something wasn't right. The leather was heating up too fast; he knew it was going to begin to smolder, then tear apart, if he kept to the pace he'd set.

Either he'd fall before the mats, over thirty feet onto packed earth, or he'd be flung forward when the leather broke, and he'd hit the pole full force. The wall was there, and he held his breath while he cleared the bricks cleanly, but the smell of burning leather was everywhere. There was no way to stop, short of grabbing at the cable with his hand, but that would only burn like hell and probably make him fall sooner.

Suddenly Cade knew what he was going to do. He was going for the odds, the safest way out of it, just praying that he would survive. He spotted the mats, and as he felt the leather begin to sag ominously, he took a deep breath, then let go, literally diving forward. With the speed he'd built on the cable and the roll of his body weight, he figured he'd make it to the mats.

He reached out, felt his hands hit the plastic, he did a forward flip and rolled onto the piled mats, landing on his stomach. For a second he didn't move. Then he twisted his head to get air, tested his arms and legs and sent up a silent prayer of thanks that he seemed to be in one piece. Slowly he eased himself to his knees, pushed to his feet and stood in the middle of the mats.

People were running toward him, Walters was yelling, but Cade didn't really see any of it. All he saw was Megan, first running, then stopping dead in her tracks, letting the others surge past her.

And he knew she was the reason the gag had all gone to hell. He hadn't double-checked the amount of solution on the leather piece before the gag, a major lapse for him—a lapse caused by thinking about her. Then, when push had come to shove, he hadn't had the moxie to take that gamble, to hang in there for a few more seconds, the last chance that could have saved the gag from being a waste of film.

All her words about Adam, about the security he needed, had been there, prodding at him. He wouldn't be any good to the boy if he was a cripple or laid up for months with broken bones. Megan had caused him to think that. Not only was she a major distraction, she was responsible for changes in him that he could barely comprehend.

Megan had scrambled down off the roof of the motor home, hit the ground and run with the crowd toward the mats. Her heart pounded sickeningly in her ears, and her chest was so tight, she couldn't draw in air. Then Cade had gotten to his feet, and she'd stopped dead.

Leon rushed past her, but she didn't move. She watched Walters right behind Ross at the mats, yelling to the ambulance crew. The people all around seemed to blur together.

Megan swallowed the sickness at the back of her throat. Then Cade raised both hands over his head, and she felt such a rush of pure relief that she almost fainted. He stood on the mats while everyone cheered and clapped, then moved to the side and neatly jumped to the ground. *He's all right,* she told herself over and over again as she forced air into her lungs, not about to figure out why her relief was so immense, beyond the fact that Adam still had a dad.

As the crowd began to disperse, everyone going back to their stations, she could hear Cade speaking to Ross. "Damn it, the treatment wasn't thick enough, and the leather burned through."

Ross nodded, looking up at the cable, then at the piece of leather Cade still had wrapped around one hand. "Who'd have figured?"

"I should have," Cade said with disgust. He threw the remnant onto the ground. As the men from the ambulance headed off, Cade unzipped the jumpsuit, stepped out of it and motioned to a young stuntman behind Ross. "Could you get my jacket?" he asked. "I left it with Jerry." The stuntman disappeared, and Cade tugged pads off his knees and elbows, then tossed jumpsuit and pads to the ground on top of the leather.

"It should have worked, Cade," Ross told him, "you set it up beautifully. Just a slide down, then about fifteen feet from the ground, let go and fall onto the mats."

"Yeah, and it will work. I just need to double-check the leather solution, or maybe overlay the strap with something else, something that can take more friction." Cade ran his fingers through his hair, then took the jacket from the man who brought it to him. As he shrugged into it, he caught sight of Megan again.

She was standing still, watching him, and looked deathly pale, with a pallor that emphasized the blueness of her eyes and the deep copper of her hair. Then he saw the way her hands were clenched.

The very thing he'd told her wouldn't happen had almost happened. Everything she feared had almost materialized. He swallowed hard, fighting his own uneasiness at what could have been, what he probably would have done before she walked into his life. He knew he had to talk to her, to make her listen and understand. But as he started toward her, she turned from him and hurried off in the opposite direction.

He stopped and watched her head toward Walters's motor home, then disappear behind it. He ran a hand over his face and knew that for everyone concerned, this near accident was the worst, the absolute worst.

"What're you looking at?" Ross asked from beside Cade.

"The doctor. She took off. All she's been talking about is how dangerous this job is, and now she's got the proof. I don't know what to do," Cade admitted. "But she's got my future in her hands—one way or another."

"Explain things to her, how the leather needed more protection. It's an honest mistake, certainly not your fault."

Cade stared at the motor home. "It is my fault. I should have known, I should have checked. And as far as Dr. Lewis is concerned, I gambled and almost lost."

"Yeah, but you didn't. I promised Walters the gag today, but I'm not so sure now."

Cade looked away from the motor home and back to Ross. "Hell, I'll do it today. Just give me a bit of time to figure out something else to use with the leather."

Walters came up at that moment. "Did I hear that right, boy?"

"Yeah," Cade said. "I'll get it done. Give me ten minutes to take care of something, then I'll get back to it."

"Sure. Take what you need. I just hope to hell it works this time."

"Yeah, me too," Cade murmured, and hoped to hell his life was going to work out, too.

Megan walked away from Cade on shaky legs and didn't stop until she had the huge motor home between herself, the man and the ugliness of the scene she'd just witnessed. Once out of sight, she stopped, leaned back against the sheet metal side for support and pressed her hands to her eyes.

God, what had happened back there? Why had she felt such all-encompassing terror when she saw the way Cade was plummeting toward the pole, when Ross swore and exclaimed, "He's lost it! My God, he's lost it!"

Her fear had been so enormous that even now she couldn't begin to absorb the magnitude of it. It was still there, a living, horrible sensation in the depths of her being—an emotion she had never felt for another person—not even Frank, when he'd finally been arrested.

That didn't make sense. None of it did. And gradually anger began to edge out the fear, anger at herself for reacting as she had, and toward Cade for putting her through this. All of a sudden she wanted to run and find him, to hit him and scream at him.

But why? It wasn't as if he was any more to her than part of her job, or any more to her than any other human being. As soon as the thought formed, Megan knew the enormity of the lie she was telling herself. Somewhere, sometime, he'd stopped being the father of the child Adam, a stuntman and a stranger. He'd become more, so much more. Yet she couldn't allow that to be. She couldn't let caring become reality. That was too close to loving someone. And she never wanted to love a man like Cade Daniels.

Even though the memory of his touch was a living thing, that didn't mean he could be part of her life or take part of her heart. Her heart? That thought brought her up short, and she had to admit that maybe it was too late to keep all of her heart untouched. But she'd do her best to make sure she escaped with as much intact as she could.

"Megan?"

As if her thoughts of him had conjured up his presence, when Megan opened her eyes, Cade was less than two feet away. The bright sun at his back shadowed his eyes and expression, but didn't lessen his impact on her. Breathing became hard and her heart started its erratic beat again, thundering against her ribs and filling her ears. She didn't want to talk to him now.

She kept her back to the metal wall of the motor home and found she was capable of saying one word. "What?"

His shoulders were hunched to the cold, and high color touched his face. "I need to explain."

"No." She shook her head and started to turn, to walk away and put distance between them. But Cade stopped her abruptly when he pressed his hands flat on the sides of the motor home, just above her shoulders. His body formed a barrier that prevented escape, yet he didn't actually touch her. She stood very still, not wanting any contact.

"Oh, yes, I do need to explain," he said in a low, intense voice.

How she wished that the anger she'd felt moments ago would come back to rescue her. But it didn't. Only the anguish of the eternity before Cade had stood on the mats, unhurt, came back and hit her full force, like a fist driven into her middle. "What . . . what did you want to explain?" she asked in a voice so tight that she barely recognized it as her own.

"What happened back there," Cade said, his arms a prison that was making it hard for her to think straight, "was my fault. The stunt was planned and set, then I screwed up."

She licked her cold lips. "The way you did to get those scars?" she asked.

His eyes narrowed, the only sign she'd made a direct hit with her question. "I guess so. But I learned from the mistakes, and I never repeated them. And I won't repeat the mistake I just made, when I do the stunt again."

She stared at him, unable to believe her ears. "You're what?"

"I'm doing it again and I'll do it right."

"And it's going to be foolproof this time?" she managed.

"I wish I could say it would be, but all I can say is that another foul-up is unlikely."

"So you'll take the chance?"

"I have to."

She rested her head against the metal and exhaled harshly. "Do you want Adam to grow up with that? You'll do a stunt again and again, hoping you won't be hurt or maimed or killed?"

"No, but I . . ."

She sucked in air, meeting his dark gaze and wishing she still had her sunglasses on. "How can a child live like that, Cade, never knowing what he'll have tomorrow? Not knowing where he'll be or who'll be there for him? It's not fair. It's wrong for a child to lose his childhood, because of what his parent chooses to do with his life.

"Children don't have any say in it, any choices. No one asks them and it's wrong, really wrong, and horribly damaging," she said in a fierce whisper, the fire of tears at the back of her eyes. She gulped in air, and finished in a rush. "And to ask a child to love you, no matter what, to make you the most important thing in his life, then to kick his foundation out from under him, just when he starts to trust you, when he starts believing in you . . ."

As the echo of her words died, she choked back the tears she didn't want to feel, the tears she didn't want to fall.

Cade stared at her—hard. Then he moved even closer and spoke softly, for her ears only, as the warmth of his breath brushed her cold face. "I thought we were talking about Adam. Not about you, not about your pain or what you went through with Frank."

Damn him! Why had she ever told him about Frank? "Leave my life out of this," she muttered.

"How can I, when you won't? You're still fighting old wars, and you aren't even close to winning."

"You don't know what you're talking about."

"Yes, I do. I've been there."

Megan didn't want to hear anything else from Cade. She just wanted to get away from him. Abruptly she hit his arm with her hand, broke free and ducked past him.

"Megan?" he called as she hurried away.

But she didn't stop. She kept going, the tears falling silently, blurring her vision as she left Cade behind, along with everything he'd said.

"Megan?" Cade called again as she neared the ambulance and passed it.

She didn't turn. She only walked faster, one hand pressed to her mouth, the other clenched at her side. Then she was at the corner of the prison wall and went around it to the right. With the fence as a shield, she stopped and swiped at her eyes, then fumbled in her pocket for her sunglasses.

"Dr. Lewis?"

She slipped on her glasses, then turned and saw Walters hurrying toward her. When he stopped in front of her, there was no smile on his face. A first for the man, as far as Megan knew. "I'm glad you're still here. Gus said he saw you walking this way." He frowned at her. "After our talk this morning, I've got a feeling that you've prejudged everything. I wanted you to know that Cade did the smart thing. He let it go. He made the best of it, and he didn't get hurt."

"He could have gotten killed."

"So could I, if I ever fall out of my crow's nest." He cocked his head to one side. "I can imagine what you thought when Cade took that fall. But he's fine. If anyone can work it out, he can."

"Is that what you wanted to say?" she asked, needing to be gone, not wanting to talk to this man at all.

"I guess I'm trying to say, I hate watching Cade lose everything without having a fighting chance."

She shook her head. She didn't want another "Cade's the best" pep talk. "I'm giving him a chance. That's why I'm here."

"I hope so," he murmured. "That kid means a lot to him. And this life means a lot to him."

She looked right at Walters. "I guess it comes down to which means the most to him, doesn't it?"

"He has to choose?"

"That's up to him. Right now I need to get back to Dedrick."

"The limo's over there near the main trailer, and my driver should be close by. Find him and tell him I said to take you where you want to go." He studied her. "But maybe you should stay and watch Cade redo the stunt."

Just the idea made her sick. "No, I don't think so." She wasn't going to watch Cade take a chance on dying again. She couldn't watch someone she cared about do that.

She stiffened inside at the unerring track her thoughts had taken. She cared about Cade Daniels? Didn't she care about all her clients, about all her cases? The answer was yes to both, an inescapable yes that she cared about Cade Daniels in a way that had nothing to do with the case.

That brought everything into focus. As a professional, she knew what that meant. "I'll see you later," she said and walked away to find the limousine for the ride back to Dedrick.

Two hours later Megan was on the phone after finally making contact with Rose. She stood in the window of the hotel sitting room, watching the street fill with dusk and the snaking lights of cars. There seemed to be a lot of people on the streets tonight, then she realized it was Sunday. Maybe there was a town tradition of cruising at the end of the weekend.

She held the phone tightly to her ear, not facing the fact that she wasn't watching the cars, but really watching for Cade to come back. She just wanted to know he was in one piece. Rose had been talking on the other end of the line, but Megan wasn't sure what she'd been saying.

"I'm sorry. What did you say, Rose?"

"I was asking why you said this was so important, when you left the message on my machine? I mean, it's all really interesting about Dedrick and the prison and the movie, but what's wrong?"

Megan closed her eyes and rested her forehead against the coldness of the windowpane. Now was the time to do what she'd known she had to do since talking to Walters. "I need to withdraw from this case."

"You what?"

"I need you to contact Brad at home as soon as I hang up, and tell him I'm off the Daniels-Sinclair case as of . . ." She looked at the luminous dial of the clock in the dim light of the room and subtracted two hours. "As of 5:00 p.m. today, Los Angeles time."

"What's going on? You've never dropped a case before."

"I found out that I can't be impartial. I thought I could be, but I can't."

"This is going to play havoc with the timetable on the case."

"Explain to Brad that personal prejudice prevents me from giving an impartial recommendation. That's all it's going to take." She closed her eyes so tightly that she saw bright colors behind her lids. "And tell him I'm not taking any more cases for a while. I have things I have to straighten out for myself, before I take on more work."

Rose was silent for a long moment, then asked, "If he needs consultation on this case?"

"Tell him I'm not available. I'll be back tomorrow, if he needs to talk to me personally."

"Are you sure about this? Are you sure you can't look past your bias to see things objectively?"

Megan simply couldn't look past Cade Daniels. That seemed so simple when she admitted it to herself. She couldn't have any sense of impartiality when she was working on a case with a man who, if he was different, would be so easy to love.

That thought brought her up short and she straightened, her eyes opening wide. But she didn't see the night through the glass. Instead she saw him over her, his eyes dark with passion, felt his touch, burning paths of fire on her bare skin.

"Hello? Are you still there?" Rose inquired.

"Yes, I'm here," she said softly. "I was just...I have to go. Please, Rose, just call Brad and explain for me. I'll be back on the first flight out tomorrow morning and I'll come right to the office, probably no later than noon."

Before Rose could ask any more questions, Megan said goodbye and hung up. She should have felt relief that an unbearable load had been lifted from her shoulders, but didn't. She was no closer to understanding herself or what was happening than she had been before the phone call. All she really knew now was that she no longer had any conflict of interest where Cade Daniels was concerned.

As she turned to face the shadowed room, she heard footsteps coming down the hall. She tensed, waiting. Then they stopped outside her door, the lock clicked and the door swung open.

Backed by the glow of the hall lights, Cade stood in the entrance, a man of shadows, a silhouette, but obviously in one piece. And Megan's relief was almost greater than it had been this afternoon, when he'd escaped unhurt from the aborted stunt.

He stood very still, his lean frame clearly etched by the back lighting. "It's done."

"You...you're all right?" she managed, rooted to the spot by the windows.

He came into the room, then swung the door shut, closing out the light. Through the shadows he spoke to her in a low voice. "I'm fine. The stunt's in the can. But it still didn't go right."

She clutched her hands tightly in front of her, unnerved to feel the unsteadiness in them. "What didn't go right?"

"The whole gag," he said, coming closer, slowly, surely, until he was within a few feet of her.

Even in the darkness she could make out the tension in his stance, in the angle of his shoulders, the way he held his head. "But you . . . you didn't get hurt, you said."

"No, I didn't. Just a few rope burns, but nothing serious."

"Then what went wrong?"

"Adam," he said, then after a long pause, "and you."

"I . . . I don't . . ."

"No, you don't. But I do," he whispered. He moved another step closer, until she could feel his body heat brush her cold arms. She inhaled the freshness of the night that clung to his clothes and heard him take a deep, rough breath. "I need to explain something that I finally realized."

She wanted to ask what, but when she could force words past the tightness in her throat, she could only say, "I need to explain something to you, too, a decision I've made."

He hesitated, then touched her on the shoulder. The contact riveted Megan to the spot. "Let me tell this first, or I won't get it out. All right?"

When she nodded, he drew back, breaking the contact, but not moving away from her. She watched him, beginning to make out his features in the dim light that left dark shadows around his eyes and throat.

He took off his jacket and tossed it onto the couch without ever looking away from Megan. She heard him take in a deep breath, then softly exhale. "Part of my success at this job has always been the ease with which I can shut out the world. I stop thinking about anything and everything expect the gag. I focus completely. That's why I'm good. That's why I've never had a major injury. It's a talent. A gift, maybe."

"Why . . . why are you telling me this?"

"Because today, doing that gag, one that should have been something I could do blindfolded and half-asleep, I screwed up. I didn't check something as simple as the way the treatment for the leather would heat up over the cable run, the first try. I pushed off too late the second time, but made it work in the end. I went through the motions, through the basics, without really seeing what I was doing."

"Why?" she asked, making herself take a breath. Then she wished she hadn't. She inhaled the scent of maleness that clung provocatively to Cade.

"At first I was worried about Adam, about the cold he has, then it all got tangled up with you. What you said when we talked earlier about Frank, how you looked, how you felt last night when you had the nightmare. How I kissed you and held you, and how it went from comforting you to wanting you." He held up a hand. "I'm not apologizing for that. I can't. What I want you to understand is that you've invaded my mind the way no one else ever has. You've made me think differently, act differently, and I screwed up because of it."

Megan stared at Cade. How could she listen to this and not want to touch him and have some contact? How could she stand here and deny the strength of her feelings for him? As if it had a life of its own, her right hand slowly lifted and touched his jaw, felt the bristling of the beginnings of a beard and the heat in his skin. Then her finger took an unsteady journey to the pulse that beat wildly just under his ear.

"I . . . I need to tell you, to explain," she breathed.

"Later," he said on a rough whisper as his hand rose to cover hers. "All I want right now is to touch you, to kiss you, to hold you and know that everything is still here, that the world is still here and you're in it with me. I've been alone all my life.'' His hold tightened on her hand. ''Megan, I don't want to be alone.''

She felt a shudder go through her body as she realized that there was no way she could walk away from Cade right now. There wasn't enough moral strength in her to leave. She wanted him. She wanted to be with him, even if it was just for now, just for this night. There were no illusions that he would be the man she could build a life with. He wasn't even close, but there was no denying that she wanted him and loved him.

Without a word she stepped into Cade's arms, into a smothering, tight embrace, something more real than anything she'd known in her life. She didn't stop to think about the consequences. She refused to. Not now. Not for a while longer. He couldn't be hers forever. She knew that, but just for tonight she was going to follow her heart and not her head.

Megan just accepted the fact that in the short time she'd known Cade, he'd gone from being a case number to a person who had captured her heart, who stirred age-old feelings, deep in her being.

She lifted her face to him, offering her lips, and when his lips found hers, she was overwhelmed by a wrenchingly stark need to deepen the kiss, to hold and be held. To forget, yet remember. She opened her mouth to him, wanting his invasion, tasting him and letting his essence seep into her soul.

Her body swayed into his, fitting neatly into his heat and strength; she felt his hand at the small of her back drawing her hips against him. The stirrings that she could feel so firmly against her pelvis made a gasp well up in her throat. Then his tongue thrust deep into her mouth, sweetly, hotly, proprietorially.

She knew that she couldn't just touch him, couldn't just kiss him and see what there was. There was no turning back now. Tonight she'd have Cade, know him, and take the knowledge with her for the rest of her life.

Passion came as suddenly as it had come last night, but now it was more complete, not at all dulled by the remnants of bad dreams and pain from the past. It was all consuming, all encompassing, and all the reality she needed right now.

She wanted to be closer to the man, to feel him against her, and tugged at his shirt, freeing it from the waistband of his jeans. When she fumbled with the buttons and couldn't make her fingers undo them, she tugged and heard a popping, then his shirt was open. She touched his chest and felt his heart beating frantically against her palms.

She moved her hands on his bare skin, felt his nipples tighten, then heard him groan, a vibrating sound against her lips and hands. She felt the scar, a rough line on the smoothness of his skin, and pressed her lips to it, wishing it were in her power to keep him from ever having something like that happen to him again. But nothing was in her power, except to have what Cade was offering her.

When she looked up at him, Cade framed her face with his hands, touched her lips with his, then looked down at her with eyes as dark as the night. For a long moment they stood like that, then without a word, Cade swept her up into his arms and she clung to him. She buried her face in the heat of his neck, tasting the vague saltiness of his skin with her tongue.

As he carried her into the bedroom, he whispered against her hair. "I've wanted this since the first time I heard your voice on the phone. Then I saw you at my door." His lips caressed her forehead. "Lord, the sight of you made me dream dreams I've never known before."

It was the same for Megan, a passion that had flared from that first moment of contact, something she hadn't wanted to recognize or name.

In the shadows of the bedroom, Cade fell with Megan into the coolness of the bed linen, then his hands found the buttons on her shirt. Bracing himself on one elbow, he looked down at her and slowly began to undo them. One button, then another . . . She held her breath, then with two to go, couldn't bear it anymore. She quickly undid them and Cade moved aside the fabric with the tip of one finger. That same finger brushed across her nipples, making them swell and ache. All of Megan's attention was on the incredible thing that was happening to her.

With just a touch this man struck chords in her that made her feel on fire and chilled at the same time. He made her yearn for what might be and grieve for what could never be. She reached up to Cade, circling his neck with her arms and drew him down to her. But instead of the kiss she wanted, that filling and tasting, he brushed her lips with his tongue, gently tracing their fullness.

She had assumed that Cade would be a self-absorbed lover, a man who took women and didn't bother with their needs. But that wasn't the truth. He was gentle, tender in a heartbreaking way, his tongue skimming over her, sampling, teasing, sweeping over her most sensitive spots.

And soon he had her shirt off, her bra discarded, then she lifted her hips and he slipped down her jeans. With a flick of his hand they flew off the bed, to be lost in the deep shadows. His fingers found the elastic of her panties, and the flimsy excuse for a cover was gone.

His body heat seemed to flow around her, soothing and gentle, yet giving promise of the fire she knew was in Cade. His hand stroked her belly, moved lower and when he touched the apex at her thighs, the fire was everywhere.

"Oh, yes," she groaned, shuddering involuntarily under his touch, lifting her hips again, offering herself to him.

Then without warning he was gone, and she opened her eyes to see only his shadow in the room. He stripped out of his clothes in moments, fumbled for protection, then came back to her, bracing himself over her, looking down at her.

Cade was experiencing a driving need for this woman, raw, sexual desire, which was so mingled with real caring and an almost magical sense of wonder that he almost couldn't move for a moment.

Then she was whispering his name, her breath hot on his skin, and her hands moved on him, lower, lower, until she found the source of his strength and heat. The groan that tore from his throat vibrated around them as his head arched back. He gasped in a breath and looked down at her once more. His desire was echoed in her response, in the turgid tips of her breasts, in the rapid breathing that seemed to match his own, and he found her mouth with his. It was a living, burning contact that felt as if it could give him life.

He had thought of her healing, and as she moved under him, opening her legs to him, inviting his possession, he knew that this woman could make everything right. If he entered her, he wouldn't ever turn back.

He ached for her, and when he tested her, felt her heat against his, when he heard her whisper, "Yes, please, yes," he took her. In one swift movement he knew what it was to be surrounded by, to be possessed by a woman.

He felt her nails biting into his back, the thrust of her hips to be closer to him than was humanly possible, and control was a thing of the past for Cade. Her legs came up to circle his hips and she began to match him, thrust for thrust. He heard her soft sighs, then felt her tighten around him, and moved harder, deeper. She gasped, her head thrown back against the pillows, then Cade felt himself begin to explode when Megan quivered and tightened yet again.

He was lost to the world, anchored only by this woman, and felt every shard of sensation soar through his body. He cried out, his head back, then, when he thought he would die, he knew that he had never been so whole in his life.

Chapter 12

Megan stirred in the deep shadows and immediately knew where she was. She could feel Cade's heat against her, hear his steady breathing. She shifted just enough to be able to look at him. Instinctively she reached out, touching his chest with a feathery caress, then his throat, as if she could memorize the feel of him under her fingertips. Memorize. That meant there would be an end to this, and she didn't want to think about endings, not until the morning, when she flew back to Los Angeles.

Memorize. The suggestion of strong features in the softness of night. The dimples, the cleft in his chin, the roughness of the coming beard. Remember. When Megan touched his lips with the tip of her finger, she felt his exhaled breath caress her skin. Then his hand was on hers and his eyes were open, dark and unreadable.

Slowly, gently, he drew her hand down to cover his heart. Yes, she would remember this. Forever.

"Why didn't you wake me?" he asked in a whisper.

"I was just watching you sleep," she said honestly.

He brushed her forehead with his lips. "You never told me what it was you wanted to say when I came back."

She shifted, resting her head in the hollow of his shoulder. "I called my assistant, Rose." She trembled when his hand started tracing whisper-light patterns on her bare shoulder. "I'm off the case. I withdrew."

"Can I ask why?" he said, stilling his hand.

She closed her eyes. "Because there was no way I could be objective about you anymore. Professionally, at the least, it would be a conflict of interest."

She could feel the beat of his heart speeding up. "So you can do what you want?"

She tried to laugh, but the sound came out weak and shaky. "I guess so."

"Great," he whispered and pulled her more tightly to him. She could feel his need of her growing, echoing her need of him. Then he was touching her, caressing her, and an insatiable fire was there, engulfing her. And when Cade kissed her, when his mouth claimed hers, the fire flared to an all-consuming height. Now he was over her, his voice soft, driving around her, murmuring words she could feel in her soul. Then he was filling her again, giving her the completeness that she had never known before. She held to him, her arms around his neck, her legs circling his hips. And she moved, faster and faster, echoing his thrusts until she felt the world become perfect—perfect feeling, perfect sensations and perfectly whole.

She cried out at the same time Cade did and wondered if she had ever loved anyone before this man. Wondered just what she was going to do when she had to leave him.

Megan woke again just before dawn and lay very still. She didn't turn to Cade or touch him, but glanced at the bed-

side clock. Five-thirty. She had to go, had to walk away, and
before she could do something foolish like reaching out to
Cade and cuddling into his heat and strength, she carefully
slipped out of bed. She picked up her robe from the footboard, then stepped into the sitting room.

Quietly closing the bedroom door, she let out a breath,
then crossed to the couch and snapped on the low sidelight.
Picking up the phone, she got the front desk, had them
connect her with Love Field and asked for a seat on the first
flight to Los Angeles. There was a vacancy on an eight
o'clock flight out, nonstop. She reserved her seat, then
pushed the Disconnect button and called the desk again, to
make arrangements for a taxi at six o'clock to take her back
to Dallas.

When the man assured her the cab would be waiting, she
thanked him, hung up and went back through the bedroom
to the bathroom. But as she was about to pass the bed, Cade
stirred, shifting onto his side, and made a soft sound of
sleep. She stopped at the footboard and looked at him. In
the glow of the small light that spilled in from the sitting
room, she could see that sleep had eased the tension in his
face, making him look somehow vulnerable. And it made
her heart hurt to think she would never see him like this
again.

Quickly she turned from him and hurried into the bathroom, closing the door behind her. She dressed in dark
slacks, a white silk shirt and low heels, then ran a brush
through her tangled hair and caught it low at her neck in a
silver clip. She avoided looking at herself too closely, not
wanting to confront the growing pain inside her that she
knew would be beginning to stamp itself on her expression.

She went quietly back into the bedroom to get the rest of
her things, then packed her garment bag in the bathroom.
She snapped it shut and took one last look around the old-

fashioned bathroom, then went into the bedroom for the last time.

Cade hadn't moved; his breathing was still deep and regular. Without stopping, she walked into the sitting area. After closing the bedroom door, she put her bag by the entry, then saw her jacket on the couch.

As she crossed to get it, she heard the bedroom door click open, and didn't have to turn to know Cade was there.

"What are you doing up?" he asked, his voice still touched with the remnants of sleepiness. "It's not even light outside."

Megan couldn't move at first, afraid to face Cade, then knew she had to do it. She had been going to run away, to leave before there would be a confrontation, but this might be for the best. Steeling herself, she turned and saw Cade in the bedroom door. He was leaning one shoulder against the jamb, arms crossed on his chest, and was only wearing his undershorts.

Why hadn't he stayed asleep? Why did he have to stand there, disheveled, heavy-eyed, and looking more sexy than any man had a right to be? She touched her tongue to her lips. "I have to go. I've got things to do."

"Go where?" he asked without moving into the room.

"Home. To Los Angeles. I'm finished here."

He straightened as she spoke, then walked slowly toward her. With nothing on but the brief shorts, he was truly indecently exposed, and was making it hard for her to keep any semblance of control. Thank heaven he didn't touch her when he got close. "You're leaving? Just like that?"

"I have to get back. I'm..." She nibbled on her bottom lip. "Cade, I can't stay here."

"You can't go," he said simply.

"I have to." She clasped her hands tightly in front of her in an effort to keep herself from reaching out to touch the scar on his shoulder, or to feel his sleek heat under her fingers. "This was a mistake. It really was, and I'm sorry. I...I have to get on with my life."

"And what happened between us doesn't mean a thing?"

She couldn't say that. She couldn't lie, when she knew she would never forget this man. "It was...was..."

"An impulse. A diversion. Is that it?"

Megan took a step back as she realized that anger was beginning to smolder in his eyes. She hadn't really expected this. Not from a man who had walked away from women all his life. "You should know all about diversions."

"That's a cheap shot," he muttered. "You know about my background, about what I've done. I'm not proud of a lot of it, but I never jumped into bed with a woman simply for a diversion."

"I didn't mean..." She let the words trail off. She needed to say the right thing, but had no idea what it was.

Cade held up one hand. "Stop, right here. Let's backtrack and figure out what's wrong."

"Cade, I..."

"I came up here last night to tell you that—" he shook his head "—to tell you that I'm falling in love with you, I guess."

No, she didn't want to hear this. It was all she could do to keep from pressing her hands to her ears. "Stop, this isn't—"

He kept talking as if she hadn't said a thing. "We're together, in every sense of the word, and now you're packing up and leaving." He came even closer, his voice dropping to a rough growl. "I'll be damned if I'll let you just walk out of here."

And she'd be damned if she was going to stay. "I can't stay."

"I want you here with me," he said, his voice uneven with emotion. "Be with me. Let me love you."

She swallowed hard. "Cade, I've lived my life with a man who gambled away everything, finally his freedom. I can't start that all over again. I won't."

"What? That's what this is all about? You've got your father and me all tangled up in some crazy fear?"

Megan felt sickness in the back of her throat. "You're like Frank in a lot of ways, except you gamble with your life. I can't live with that. I won't, Cade, I won't."

He reached out to her, but when she flinched and drew back, he raked both hands through his hair, then ran them down over his face. She heard him suck in air, then exhale it in a rush. "Doc, for being a psychologist, you don't know much about yourself at all."

"What are you—?"

"I've got a high school education, a few years of college, but I can tell you're still fighting old wars. You've never let go, never put an end to what Frank did to you." He leaned closer to her, his breath hot on her skin. "You've made Frank some god who you can't fight, so you run from him. You try to cut him out of your life, but he gives you nightmares. You've never faced down your enemy and had a victory."

She felt anger burn through her, then die as suddenly as it came. She felt weak and did her best to keep the tears that burned behind her eyes from falling. "This isn't a war, Cade. It's my life."

He drew back, his face closed, eyes hooded. "And you want to walk out of here alone and turn your back on what we could have together?"

"I have to," she whispered unsteadily. "I have to."

She could sense him withdrawing from her, something that should have made things easier, but instead she felt isolated and more alone than she ever had in her life. "Can I ask you something before you leave?" he asked abruptly.

She bit her lip and nodded, not able to get any more words past the lump in her throat.

"Were you going to recommend that I get Adam or not?" he asked.

She shook her head. "It doesn't matter now."

"Oh, yes, it does. It does to me. What were you going to recommend if you stayed on the case?"

She moved farther from him, her eyes burning, but free of tears. "What do you think?"

He turned away from her, crossing to the windows and staring out at the rising sun. Without looking back at her, he said in a low, rough voice, "Because of what you've gone through, you were going to make sure I didn't have my son."

"It doesn't matter now. I have no say in it."

He turned to face her again, his expression bleak. "Will you try and influence the next psychologist to take your place?"

"No, of course not. I took myself off the case."

He came back to her and reached out, ignoring her jerk when he cupped her chin in his strong fingers. "You're so wrong about everything, Doc. And you've lost more than you'll ever know. I hope for your sake that someday you'll be able to get rid of your nightmares."

She licked her lips, hating the contact as much as she hated the burning urge to hold Cade and never let him go.

"Either win your war or surrender," Cade growled. "But for heaven's sake, get it over with."

She jerked free of his touch. "You aren't making sense," she muttered, rubbing at her chin where he'd touched her.

"Maybe I'm not. Maybe I'm dreaming and this is my nightmare. Maybe I'll wake up and find out that you're still in bed with me, that all I have to do is reach out and touch you, that life is good and the world is right."

Megan turned quickly and scooped up her jacket and purse, then crossed to the hall door. She picked up her bag, then, without looking at Cade, murmured, "Goodbye."

But before she could reach for the door, Cade was there, his hand closing over her upper arm and tugging her around, until she had no choice but to look at him. His dark eyes burned into hers, a mixture of anger and pain searing through them. "Goodbye," he whispered roughly, then bent and kissed her, a fierce, hard kiss.

He let her go, then turned and walked away into the bedroom.

Megan stared at the wooden barrier as he slammed it after him, then heard another door close and water start to run. With a shaking hand she reached for the knob and pulled open the door to the hall. She couldn't go back to the sort of life she'd had with Frank. Not even for Cade. Without looking back, she left.

Cade stayed in the shower, letting the warmth of the water run over him, but nothing could touch the coldness inside. He couldn't believe what had happened. In the space of a week, Megan Lewis had taken him higher than he'd ever gone, and plunged him into depths he didn't know if he could ever escape.

He loved her. It was that simple, that painful. And she'd walked away from him. Frank. The name circled in his head, around and around. Because of a man Cade had never known, his whole life was torn up. He closed his eyes and stood under the water, trying to clear his head to decide what to do now.

One thought came to him with a clarity that shocked him. He had to go after Megan. He couldn't let her go. When he turned off the water, he realized the phone was ringing. Grabbing a towel, he wrapped it around his hips, hurried into the sitting room and reached for the phone.

"Yeah?" he said.

"Cade, Doris. I hesitated to call you, but I thought you should know that Adam's in the hospital. His cold went into pneumonia."

Cade felt as if his world was falling apart around his ears. And even a stiff drink wouldn't help set it right. "Why in the hell didn't you call earlier? Doris, damn it, why?"

"We thought it might not be too bad, that he'd be out before you needed to know. But he's running a high fever. He's so sick, Cade."

Cade tried to think. "I'm coming back."

"No, you don't have to. I'll call you and let you know what happens."

"I won't sit here and wait. What hospital is he in?"

"Children's Pediatric in Los Angeles."

"I'll be there as soon as I possibly can get there," he said, then hung up.

For a long moment he stood without moving, trying to absorb what was going on. He had to get to Adam. He'd fly back and be with Adam, then try to find Megan and make some sense out of what had happened.

He picked up the phone again and called Leon's room. When the man answered in a voice thick with sleep, Cade said, "Leon, Cade. I'm going back to L.A. My son's sick. He's in the hospital. Do you know if Walters's jet's still at Love Field?"

"Yeah, it sure is."

"How can I get in touch with Walters?"

"I'll do it. You just get yourself to Love Field. It'll be waiting for you when you get there."

"Thank you. Tell Walters I'm out of here until he hears from me."

He put the receiver back, then called the front desk. "I'm going to be gone for a few days. Keep my room for me, and I'll let you know when I'll be back."

"Yes, sir," the clerk said. "Is there anything else you need?"

"A taxi."

"Sorry, we've only got two, and one left here about ten minutes ago with a lady in it, going to the airport. The other one should be here pretty soon."

"Fine, call me when it arrives," he said and hung up.

Less than four hours later, Cade was getting out of a taxi in front of the children's hospital in Los Angeles. He hurried up the sweep of stairs to the entrance of the towering, glass and steel structure, went into the lobby and found out that Adam was on the tenth floor.

He jogged to the elevators and rode up to the tenth floor. As he stepped out into the corridor, he turned to the right and saw Leo Sinclair at the nursing station, less than twenty feet down the corridor. His ex-father-in-law was a tall, strapping man with silver hair, who always seemed to be controlled, maybe even a bit cool. But now he looked intense, strained and older than his sixty-two years.

When he spotted Cade, his expression only tightened even more. "I didn't know if you'd come or not."

"He's my son, Leo. I can't lose him," Cade said honestly as he set his tote in front of the nurse's desk. "You should understand that better than anyone."

The older man nodded. "I do, Cade, I really do."

Cade turned to the nurse in charge. "I'm Cade Daniels. My son Adam was admitted here yesterday. I want to see him."

"So, you came after all?" Doris said as she hurried up to the desk.

"I told you, I had to, Doris."

Doris looked at Cade, then at her husband. As Leo slipped his arm around Doris's shoulder, the woman shook her head. "Of course you did."

"Thank you," Cade said simply, then asked the nurse, "Where is my son?"

"He's down the hall, the third door. He's in a private room."

Cade was heading down the hall before the woman had finished talking and found the room. He went inside, into a pale green space with cartoon characters decorating the walls and a single window at the far end that let sunlight flood in. But there was still an almost sad tone to the area. And that was emphasized when Cade saw the single crib against the side wall, a dresser on its left and a monitor that beeped to the right.

A doctor was bending over the crib, and Cade hurried across to him. "Doctor?" he said and the man straightened and turned around.

As the physician moved to one side, Cade could see Adam. It made his heart lurch to see the child, who had appeared so full of life, so healthy just days ago, lying still and pale between the white sheets. His eyes were closed, the lids as thin as parchment and his tiny hands lay limply by his side. The thin sheet over him moved ever so slightly with each breath he took.

Cade felt light-headed for a minute, then went closer and reached out to grip the top rail of the metal crib.

"Are you Mr. Daniels?" the doctor said.

"Yes, I'm Cade Daniels," he said without looking away from Adam. "What's going on with my son?"

"He's got pneumonia. His lungs are congested. He's running a high fever. He was on oxygen for a while, but he's breathing a bit easier now."

Cade looked at the other man. "He's getting better?"

"I didn't say that. He's a bit clearer, but the fluids can build again. That's why we're monitoring his respiration." The doctor hesitated. "Adam's condition is serious, very serious, but we should know more in the next twenty-four hours."

"Can I stay?"

"Yes, go ahead, but he won't know you're here. He's unconscious from a combination of the medication and the fever."

Cade closed his eyes for a long moment, then asked in a low voice, "Does he have a chance?"

The doctor shrugged. "He was healthy before this happened. He's got a good chance." He looked back at Adam. "I've seen children worse than Adam come right out of it, but . . ." His voice trailed off.

"I understand," Cade murmured.

"Believe me, there isn't a lot you can do for him right now."

"I know," he said, then added, "but I need to be here with my son." Cade reached for the nearest chair, slid it over beside the crib, then dropped onto the green vinyl seat and sat forward. Carefully he reached between the metal slats and took Adam's hand into his own.

"It might be a long time before there's a change," the doctor said.

"I'll wait."

Megan didn't go to the office when she got into Los Angeles. Instead, she picked up her car in the parking lot and drove toward the ocean. When she hit Coast Highway, she turned north toward Malibu.

All the way back she'd done nothing but think about Cade, about what he'd said and about her life. She couldn't help others while she was so mixed up in her own life. She drove along the coast, thinking, crying for no reason, then finally parked at a lookout point near Ventura.

She sat in her car, watching the ocean, feeling fragmented and incomplete. Then she saw pay phones near a beach patrol building. She had to call Rose.

Getting out into the chilly ocean air, she hurried to the phone and put in the call.

When Rose heard her voice, Megan couldn't get in a word edgeways.

"Where are you?" Rose asked. "It's past noon hour and they're really put out at court. Brad thinks this will throw the whole case back at least three months, before they can get another court date."

"I'm at the beach," Megan finally said when Rose stopped talking to take a breath. "And I'm not coming in. I'm taking some time off. Go through my cases and see what you can put off for a week or so. I'll be back in touch, or you can leave a message on my machine at the house. I'll monitor it."

"Before you hang up, there's something you need to know about."

"What's that?"

"Your father's parole hearing has been moved up to tomorrow at ten in the morning."

Megan closed her eyes and pressed her forehead to the cold metal front of the phone. "Did he call?"

"Yes, and he kept calling until I took the call. I told him you weren't here. I didn't know when you'd be back, and you weren't likely to contact him."

"And?"

"He hung up on me."

That was just like Frank. If he couldn't get someone to give him what he wanted, he'd cut them off. "Thanks for telling me," she said in a low voice. "I'm sorry you had to deal with him like that."

"I didn't mind. I'm just wondering if he really thinks you'll be there."

"Sure he does," Megan said. "He thinks I'm going to cave in, testify for him and make things right." She found her vision blurring with tears. "But I can't make anything right. Not even my own life."

"What?"

"Nothing. I need to go." She swiped at her eyes. "I'll be in touch."

"Cade?"

He heard Doris Sinclair's voice and closed his eyes for a minute. Then he let go of Adam's hand, stood and turned to see the older woman coming toward the crib. "Is there any change?" she asked in a tight whisper, her lips trembling.

"No, nothing." Cade ran a hand over his face. "What time is it?"

"Just after five."

"It feels as if I've been here days instead of just hours."

Doris came closer and as she looked down at Adam, tears filled her eyes and spilled down her cheeks. "The poor baby. I couldn't . . . bear to lose him . . . too."

Cade put his arm around Doris's shoulders and gently drew her to him. At first the older woman was stiff in his arms, then she seemed to collapse against him while she softly sobbed.

Cade almost envied her the ability to cry, to find some release for her emotions. All he could do was sit in this chair, watching his son and being afraid that the two most important people in his world wouldn't be there for him.

Doris finally moved back and dabbed at her eyes with a hankie she'd been holding. "Why don't you go and get something to eat, Cade, or some coffee or something? I'll stay with the baby."

"Are you sure, Doris?"

"Yes, I'm sure," she said and went around him to sit in the chair he'd just vacated.

Cade rotated his head to try and ease the bunching of his neck muscles, then looked down at Adam. "If there's any change at all, you'll get me, won't you?" he said to Doris.

"Yes, I will," she replied softly as she pressed the hankie to her eyes again.

Cade hesitated, then turned and strode toward the door. He asked the nurse where the pay phones were, then headed down the hall toward the bank of phones outside a waiting room.

It took him several tries before he finally found Megan's listing in the phone book, then he pushed a quarter into the coin slot and dialed the number. It rang twice before a woman answered it. "Dr. Lewis's office. How may I help you?"

Cade didn't know where to begin. "I'm looking for Dr. Lewis. It's important."

"I'm afraid she isn't in right now. Can I take a message?"

He closed his eyes. "Are you Rose?"

She seemed taken back, then said, "Yes, I'm the doctor's assistant."

"Then you know who I am . . . Cade Daniels."

"Oh, yes, Mr. Daniels. How can I help you?"

"Get me in contact with the doctor."

"Is there something wrong?" she asked politely.

"Wrong" didn't even begin to cover it. "Yes, I really need to talk to her."

"I'm so sorry. She's out of contact right now. She—"

"Didn't she get back from Texas today?"

"Yes, but she didn't come in to the office. She's taking some time off to get a much needed rest."

"Is she all right?"

"I think so. She had some bad news today and—"

"About Frank?"

"She told you about him?"

"Yes. What happened?"

"His parole hearing's been moved up to tomorrow."

He closed his eyes. And Megan couldn't face it. "Do you have any idea where I could find her?"

"None, I'm sorry. But I can take a message. She said she'll check back with me."

What could he say? What would make a difference, if Rose got the message to her? Then he knew. "Just tell her that I love her."

"I beg your pardon?"

"I love her and I need her."

"Yes, sir, I'll give her that message," Rose said with audible enthusiasm. "Does she know where to reach you?"

"She can find me. And thank you, Rose."

He hung up, then leaned back against the phone and closed his eyes. He needed some food, some coffee and he needed Megan. He wished she was with him here and now. He wished he could hold her and have her heal his wounds.

He straightened and exhaled in a rush. It didn't do any good to wish like that. If wishes worked, he'd have a healthy little boy and Megan in his life.

Chapter 13

It was just after midnight when Cade stirred from a restless sleep on the couch in the waiting area near Adam's room, and saw Doris and Leo standing over him. He was instantly awake, awkwardly sitting up and almost afraid to ask, "What is it?"

Doris dropped to his side and touched his arm. "Cade, the baby's going to be all right. His fever broke and his lungs are clearing."

Cade stared at her, then looked up at Leo. "He's out of danger?"

"Yes, he is. The doctor expects a full recovery."

For a minute Cade felt incapable of moving, then sank back and rested his head on the cushions. He stared at the ceiling over him. "Thank goodness," he whispered as relief flooded through him.

"He's awake and even eating," Doris said.

Cade exhaled, then sat straight again. "I need to see him."

"Of course, but first Doris and I want to talk to you, Cade," Leo said.

He looked again at Leo, seeing the exhaustion from hours at the hospital that had left him a drained version of his usual self, then at Doris. Even though she was pale and obviously ready to drop, she was gazing at him intently. He didn't have it in him to fight them, to go back to the adversarial roles he and they had always had, roles that had been set aside for a time, while Adam was in danger. He needed to see Adam and find Megan, then he'd do whatever he had to do. "I'm tired," he said.

"We all are," Leo said, and unexpectedly reached out to put his hand on Cade's shoulder. "But this is important."

Cade sank back into the couch. "All right," he said. "What?"

Megan drove. She went north up the coast, stopped when she couldn't drive anymore, then on the second evening, stayed at a small motel on the ocean, just north of San Francisco. She stopped her car in front of the office, got out and went in to get a room.

When she stepped through the glass door into the reception area, a bell rang in the distance. Megan moved into the space, a tiny room cut in half by a desk that went from wall to wall. As she approached the desk, a woman came out of a back room and smiled at her.

"Good evening. Welcome to the Surf's Up Motel."

Megan laid her purse on the desk. "I need a room."

"Are you alone, or is someone with you?" the woman asked.

"Alone," Megan said, and the word struck her. Alone. She was totally alone, by choice.

"That's fifty-two dollars and five cents with tax," the woman said as she began to fill out a card. Then she pushed it across the desk to Megan. "Name, address, phone and license number."

Megan picked up a pen that was secured to the desk by a thin chain and began to complete the spaces.

"So, you on vacation or just traveling through?" the woman asked.

"Just traveling through," Megan murmured while she wrote.

"Getting away from things?"

Megan stopped writing and looked up at the woman. "Excuse me?"

"I just asked if you were getting away. You know, taking a breather, leaving things behind to get a break."

Megan looked back down at the card. "I..." The pen was poised, but she didn't finish writing. She was running away, getting into her car and driving, just the way Cade had said he'd done before. The way she had over two years ago. And it wasn't doing a bit of good.

She couldn't hide from the possibility that Frank could be getting ready for release on parole, and she couldn't hide from the fact that she was alone because she'd walked away from Cade. This wasn't working. The war was following her.

She finished filling in the card, then handed it to the woman. "I'm only going to be here for a few hours." She just needed to rest, to get her thoughts straight, then get on with her life.

The woman gave her a key, and Megan went out into cool night air, filled with the pungency of the nearby ocean. She went to her room, stepped inside and knew what she had to do. She had to put an end to her war. Maybe she wouldn't claim victory, but it would be over finally.

At ten o'clock the next morning Megan was in the visiting room at the Northanger Facility for Men, just outside a small California town, two hundred miles north of Los Angeles.

The prison wasn't anything like what she'd expected. No gray dinginess, no high walls with barbed wire, no heavy, metal bars. Northanger looked like a college that had seen better days, with rolling lawns, brick buildings dotting the hundred-acre plot of land, windows of clear glass and only a six-foot-high chain-link fence on the perimeter. But the attendant who had brought her from the front desk to this room stayed. The man closed the door and stood with his back against it, while Megan went farther into the room.

There was only one other person there—Frank. He wasn't the man Megan remembered.

He was by the windows, his back to her. He seemed smaller, less imposing than she remembered, his hair thinner and much grayer than it had been. Dressed in a plain white shirt and dark slacks that looked like casual wear, not prison garb, he was as thin as ever.

"Frank?" she said, as she went toward the long table in the middle of the room.

"You can visit for fifteen minutes," the man by the door told her. "Just stay on your side of the table, and no touching."

Frank turned slowly and saw Megan; she could read the shock on his face. Then it was gone, replaced by the smile that Megan had seen enough over the years. Frank Lewis was getting into his likable mode. "Good to see you, girl," he said as he came to his side of the table. "It's been a long time."

"Over two years," Megan said, not moving, then blurted out, "Did you make parole?"

His face tightened, the "nice guy" mask slipping for a moment. "No, they won't let me out," he said, then the

smile was back. "But I knew you'd come. I just knew it."
He tapped his shirt over his heart. "I felt it in here."

All Megan felt in her heart was relief that he'd been de-
nied parole, that he hadn't been able to con the authorities.

"Come here, girl," Frank said, motioning Megan to the
table. "Sit. Let's talk. We've got a lot to say."

Megan almost turned and left, but knew she couldn't. She
did have a lot to say to Frank, and it had to be said now. She
went to the table, sat on one of the hard, wooden chairs
facing it and looked at her father.

Yes, she'd been fighting the Frank Lewis war all her life,
but she knew now that he wasn't the enemy at all. His addiction was. Frank took a chair opposite her, leaning forward with his arms on the table.

"I knew you'd come," he said. "I knew it. You wouldn't
let me down."

Megan held tightly to her purse in her lap. "How did you
know?"

"You always did, Meggie, always. You couldn't cut off
your old man just like that. It's not in you to do that."

It wasn't. He knew that, and now she did, too. "You're
right."

"And you'll help me?"

"What?"

"Listen, Meggie, you're a professional, someone that's
respected. You can talk to the parole board. They can't deny
me parole. I've been a model prisoner in here." He looked
around the room. "It's almost killing me, but I'm doing
everything they say."

"Why did they deny you parole?" she asked.

He shrugged sharply. "Some mumbo jumbo about failure to rehabilitate."

"They think you aren't rehabilitated, Frank, that you'd
go out and do the same thing."

"That's what they said, but they don't know anything. I'd never do this again. I wouldn't, I swear to you, I wouldn't. I'd be smarter, quicker, less gullible."

"And you wouldn't get caught, would you?"

"Not again, Meggie. Never again. I swear to you, I wouldn't."

She stared at Frank; the realization came to her that she'd faced her enemy—and found an illusion. "You need help, Frank, and they can give it to you in here."

"Help?" he demanded, standing to face her across the table. "All the help I need is a daughter who'll go out on a limb for me, a daughter who cares enough to get in there and help me."

She shook her head, incredible sadness sinking into her, yet it was all overlaid with relief. "You need help I can't give you. You need to get control, to accept the fact that you're addicted to gambling, that the addiction is the root of your problems."

He stood straight. "Oh, so that's it, is it? High and mighty, doctor with money, who doesn't want to have a father who's made a few mistakes?"

Megan felt something in her snap, and raw anger flooded through her. "A few mistakes, Frank?"

He leaned both hands flat on the table, getting closer to her. "Why don't you ever call me Dad or Father?"

She stood, facing him without flinching. "Because you never were my father. You never took care of me, were there for me or let me be a child. You let gambling consume you. You let gambling take all of you, and there was nothing left for me." She was shocked that there were no tears, just a sense of cleansing with each word. "There was nothing but worry and trying to keep things together. And I'm not doing that anymore. I swear to you, I've finished with it."

He glared at her, letting his eyes skim over her casual clothes, the jeans and bulky sweater and her loose hair. "And you're doing so well alone?"

"You don't know what I'm doing. You haven't even asked, not once since I came through the door, what my life is like, what's going on in my world. It's all about you. It always has been."

"I didn't have to ask. I can see it. You're an uptight doctor who doesn't trust anyone. Someone who thinks she can go through life without caring about anyone." He suddenly grew very calm—Jekyll and Hyde. She remembered it too well. "You go ahead the way you want to go. I'll get by. I don't need you." He turned his back on her. "Now get out."

She stared at him. Why had she ever thought he and Cade were the same, that the two men operated on the same principle? Cade was so far removed from Frank that night and day couldn't have been more diametrically opposed. But she was Frank's daughter, and like her father, she'd made mistakes, horrible mistakes. She wasn't going to make another right now.

"If you ever get help, if you ever realize just what you're doing..."

He turned on her. "Get out of here, Meggie. I don't need you. I don't want you. Let's leave it at that."

She hesitated, then turned and left her father. She didn't feel as if she'd had a victory, but definitely knew the war was over.

During her drive back to Los Angeles, Megan finally could think clearly. She could understand everything. She was alone. She'd let Frank do that to her. He'd taken everything from her, including Cade. But Frank was in prison, and she wouldn't let him go on ruining her life. There would be scars, but no more open wounds.

When she reached the building where her office was located, just after five, she parked in the underground facility and went upstairs. She stepped through the front door and into the shadows. Rose was gone, and the premises were completely empty.

Flipping on the overhead lights, she crossed the reception area and went into her private office. She tossed her purse onto the chair by the door, then pulled back the drapes on the windows. The ocean was far below, being bathed in the colors of twilight. Megan sat down behind her desk, stared out the windows, then picked up the phone and called long-distance information.

"Texas, Dedrick, Texas," she said to the operator. "I need the number for Hall's Hotel."

Mr. Hall answered almost immediately. "Hall's Hotel. Horace Hall speaking."

"I'm trying to get in touch with Cade Daniels."

"Well, he's not here. He left on Monday, said he'd be back, but never showed up again."

"He's gone?"

"Yes, ma'am, in a real hurry, he was. He said he'd be back in a few days, but I haven't heard from him since."

"Thank you," she said, then put the receiver back in place.

What had happened? Had Cade left the film? Had he tried the stunt? She didn't know what to think. Snapping on her desk light, she reached for the folders lying to one side and began to go through them, hoping against hope that Rose hadn't yet sent Adam's file back to Brad.

When she found it, she flipped it open and found Cade's home phone number. After two rings, his answering machine clicked on, and when it came time to leave a message, she said, "Cade. Are you there? It's Megan. I have to talk to you. Call me as soon as you get this."

She was about to close the files, then spotted the number for Evan Rice and on impulse dialed it. After two rings a man answered. "Evan Rice. Can I help you?"

She exhaled a sigh, thankful the man was in his offices after hours. "Mr. Rice, this is Dr. Megan Lewis. I was working on the Adam Daniels case."

"Oh, yes, Doctor. Cade told me you pulled yourself off the case. I have to admit that I was worried, but it all worked out just fine, didn't it?"

"Excuse me?"

"The agreement between Cade and the Sinclairs."

"What agreement?"

"The Sinclairs decided to drop the suit and share custody with Cade."

Megan couldn't believe that anything would have softened Doris's and Leo's attitude toward Cade. "Are you sure?"

"Yes, very sure. I'm working on the agreement myself. I think after the child almost died, it brought them all up short."

Megan felt her breath leave her in a rush. "Adam almost died?"

"Yes, pneumonia, but he's fine now. He's expected to be better than new."

That was where Cade had gone, why he wasn't in Dedrick. "Cade's with Adam?"

"No. He was for two days, no sleep, no nothing, but he's gone back to Texas for a few days."

"He's on location in Dedrick?"

"Yes. He went back, right after he knew the child was all right."

"But I tried the hotel and—"

"He's staying with Rick Walters at the location. He decided it would be best to be that close, since he has a very involved stunt to do. I guess I can tell you now that it's important to him to do it."

"I know. He gave his word."

"And Walters is paying him enough to give him and Adam some security for a while."

The money. "He needs the money?"

"That's why he's back at work. Why he's willing to do what Walters wants. But he's smart, Dr. Lewis. Cade knows what he's doing. He's not foolish. Cade knows how to do stunts, believe me, and he wouldn't take the chance if he didn't believe he could do it. He wants the best for the boy."

How different from Frank. Night and day. "Yes, I know he does."

"Is it important for you to reach him?"

It was just a matter of her life. "Yes, very important."

"Well, he'll be calling in to me about the papers. I can tell him you need to talk to him."

"That would be great," she said.

"Is there any message I can give him for you?"

She almost said no, but thought better of it. "Yes, please. Just tell him the war's over."

"Pardon me?"

"The war is over. He'll understand."

"Sure, of course," the man said. "Anything else?"

"No, just that I need to talk to him as quickly as possible."

Megan hung up and sat alone in her office for a long time, before reaching for the phone again. She was beginning to feel liberated, free for the first time in her life, and also totally centered. She didn't want to sit here, waiting for things to be set right. She wanted to make sure they were.

* * *

Cade sat in the stunt car, protected by a helmet, knee, shoulder and elbow pads. He stared at the slanted ramp that had been disguised as a concrete embankment, about fifty feet from the wall of the warden's house.

The midday sun was bright, making his eyes water, and he closed his eyes for a minute. But as soon as he did, he saw Megan the last time they'd talked. How he wished he hadn't let her go. How he wished he'd stayed with her, until she could admit that she was afraid to love, that she was so scarred by Frank that she couldn't even trust herself, let alone him.

Cade opened his eyes and tried to focus on the gag. He knew the speed, the split second when he should hit the ramp, fly over the fence, then fly, roll and skid into the governor's car. He knew it like the back of his hand, because he'd gone over it, over and over again.

But he felt unsure, and knew he couldn't afford to have those feelings when he went for broke. He felt uneasy. Adam really did need him, and he needed Adam. The eternity in the hospital had proven that to him a hundredfold.

When this was over, he was going to go back to find Megan, make her listen, try to convince her that he could love her and make her happy, even if he was a performer in the circus who got shot out of a cannon on a regular basis.

Actually he had a game plan, a trump card he could use that might make her listen to him. Above all, she had to believe that he loved her and wouldn't ever do anything to hurt her.

"Cade?" he heard in his earpiece.

"Yeah, Ross?"

"All set. Just waiting for you to give the High sign."

He started the car, let it idle and stared at the ramp. Hit it, maintain speed, keep the car level, then go into a roll. It was simple, timing, planning. Just do it. Just do it.

He heard Ross in the earpiece again. "Cade?"

"Yeah."

"Leon just got back from town, and he says there's a message for you. Evan called, said the papers were drawn up. No problems. And let me read this, to make sure I have it right. Evan says he got a call from the doctor, and she says to tell you, 'The war's over.'"

"What?"

"Dr. Lewis said, 'The war is over.' That's the message."

Cade sank back in the seat for a minute. She'd done it. She'd won. She'd faced the enemy, and Frank Lewis was no more.

"Does that make sense to you, Cade?"

"Yes, it does," he answered, then knew he was ready to do the gag. "It's time to go for it."

"Good. I'll give you the countdown, then do it your way, Cade."

"Got you."

She'd won the war. He almost laughed out loud as he revved the engine of the stunt car. "One thousand five, one thousand four," he heard in his earpiece. "One thousand three, one thousand two, one thousand one...and...now!"

Cade exhaled, pressed the accelerator to the floor and never took his eyes off the ramp as the car rushed forward. With a quick glance at RPMs and speed, Cade hit the ramp and in that second, knew he had it licked. The car went flying into the air, clearing the fence, then Cade set off the small explosive underneath. He felt the car go into a roll...once...twice...three times, then it landed on the lawn on its wheels, skidding in the right direction.

The governor's car was there, the position was perfect, the impact came. He felt the jar of the stop in his bones, but kept the wheel straight. The stunt car ground through the second vehicle, shuddering to a halt on its side on the steps of the house.

Cade sat very still for just a moment, threw off his helmet, then pulled himself out the window and jumped to the ground, running to the west side of the house. "Clear," he said into his mouthpiece, and in the next moment, the two tangled cars exploded in a fiery ball.

Cade stopped out of camera range, turned, saw the plume of smoke and flame soar into the Texas sky, then heard the whole area erupt into spontaneous cheering and applause.

"It's a wrap!" he heard Walters boom over the other noise. "That's a print! A real score!"

"Perfect," Leon said as he jogged over to Cade.

Cade nodded. "Yeah, perfect," he repeated as he stripped off the orange jumpsuit and pads. He handed them to Leon, then took his jacket. "And done."

He turned to go to Walters, to tell him that was it. He was out of here and on the first flight to Los Angeles, but it wasn't the red-haired man he saw. It was Megan, getting out of Gus's van, her hair burnished by the noontime sun, her slender figure in jeans and a heavy, cabled sweater, looking slight and delicate.

He stood very still, watching, waiting, certain he was dreaming as she came toward him with excruciating slowness. First she was within ten feet, then five, and finally right in front of him.

She looked up at him, the blueness of her eyes a perfect match for the sky overhead. "Did you get my message?" she asked in a voice just loud enough for Cade to hear.

He nodded. "Yes, I did."

"You . . . you did that stunt very well."

"Thank you."

"What are we talking about?" she said.

"I don't know. It's up to you."

"I . . . don't know where to start, Cade."

"Then let me make it easier for you, Megan. I love you. No matter what I do for a living, I love you. I've never loved anyone like I love you."

She smiled, a brilliant expression, then was in his arms. "Oh, God, do you really?"

"So much, I ache from it. Don't you believe me?"

He felt her stiffen a bit. "I never . . . I never felt loved."

The bald admission stunned him and broke his heart. God, he loved her more than life itself, and she wasn't sure of it. He tipped her face with one finger until she was looking into his eyes. "Then know right now that you're more loved than any other woman on this earth. And I'll love you forever. If you'll have me and my child?"

Tears welled up in her eyes, making the blue shimmer. "Have you? Cade Daniels, I just fought a war for you. I came to Texas on a plane that, I might add, saw more than its share of turbulence, and I watched you do your stunt. Have you? I'll never let you go."

Epilogue

Sometime during the night Megan woke and knew she'd finally found the place she'd been looking for all her life—Cade's embrace. She felt him holding her, his heat running the length of her body, and could feel the vibration of his heart against her breasts.

"Cade?" she said softly through the shadows.

"Mmm," he breathed, his hand gently rubbing her arm.

"Are you awake?" she asked, tracing the line of the scar on his shoulder. She felt the response in him to her touch, the way he shifted toward her, the weight of his leg over her thighs. Would she ever have enough of this man? Would she ever feel satiated, able to walk away?

The answer came with a certainty that burned itself into her soul. Never. Since they'd come back here from the prison, they'd made love and they'd loved, each experience more intense and more satisfying than the last.

Now Megan had to say the words, to set things straight, so she could put the past behind her, once and for all.

"I'm sorry I wasn't there for you when Adam was so sick. I had no idea, or—"

He touched her lips with his finger. "Hush. You didn't know. And it worked out. He's fine. Doris and Leo have ended their war, and we're going to raise Adam together." His finger moved to touch the tip of her chin. "I want to do that with you."

"I want that, too."

"And speaking of wars, I guess I've finished one of mine, too. I've decided that Ross is pretty smart. He knew when to get into coordinating and away from stunts. I'm going to do the same thing, going together with Ross and two other former stuntmen to form a business. We can plan, do layouts and train new stuntmen."

She didn't want him to give up what he loved for her. "You have to do what you need to do," she said. "If it's stunts, I can deal with it. I really can."

"But I can't. I don't want to take any chance of leaving you and Adam, before we've been together for at least fifty years." He kissed her quickly. "I'm not swearing off it altogether, mind you, but I'm going to be management instead of worker from now on."

She snuggled into his side, sensing such a link with this man that she felt as if she had become a part of him. "Then there's my war," she said softly.

"What about it, love?"

"I saw him, Cade."

"I know," he whispered, tightening his hold on her ever so slightly. "And?"

"He's just the same as he always was. But I'm changed. I can see that you were right. I faced him. I told him how I felt and I walked away. I'm his daughter, but not his child. The war's over."

"And you won."

"The peace is secure," she said.

In the silence of the room Cade took Megan, the two of them coming together with nothing but their love. And they spent what could have been an eternity—or the single beat of a heart—showing each other how deep and abiding that love could be.

* * * * *

Silhouette Sensation

COMING NEXT MONTH

THE LIGHTS OF HOME
Marilyn Pappano

Eight years of waiting were over, and Jess Trujillo was coming home. Home to the town where he'd been born, and home to the only woman he'd ever loved, Caitlin Pierce, who had betrayed him just when it had counted most.

The chemistry between them was still strong, but Jess would never let himself love Caitlin again. However, that didn't mean he didn't want her in his bed—or his ring on her finger!

NIGHT SHADOW
Nora Roberts

A solitary figure robed in black was fighting a single-handed battle against crime. Nothing—not even love—could deter the man called Nemesis from his mission.

Deborah O'Roarke owed Nemesis her life, but she could not accept his methods of achieving justice. Still she felt a disturbing desire for this mysterious stranger who lived in the shadows. Who was he?

Silhouette Sensation

COMING NEXT MONTH

BLACK HORSE ISLAND
Dee Holmes

Keely Lockwood was determined to turn her father's dream of a refuge for troubled teenage boys into reality, but she had only one month in which to do it—and she needed Jed Corey.

Once a street-tough kid, Jed had been her father's greatest success. But now he was a dangerously attractive man who thought she was the wrong person for this job.

It was going to be a summer neither one of them would ever forget...

A LOVING TOUCH
Joyce McGill

Victoria Shelton's special gifts had never brought her anything but pain, so Michael Gallagher's urgent request—that she use her psychic abilities to help him find his missing friend and partner—was out of the question.

It wasn't easy to say no to a man as compelling as Michael Gallagher. But surely, even though he was desperate, he wouldn't seduce Tory just to change her mind...would he?

Zodiac Wordsearch Competition

How would you like a years' supply of Silhouette Sensations ABSOLUTELY FREE?

Well, you can win them! All you have to do is complete the word puzzle below and send it to us by 30th June 1994. The first five correct entries picked out of the bag after this date will each win one years' supply of Silhouette Sensation romances (four books every month - worth over £90). What could be easier?

S	E	C	S	I	P	R	I	A	C	F
U	U	D	C	A	N	C	E	R	D	I
L	E	I	N	I	M	E	G	U	S	R
C	A	P	R	I	C	O	R	N	U	E
S	E	I	R	A	N	G	I	S	I	O
P	O	P	W	A	T	E	R	W	R	I
L	G	A	H	M	A	T	I	T	A	P
U	R	R	T	O	U	H	I	S	U	R
T	I	B	R	O	R	E	N	G	Q	O
O	V	I	A	N	U	S	A	T	A	C
I	O	L	E	O	S	T	A	R	N	S

Pisces	Aries	Leo	Earth
Cancer	Gemini	Virgo	Star
Scorpio	Taurus	Fire	Sign
Aquarius	Libra	Water	Moon
Capricorn	Sagittarius	Pluto	Air

Please turn over for entry details

ow to enter

overleaf below the word puzzle, are hidden find them by reading the letters forwards, down, or diagonally. When you find a word, circle it or put a line through it. After you have found all the words, the left-out letters will spell a secret message that you can read from left to right, from the top of the puzzle through to the bottom.

Don't forget to enter your name and address in the space below then put this page in an envelope and post it today (you don't need a stamp). Competition closes 30th June 1994.

Silhouette Competition
Freepost
P.O. Box 236
Croydon
Surrey CR9 9EL

✂ -

COMZW

Hidden message

_____

_____

Are you a Reader Service subscriber?   Yes ☐   No ☐

Ms/Mrs/Miss/Mr
_____

Address
_____

_____

_____

Postcode
_____